He'll fight

FOR HER

New York Times & USA Today Bestselling Author

CYNTHIA
EDEN

CHAPTER ONE

The suits were giving her a headache. Kathleen "Kat" O'Shaughnessy kept a brittle, polite smile on her face—after all, she'd had plenty of practice at being fake during her life—as she strode off the elevator. Of course, the two men immediately moved with her. Suit Number One and Suit Number Two. Everywhere she went, they followed. No, not followed. One led, one followed, and she was sandwiched in the middle of her particular hell.

"Is there a specific reason," Kat asked as she made sure her voice was all nice and easy and polite, "why we are sneaking into this building after midnight? I mean, call me crazy, but I figure normal business hours are probably more like nine to five."

No smile from either man. No response. They were driving her insane.

So maybe they were still mad at her. Was it really *her* fault that things had gone down so poorly earlier that day? She didn't think so. Well...maybe.

Suit Number One opened an office door for her. He had a name. Bryan. Bryan Brisk. Suit Two had a name, too. Tom Wayne. Special Agents with the FBI, both of them. Men with badges and guns and zero sense of fun.

"There's been a change of plans," Agent Bryan Brisk announced as he stood next to that open door. "Your protection detail is changing."

Changing? Her heart kicked with a fast lick of excitement.

"You like rule breaking," Bryan added in that slightly uptight New York accent of his. "Then we'll give you someone who can make sure you stay in line."

She smiled at him. "You *are* mad. You said you weren't, but you lied. I can tell. You're angry." Kat could feel Tom Wayne practically breathing down her neck. Someone really needed to learn the concept of personal space. She turned toward Tom and shooed him back. *Space,* she mouthed.

His eyes narrowed. She winked. Then focused on Bryan once more.

Bryan was thin and tall, with hair that she *knew* he had to get salon lightened to that particular blond shade. His teeth were almost too white, and she was pretty sure *by-the-book* was his catchphrase. He never smiled. He never cracked a joke. And she was fairly certain she'd almost given him a heart attack earlier that day.

"Bryan..." She sighed his name and put her hand on his shoulder. For the moment, she ignored the open office door and anyone who might be waiting inside for her. "I just needed a walk."

"*You were gone for two hours.*"

"It was a long walk. And I found a bakery. What did you want me to do? *Not* eat the brownies?" Talk about a crime.

A little muscle under Bryan's left eye twitched. "You're under federal protection. You are *not* supposed to go out and eat brownies. You are not supposed to disappear for hours at a time—"

"Two hours, only two."

"Your life is in danger, but you act as if everything is a freaking joke to you."

No, it wasn't a joke. Nothing about her life had ever been a joke. If only. Her chin notched up. "I don't like the tone, Bryan. Not at all." Kat sighed. "And just when I thought we were starting to be friends."

"Friends?" Bryan seemed to strangle on the word.

"I brought you a brownie back, didn't I?" Talk about ungrateful. She'd brought them *both* brownies.

Bryan's mouth opened. Closed. He was going to say something but she'd just caught movement beyond the open door. Because she didn't want to deal with Bryan right then—*the jerk has no idea who I am or what I think is a damn joke, he hasn't lived my life and seen the shit that I have*—Kat rolled back her shoulders and strolled inside. She was wearing two-inch heels. Expensive and stylish, just like the rest of her outfit. The slacks and black cashmere sweater had been carefully selected from a boutique in Paris. The pearl necklace she wore had belonged to her mother, a woman who had *always* looked and acted like perfection.

A woman very different from Kat.

When she entered the office, silence reigned.

Wilde Protection and Securities. She'd noticed the name of the company. Located at the tip top of the Atlanta high-rise, Kat figured she had to be in the big boss's office. And...*bingo.* That had to be the big boss sitting behind the desk. Young and handsome, with his face carefully expressionless...she was sure that was the guy her suits were there to meet.

But Kat's gaze was drawn away from the big boss and over to the other man. To the guy who stood back, hanging near the large floor to ceiling windows that overlooked the city. The mystery man was huge, tall and muscled, and his arms were folded over his massive chest. He wore jeans and a black t-shirt, one that looked like it was going to lose the battle against his muscles. A battered leather jacket was on the chair near him. The guy's dark hair was too long. A beard covered his hard jaw, and his dark eyes were pinned right on her.

Yum.

No, no, that was *not* the response she should have. He wasn't sexy—not typically sexy, anyway, like the fellow sitting all snug and safe behind the desk. The big bruiser she was currently locking eyes with—he just emitted a kind of raw power that pulled at her senses. That made her want to get a little closer.

So she did.

She headed straight for him. As she closed in, Kat was sure those powerful shoulders of his stiffened. *Hello, new toy.* She extended her hand toward him. "Hi, there." She made sure her smile stretched. "I'm Kat."

He looked at her hand. Looked at her. Didn't take it.

She wiggled her fingers.

He shook his head.

And she liked him even more.

"We can shake later." Obviously, there would be a later. She tipped back her head and enjoyed staring up at him. She stood at five-foot-eight, and with her heels, she had some nice, extra inches. But this mystery man was way taller, and she liked that about him.

If only they had met under different circumstances. The kind of circumstances that didn't get a person killed.

I know I'm living on borrowed time. Seven days. That's all I have left. If that. When a woman was facing off against the grim reaper, she tended to get a little desperate.

Kat was way past the *little* part, and into full-on *a lot* land.

"Ah, excuse me."

Her head turned.

The boss behind the desk had stood. He motioned to the chairs near him. "Why don't we all get seated so we can discuss this case?"

This case...he meant her. She was the case.

Taking her time, Kat headed for one of the offered chairs. Surprise, surprise, Suit Number One took the seat to her left. Suit Number Two got the one to her right. Then they pulled their chairs even closer to her. She shot them a disgruntled look. Did they really think she was going to try running right then? No.

She'd wait until *after* the little meet-and-greet to make her escape. She settled herself in, crossed her legs, folded her hands in her lap, and got ready to do what she did best—play the game.

She'd been playing this particular game her entire life. A little game she liked to call...

Trust no one and keep your ass alive.

She thought the title was rather catchy.

***

The woman was too damn beautiful.

Rick Williams didn't move from his position near the windows. He kept his arms crossed over his chest, kept his eyes on his target, and tried to act like his heart wasn't doing a freaking triple-time rhythm in his chest. When she'd walked into the room, when she'd glanced at Eric, dismissed him, then turned her gorgeous, emerald gaze on Rick...

I forgot my own name for a minute.

Absolute perfection. That's what she was. From the top of her dark hair—a long, thick mass that cascaded over her shoulders—down her curving body. God, those curves...

Her feet were sexy as hell in her heels. She didn't swing her feet though. Didn't move at all as she sat statue-still in the chair. Her face showed mild curiosity. What a face. Creamy skin. Cat eyes that had been accentuated by dark shadow. High, arching brows. Blood red lips. A cute little mole near her mouth and—

"Why am I here, exactly?" Her voice was husky and warm, sensual, and designed to take a man straight to his knees. "I thought I already had protection." Her gaze darted to the two men who sat beside her. Way too close to her, in Rick's opinion.

It was the blond guy who cleared his throat and responded to her question. "The federal government believes that your protection detail needs to be enhanced."

She nodded. "Oh, you mean...because someone broke into my hotel room today and littered it with bullets? And if I *hadn't* just happened to be out on my brownie run, I would have been slaughtered in my bed? Is *that* why you think my detail needs to be enhanced?"

Her voice stayed cool and calm the whole time, but Rick—he felt *anything* but cool. The idea of someone shooting at her enraged him.

And what the hell did she mean about a brownie run?

Before anyone could speak, she gave another nod. "Yes, I do agree...some *enhancement* is required." She turned her head toward Rick. Winked at him. "I'm guessing you're the man for the job."

If he hadn't been standing in front of the window, he would've looked over his shoulder to see if she'd just winked at someone else. Because women who looked like *her* didn't normally flirt with guys who looked like him. Women like *her* were supposed to go for the jerk suits next to her. Those perfectly dressed guys with their capped teeth and their styled hair. The woman sitting so poised in that chair oozed money and charm, and she was supposed to stick with the fancy boys.

Not go slumming it with him.

But then again...if the stories about her were true...

Eric cleared his throat. "Ms. O'Shaughnessy...my name is Eric Wilde, and you're in my security company."

"We don't need to be formal. My name's Kathleen—"

"Kathleen—"

"But I go by Kat. Feel free to call me that." Her gaze slid back to Rick. "You can call me that, too."

He didn't move.

Her smile stretched. "And what's your name?"

Rick didn't respond.

He could've sworn that her eyes actually danced with glee. She licked her lower lip and murmured, "I do love the strong, silent type."

"*Kat,*" the blond next to her said her name with a rush of annoyance. He reached out and curved a hand warningly around her wrist.

Rick growled.

He didn't mean to growl. Normally, he was a bit more civilized than that. *A bit.* But he didn't like the jerk's tone. And he liked it even *less* that the fellow had his hand on Kat.

The tension in the room seemed to thicken. Eric swiveled his head toward Rick and frowned.

The two stiffs in their suits also turned their attention to Rick. The blond kept his hold on Kat's wrist.

"Remove it," Rick ordered.

Kat's brows lifted.

The blond didn't obey the order.

Anger twisted inside of Rick. Unexpected. Unwelcome. He took a quick step forward—

"Remove the hand, Bryan," Kat instructed. "Do it now."

Bryan removed the hand.

Kat kept staring at Rick. "I like your voice. It's deep and rumbly and—"

"It reminds you of a freaking grizzly bear," Rick *rumbled,* dammit. "I've been told that before."

She blinked. "No. I wasn't going to say grizzly bear." She gave a little wince. "Bears don't talk. I don't know who told you that they did, but that person was lying."

He would *not* smile at her.

"But I do find your voice very sexy."

The redheaded agent sighed. "Here we go...Mind games, twelve o'clock."

"*Ahem.*" Eric slapped his hands down on his desk, obviously ready to take control of the situation. "Agent Brisk, why don't we get focused on the matter at hand?" He glanced pointedly at his watch. "I have a family at home, and I don't particularly enjoy leaving them in the middle of the night."

"I understand you saw us as a favor to my boss," Bryan Brisk began. "And I appreciate your time. And your discretion."

"Discretion is of the upmost importance with this case." The redheaded agent leaned forward. *Tom Wayne.* Rick had been briefed on both men before they'd walked inside with Kathleen—Kat—between them.

Bryan tapped his fingers on the edge of Eric's desk. "I'm assuming you gentlemen know who she is."

Because he was watching Kat, Rick saw her shoulders stiffen right before she announced, "*She* has already introduced herself to everyone, so, of course, these two fellows know who I am." Her head swiveled toward Bryan. "Do keep up."

Oh, she didn't like that fellow. Obviously. There had been enough bite in her voice to leave a mark.

Rick decided to edge closer. *Not* just because he wanted to catch her scent again. Though he was pretty sure she'd smelled like rich vanilla when she'd stood in front of him. As he approached her, Kat's attention shifted to him. He rather liked having her eyes on him and not on Agent Bryan Brisk. Staring into her eyes, Rick said, "Everyone on the East Coast knows who Kathleen O'Shaughnessy is."

Her lips curved. Her gaze remained steady on him. "Are you a fan?" A little flutter of her insanely long lashes. "I have to confess, I have gotten a few stalkers now that the world knows who I am..."

"A mafia princess," Rick drawled. He was tired of her perfect facade. He wanted to push until the porcelain broke, and he saw the real woman. "A beauty queen raised in the middle of drugs, sex, and violence."

Her smile didn't waver. Neither did her gaze.

So he kept talking. And closing in. "The only child of Antonio O'Shaughnessy. Protected and pampered your whole life, you lived rich and high on·your daddy's blood money. But dear old dad was gunned down last year, and now your house of cards has crashed."

She looked away. Focused on Agent Brisk. "He doesn't like me."

Rick stilled. Had her voice trembled? Surely not.

"Bryan, why are we here if you're just going to make me talk to a jerk who doesn't like me?"

"Ahem." Rick cleared his throat and waited for her incredible eyes to come back to him. When they did—

Shit, what was I saying?

She looked expectantly at him.

Eric's chair squeaked as the wheels rolled back, and he stood. "You're here," Eric pointed out, "because Uncle Sam called in one big-ass favor from me. Ms. O'Shaughnessy, it seems you keep dodging the federal agents who are supposed to be keeping you safe as part of the Witness Protection Program. Since you won't play by the rules, you're getting your very own twenty-four, seven civilian guard."

She held up one delicate hand—one delicate finger. "We should be clear on a few things. One, I'm not in Witness Protection. Not yet. See, I only get that golden pass *after* I testify in court. That's why the two escorts I have tonight are FBI agents and not U.S. marshals." Another finger lifted. "Two, I don't remember requesting my 'very own twenty-four, seven civilian guard' but I do thank you very much for the offer."

Rick leaned one hip against the side of Eric's desk and glowered down at her. This job was going to be such a pain in his ass. Call him psychic, but he could already tell. "It's not an offer, sweetheart. It's a done deal."

Her delicate nostrils flared. "Are we dating?"

Rick blinked. "Uh..."

"Dating? Fucking? Hooking up every now and then for a quickie in the dark?"

The images that popped into his head...

Yes, please.

"We're not," she said, while every muscle in his body tightened. "So drop the endearments. Unless *you* want to be sweet cheeks."

Yeah, this job was going to be a *major* pain in his ass. "Do I look sweet?"

Her cute little pink tongue swiped over her lower lip. "Sweet enough to eat."

His jeans were too damn tight.

"Stop messing with him," Bryan groused as he leaned toward Kat. "He hasn't even started the job yet, and you're trying to scare him off."

"I don't scare off easily." The agent was too close to her again. "Where the hell were you, buddy, when her hotel room got shot to hell and back?"

Bryan shook his head. "What?"

"Her hotel room." Rick rolled one hand in the air. "My boss Eric here...he said *your* boss called him because you're doing a piss poor job of keeping Kat safe. She was almost killed tonight, and the FBI can't afford to lose her." And he had a really bad feeling in the pit of his stomach about why the FBI was going to a civilian contractor instead of continuing to use one of their own...

Bryan swiped a hand over his face. "I stepped out to make a phone call, all right? I thought she was in, safe and sound—"

"We both did," Tom Wayne interjected. "And we have *no* idea how her location got compromised. But we're here now because we were told to deliver her to this location." A rough exhale. "And then to walk away." Tom actually sounded relieved as he delivered that last bit of news.

Shock flashed for a moment on Kat's face. "Walk away? You're abandoning me?"

Neither agent spoke.

"Somehow," Kat dramatically sighed, "I'll have to find the strength to move on without the two of you in my life. It will be hard, but I'll soldier on."

A muscle jerked beneath Bryan's left eye as he fixed his gaze on Eric. "You're taking her case?"

A nod from Eric.

Bryan inclined his head toward Rick. "*He's* the bodyguard?"

That tone was almost insulting. No, there was no *almost* about it. Rick gave him a cold smile. "I'm a whole lot more than just a bodyguard."

Now Bryan rose. He moved toward Rick. Tilted his head back and stared *up* at Rick. "You swear you'll keep her alive?"

"I hate when people talk as if I'm not in the room," Kat declared. "One of the most annoying things in the world."

"I'll keep her alive," Rick promised.

Bryan gave another nod. "She's a pain in the ass, but she grows on you."

"You do care," Kat sounded amused.

Rick swung his gaze to Kat. Her life was on the line. "I *will* keep you alive." Because that was the job. *She* was the mystery job that had dragged his ass out of a very warm bed in the middle of the night. There were seven days—just seven—until Kathleen O'Shaughnessy was scheduled to testify in court. The first of *many* appearances before a judge because she was supposed to help take down some of the worst criminals on the East Coast.

She could destroy a whole lot of lives with her testimony.

And that was the reason a whole lot of people wanted her dead.

"If you're taking over her case, our work is done." Bryan rolled back his shoulders and cast a glance at Kat. "I'd like to say it's been a pleasure, but we both know that would be a lie."

"It's been more like a nightmare." Tom rose to his feet. He slapped a hand around Rick's shoulder. "Good luck, man. You're gonna need it."

Kat didn't move. "You're deserting me. Both of you."

Bryan reached into his pocket and pulled out a card. He tucked it into the palm of her hand. "We don't have a choice. Rank has been pulled." His voice roughened as he told her, "*Only FBI agents knew we were at that hotel.*"

Did Kat get what the guy was saying? Rick sure did. The case was being given to Wilde because the FBI couldn't be trusted. Someone had bought his or her way into the Bureau. Someone who wanted Kat dead.

That was where he came in. "So long, boys. Don't let the door hit you in the ass."

Bryan glowered at him.

Rick motioned toward the door. They had work to do. The sooner the FBI suits got out of there, the better.

Tom headed toward the exit first. Bryan hesitated and glanced over at Kat.

"You're...really leaving me? With *them*?" Now Kat was on her feet. "How do I know that I can trust them? I mean, who are these guys?"

Bryan rubbed a hand over his jaw. "My boss said they're the best. But if I were you, I wouldn't trust anyone completely."

Well, wasn't Bryan a fun greeting card type of fellow?

You need to go, bro.

"You have my number," Bryan muttered to Kat. "If you need me, I'm there."

Nope. Not gonna happen. The last thing Rick intended to allow was for her to call the FBI and give away her *hidden* location. Rick shoved away from the desk. He caught Bryan by the scruff of the neck and *guided* the fellow to the door. "Don't worry. You'll see her again in seven days." He didn't like the way Bryan kept shooting brooding looks back at Kat. "She'll be the one at the courthouse, singing like a bird, and getting all the bad guys sent to jail. You won't be able to miss her."

"But—"

"Security is waiting beyond this door. They'll see you downstairs." Security that had been there all along, just lurking in the shadows. Wilde agents knew their shit. They knew how to be seen and how to hide. They wouldn't be hiding any longer. "Good-bye."

Yeah, he kicked the two agents out. Rather enjoyed it, too. Then he slammed the door and spun around.

He came face-to-face with Kat. He hadn't heard her cross the room. Probably because the carpeting was too thick. Eric needed to learn how to stop overindulging with expensive things.

Kat's eyes were wide, and, for the first time, a little afraid. "They can't just leave me here."

"They can." He nodded. "They did."

"But—"

"Maybe you shouldn't have ditched them today for a...what was it?" He glanced over her shoulder at Eric.

"Brownie run," Eric supplied helpfully.

Rick snapped his fingers together. "Right. Disappearing on agents—that makes them look bad to their bosses. Then when the bad guys find your location and shoot up your bed—that makes the agents look even *worse*."

She sucked in a sharp breath. "Wouldn't it have been worse if I'd been in the bed when it was shot up? The way I see it, my brownie run saved my life."

Actually, it probably had. He intended to rely on more than blind luck when it came to her safety. Rick inhaled and pulled in more of her sweet vanilla scent. "What did they do?" Rick asked, genuinely curious. "Take one look into your green eyes and get lost? Fall for that husky voice that you know is pure sex? Did you wrap the

Feds around your little finger within the first five minutes of meeting them? Or did it take longer? Maybe you went in for a whole ten minutes before you had them wrapped up and lost in you?"

He expected his words to make her angry. He *wanted* her angry. Instead, she smiled at him.

Fuck. Tread with caution. Extreme caution. Warnings blasted in his head.

Her hand rose and pressed to his chest. "Why don't we see..." Kat murmured, "just how long it takes *you* to get wrapped up in me?"

She was dangerous. A player to her core. And he was supposed to believe that she'd really disappeared to buy brownies? Oh, hell, no. She'd been up to no good, and he would be finding out the truth about her little jaunt. Later. After all, that was part of the plan.

Some people thought she was the innocent victim. He didn't buy that particular line of BS. She was treacherous and cold, and he had to keep a very close eye on her.

"Princess," he told her, edging even closer to her. "There aren't going to be any more brownie runs."

"We'll see about that, sweet cheeks."

"But you do have one thing right...you and I will be wrapped up in each other soon. In fact, we're about to be inseparable."

"Oh, no, we're—"

His hand flew up, and he locked a handcuff around her wrist. A second later, he snapped one around his own. He'd had the cuffs in his back pocket the whole time, knowing they would be needed.

Her eyes doubled in size. Then narrowed. Became pretty much slits.

"You're insane," she whispered.

He winked at her. "I am...and for the next seven days, I'm also all yours."

CHAPTER TWO

The FBI agents had left her. Since they'd been cramping her style—and getting in the way of business that she needed to take care of—Kat wasn't exactly mourning the loss of their companionship.

But she also wasn't ready to jump on the crazy boat with the hot guy who'd just cuffed himself to her. *Play the game. Stick to your role.* Her chin notched up. "You're into bondage. That's great. Good for you, living your best life. Bravo. But I don't have time to live out your fantasy right now."

A furrow appeared between his heavy brows. She was also pretty sure that his jaw clenched. She was so tempted to pat his beard. It wasn't a thick, too long beard. It was a nicely trimmed one that hugged the hard edges of his square jaw. Made him look all sexy and yummy.

What *didn't* make him look yummy? The freaking handcuffs. Maybe under different circumstances...but right then? Hard no.

"Kathleen..." He growled out her name, all hot and dark. Her stomach did a funny flip.

She pasted her fake smile in place. Let her eyes drift over him, and, for the moment, kept ignoring the other man in the room. As far as she was concerned, the big fellow in front of her was the main threat. "Usually," Kat allowed, "I at least know a man's name before he handcuffs me." She tugged her wrist back. Pulled his with it. "You still haven't introduced yourself."

"Rick Williams."

"Was that so hard?" She tugged again. "Now get the cuffs off, and we'll talk like adults."

But Rick shook that dark head of his. The man had some wonderfully thick hair. The kind of hair that a woman could sink her fingers in.

"No can do," he told her. "You're a flight risk."

Yes, she was.

"You eluded your government agents because they looked at you and got sucked in by that beautiful face."

Now he was just being sweet. "You think I'm beautiful?"

"You know you are. You use that shit to trick dumbasses. I'm not a dumbass."

"Good to know."

"The cuffs stay on until we're in a secure location. Once we're there, I'll let you go."

Was she supposed to believe him? "Promises, promises..."

"*Enough.*"

Kat and Rick both turned at the rough voice.

"Hi, there." The man standing behind the desk smiled. "I'm Eric Wilde."

He'd already introduced himself—

"This is my office, my building, and my company. So how about you both sit down and we'll go over a few ground rules so that we can get this case going?"

How about no—

Crap. Rick was heading for one of the chairs near the desk, and since they were connected, she either got dragged along or she double-timed it and kept up. For the moment, she double-timed it. And once more, Kat found herself seated in front of Eric's desk.

This time, Rick was beside her. Leaning in all close. Well, okay, maybe he wasn't leaning in. He was just *big* so he took up a lot of space.

"I think your cuff is going to bruise my wrist," she mumbled.

Immediately, his free hand reached out and started rubbing her wrist, easing below the cuff. She jumped because the movement was so surprising and because his touch felt so good. Warm and soothing. He had callused fingertips and massive fingers, but he was being extra careful as he stroked her skin.

"Stop," she said, aware that her voice was way too husky. "I was just bullshitting."

He stopped.

Eric cleared his throat. "Obviously, you two will get along wonderfully."

She gaped at him.

Looking slightly sheepish, Eric told her, "Kat, you're in good hands—"

"I'm in cuffs. My federal protection ditched me, and now I'm trapped with you guys."

Eric leaned forward. "We're better than the Feds. I assure you, my agents are the best that you'll come across. Your safety is our priority, and nothing will happen to you before the court date."

What about after the court date? No one ever talked about that part.

Still looking all sincere and intense, Eric continued, "Your hotel location was leaked. The Feds were the only ones who knew where you were—"

"Tom and Bryan didn't sell me out." An automatic response, but...was it one that she believed?

Eric shrugged. "Not saying it was them. I have people looking into the matter right now. *Someone* at the Bureau was bought. Someone gave you up. The higher ups at the FBI don't want to take a chance of that happening again, so they turned to me."

"And turning to a civilian agency is really what the FBI does?" She wasn't buying it.

"I've worked for Uncle Sam more than you might realize. The clearance I have and that my team members have—it goes exceedingly high up the food chain."

Kat eased out a slow breath. If someone in the FBI had sold her out, then she needed to proceed with extreme caution. How many times had her father said the Feds were dangerous? But, then again, she'd thought no one was more dangerous than dear old dad. "What's the plan?"

Rick shifted in the chair next to her. "You get the package deal. I keep you hidden, keep you safe, and I kick the ass of anyone who tries to hurt you."

He sounded so confident, but he hadn't lived her life. "You don't know the people who are after me." She could feel the crack in her mask. The stupid facade that she wore all the time. "You get in their way, and *you'll* be hurt. Or you'll be dead."

She knew there was a target on her back. But why bring him into the crossfire?

"I'm not scared."

She turned her head. Stared into his dark, deep eyes. "You should rethink that."

A shrug of his massive shoulders. "You're not looking at an amateur. I can keep you safe."

Or what—die trying?

"Rick will have backup," Eric inserted smoothly. "Other Wilde agents will have his six. You'll both be monitored and protected."

Like she hadn't heard that before. Kat bit her lower lip.

"We're your best chance," Eric assured her. "And we're your only option."

No, she had another option. *Get away. Run. Hide. Become someone new and leave the nightmare behind.* Only it was a little hard to run when she was handcuffed to the Rock wannabe beside her.

So, step one for her...ditch the cuffs. And in order to do that, she had to make Rick think she was along for whatever ride he had planned. Her shoulders sagged. "I apologize for not saying it sooner, but thank you." She let her head dip forward. "It's been really, really hard and scary, and I'm grateful for the help you're giving to me. You...you don't need to cuff me, though. I'll cooperate fully."

Silence.

She risked a glance at Rick.

The man was smirking at her. "Does that shit usually work? The trembly, breathy voice? The weak, wounded posture? Because, seriously, that was a pretty good performance, only it wasn't one I was buying."

Such. A. Jerk.

And had Eric smothered a laugh? Her gaze shot to him.

He coughed. "Ah...that's why Rick is in charge of your protection detail. He's not, um, easily swayed."

"You mean he has a heart of stone." Good to know.

"I mean you won't get past his guard. He won't make mistakes. You *should* be grateful for that fact. He'll keep you alive, and that's all that matters."

She could practically feel the heat pouring from Rick's body. He was going to be her constant companion for the next week? From the corner of her eye, she took his measure once more.

Big, bad, and dangerous. Dammit, she was screwed.

And cuffed.

***

"Why are there five identical SUVs in here?" Kat's voice seemed to echo in the parking garage.

Rick tossed her a quick smile. "Because, Kat, we can't just have one car seen leaving the facility. If you were tailed here—or if your helpful FBI buddies sold you out again—we don't want to make it easy for the bad guys to follow you." He motioned toward the waiting SUVs—and toward the agents who were already behind the steering wheels. "They'll all leave at once. All go in different directions. And anyone trying to follow you will have one hell of a hard time figuring out where you really are."

Now, time to stop chit-chatting in the garage and get moving. He opened the rear door of the nearest SUV. "Ladies first."

"Bite me."

I would love to.

She climbed inside, he followed because— cuffs. Not like he could be far away from her. Not like he *wanted* to be far away. He yanked the door closed behind him. "We're moving under the cover of darkness. That makes it even harder to track us."

The SUVs were already moving. All of the drivers had their instructions. Getting Kat to a safe house was priority one. Once he had her inside and locked up, then they'd see about getting the cuffs off. Until he had her secure, though, there was no way he was letting her go. He already felt as if the woman was one moment away from jumping and running.

It was harder to jump and run when you were attached to another person.

"What's the safe house going to be like?" Kat wanted to know.

"Not the five-star hotels or the lavish mansions that you're used to, I'm afraid. But it will do."

A huff. "How do you know what I'm used to?"

Because he'd seen her file. Her very thick file. Instead of saying that, though, he told her, "Because I can read a gossip website. I saw all the pics of you and your family. The fancy cars. The expensive clothes. Everything bought with dad's blood money."

She flinched.

And he felt like an ass. "Kathleen—"

"I told you to call me Kat. It's my name. And you know what? I'm tired. It's been one hell of a day and night, and if it's all the same to you and whoever is up there driving this SUV—"

Carter was driving. Carter Styles. But Carter knew when to stay silent. This was one of those silent times.

"I'm going to sleep. Wake me up when we get to the safe house, all right?"

She turned away. Put her head against the window. Closed her eyes.

Shut him out.

"All right, princess," he murmured. "I'll do that."

Silence stretched in the vehicle. The SUVs were dispersing, just as planned. Carter drove through the city and Rick glanced back, making sure he didn't see a tail on them. The road appeared dark and empty behind him.

And beside him, Kat's breathing was soft and gentle.

Time passed. More miles. More turns and twists. They weren't heading straight to their destination. The goal was to throw off anyone who might be after her, so a few tricks were needed.

"That's really her, huh?" Carter asked, voice gruff and quiet.

"Yeah, it's her." Rick's gaze had returned to Kat.

"She's even prettier than in the photos."

Rick stiffened. "Didn't realize you were a fan."

"I-I'm not, I mean...after her dad was killed, her pictures were everywhere. Everyone remembers what she looked like when she came out of that restaurant, her father's blood on her dress."

Yes, that image had been everywhere.

"Do you think it's true that the guy killed her dad because the shooter was in love with Kat—"

"She's not sleeping, so how about we cut the chit-chat, okay, Carter?" He'd caught the faint hitch in her breath at the mention of her father. Probably not a memory she enjoyed reliving. Yes, she'd been at the restaurant when her father had been gunned down. And no, he had no clue if the shooter had been in love with her or not.

Her head turned toward Rick. He met her stare.

Carter cleared his throat. "Uh, here's our stop."

About freaking time.

Carter steered the SUV into a parking garage. Braked. "Do you need any—"

"Just get the hell out of here. I've got her." A rough edge entered his voice as he pulled Kat from the car. A moment later, she shivered as she stood next to him, and they watched the SUV's tail-lights disappear as it left the garage.

"He's a chatty one," Kat announced.

Rick grunted.

"And you're not."

He pulled a set of keys from his pocket. Hit the button to unlock their ride—

The lights flashed on a nearby sports car. Sleek and fast, but big enough to accommodate his long frame. He headed toward it—she did a quick run to keep up with him—and Rick opened the driver side door. "You need to crawl into the passenger seat."

She scrunched up that gorgeous face of hers. "Why not just take the cuffs *off*?"

"Because we're not in a safe location yet. If eyes were on Wilde, then word is spreading to look for the black SUVs. Carter will keep driving around the city, he'll leave a bullshit trail, while you and I vanish in a new ride."

"This *ride* isn't exactly low key."

"I wanted fast, so I got it."

"Adrenaline junkie," she accused. But she bent and climbed into the car. As she shimmed her way over the console, he got one fine and up-close view of her ass.

He tried not to drool. Holy—

"Hope you're enjoying the view."

He was. Only he felt guilty as shit so Rick whipped his gaze away. But then the cuff yanked against his wrist and his stare shot right back to her. She'd settled into the passenger seat. Her hair tumbled over her shoulders as the vehicle's interior light fell on her.

She cocked her head. "I expect to be given a similar view later."

Oh, did she? "Princess, you can check out my ass any time you like." He slid behind the wheel. Adjusted the seat to give him as much leg room as possible, and then had the engine purring to life. A sexy, beautiful purr.

He whipped them out of there. Flew through the city. No one was following them. No one could.

"He didn't love me."

Rick braked at a red light.

"The shooter—I didn't even know him. He was some hired hit guy. He came in, took aim at my dad, and blasted. The blood hit me, and I screamed, and he just walked away."

Fuck. "I'm sorry." The light changed, and he flew forward.

"Why?" Her voice was brittle. "My father was a monster. Everyone says so. I'm pretty sure some folks were even celebrating in the street when they found out he was dead."

Okay, that was true but... "I'm sorry because he wasn't a monster to you."

"Don't be so sure about that."

Her words were so soft he wasn't certain he even heard them. But his gaze flew to her.

She was staring out of the window. "Seven days, huh?"

He got his eyes back on the road.

"Staying with me—day and night like that—it's going to be hell for you."

"Thanks for the warning."

"My pleasure."

He wouldn't smile. "You won't get away from me, you know."

"I don't know any such thing." A pause. "And what makes you think I was even thinking about running?"

Rick thought it because he wasn't an idiot. "You shouldn't run. Not unless you want to die."

They needed to get this shit straight right now. "I'm the only thing standing between you and a bullet. You want to keep living? Then you'll play by my rules."

"I'm not really big on rules."

Like he hadn't already noticed. "Too bad. I freaking love them."

"Surprise, surprise..."

"My rules are pretty simple."

"I can't wait to hear them."

He drove through the city. After a while, it was time to turn from the bright lights. To slip away. The road stretched before him as the skyscrapers and their lights faded into the distance. "Rule one, do what I tell you."

"You mean follow all of your orders?"

That was exactly what he meant. "Follow my orders and you'll keep living." Simple fact.

"I suspect you just *like* giving orders."

"I do. But in this case, with you, I'm trying to make sure you continue breathing."

"Then by all means, do share rule number two."

She was mocking him. His hands tightened around the steering wheel. "Rule two, no outside communication. You won't be calling anyone, you won't be visiting anyone, and you sure as shit won't be taking secret messages to anyone."

A quick inhale. "I have no idea what you mean."

"Princess, do I look like some dumbass FBI agent?"

"Is this a trick question?"

"We sent Wilde agents to the bakery. Your so-called brownie run was bullshit. We know you borrowed a phone from some jerk you flirted with while you were there. We know you made a phone call. It's only a matter of time until we figure out *who* you called."

"Well, aren't you part of the most thorough security agency around?"

"We *do* try to be thorough," he allowed.

"Your rules are tiring me out."

"Too bad, because we're only getting started..." He hit the remote that had been hidden in the console, and a big gate opened. They were away from the city. Away from neighbors. On a long stretch of road. He'd be able to see anyone coming. No surprises. "Rule three, you don't bullshit me." He advanced along the winding drive that would take them to the main house.

Not a mansion. Not some sprawling estate. A simple farmhouse that had been converted into one of Wilde's safe houses. Small on the outside, but filled with state-of-the-art tech on the inside.

He parked the car in the nearby garage. Had her do her sexy shimmy to get over the seat and console and out of the driver's side. When she stood, her body brushed against his. And, yeah, she still smelled too good. She hesitated against him, and her free hand rose to press against his chest. For a moment, he enjoyed the rush of having her so close. She was beautiful, after all. A walking fantasy. But...

"Rule four..."

"Seriously? We need to talk about your rule obsession."

"You're not going to use sex to get past my guard."

She blinked up at him. The moonlight shone down on her.

"Not going to happen, princess. You can brush your body against mine, you can lick that lower lip, you can try to work me to your heart's content, but I am going to do my job no matter what."

She slipped even closer to him. Her hand moved to curl behind his neck. Her breasts pressed to his chest. She lifted onto her tip-toes. Her tongue slid out and traced along her lower lip—

And his dick shoved hard against the front of his jeans.

"Oh, Rick..." She breathed his name like it was the best sin on earth. "If I were going to work you..."

His head leaned toward her.

Her lips were *almost* touching his. He could nearly taste her.

"If I were going to work you..." She leaned up and *bit* his lower lip. A light, sensual tug that sent desire surging through every cell of his body. "Trust me, your job would be the last thing on your mind." Then she shoved against him. Hard. "But I'm not interested, and you're insulting me *and* pissing me off."

He blinked at her.

"So how about we get inside, you get the cuffs off me, and I try really hard not to kill you tonight. Sound like a plan to you?"

CHAPTER THREE

The door shut behind Rick. He clicked all the locks in place. He set the alarm. He took his sweet, God-awful time about it all...

Kat narrowed her eyes on him. The jerk thought she'd seduce him into getting her freedom? Hello, high opinion. Why did it surprise her? She'd seen the online articles that people posted about her. She knew what was said. Sure, it was crap. Lies. But...

But it hurts. And Rick, damn him, had *hurt* her.

"All right, princess, time for your freedom."

She held out her hand. "I'm not a princess."

He pulled a key out of his pocket. It had been there the whole time? Hell, she could've slid the thing out while he was distracted. Way for her to be off her game. It was just because she was tired, that was all. Running on pure fumes. She'd grab a few hours' worth of sleep, then she'd hit the ground running—literally—the next day. She would not be staying Rick's prisoner.

His fingers brushed over her wrist. He slid the key into the tiny lock. *Snick.* The cuff popped open, and her breath rushed out in relief.

Before she could snatch her hand back, his fingers were curving around her wrist. His heavy brows pulled together. "Shit, I think you are going to have a mark." His thumb swiped over her wrist.

"Probably. I bruise easily."

His gaze met hers. "I'll remember that."

What? Why? She shook her head. "You are an insane man."

"And you're a gorgeous, tricky, possibly homicidal woman."

She wouldn't argue those points. "It's good we understand each other."

He rubbed her wrist again. "I'm sorry about your bruise. I'll be more careful with you in the future."

Aw, that was almost sweet. Kat batted her lashes at him. "I'm sorry that you're an ass, and I won't be more careful with you in the future."

He nodded and seemed to take the hit. "I shouldn't have said that part about you working me."

She stepped closer to him. "If I wanted to work you, you'd be on the floor, groveling."

"Think you're that irresistible, huh?"

"I think I can tell when a man wants me." Now she let her gaze drift down his body. *Wow.* "I, uh, would say the signs are there."

"My control doesn't break. I can want you and still keep my distance."

"Can you? Then why are you still massaging my wrist? Doesn't feel like distance."

He let her go.

The cuff dangled from his wrist.

"Your room is the second one down the hallway." He pointed. The cuff bounced. "You'll find clothes, toiletries, make-up...everything you need should be waiting on you."

"Aren't you the thorough one." Not a question. She turned away.

"You have no idea." Low, rough, sexy.

Her shoulders squared. It was past time to leave Rick's not-so-charming company. She put one foot in front of the other. Moved with the grace her mother had drummed into her years and years ago. *They expect you to be trash. Show them you're not. Show them that you can be anything.*

"It's only seven days." His voice drifted behind her. "Seven days and then you never have to see me again. Just remember, you have to follow my rules."

She'd spent a lifetime following rules. Now death was stalking her. There wasn't any time left for her. *I'm going to die, and I never lived.*

She was desperate, she was scared, and she was sure as hell going to break his rules.

If she stayed with him, if she just waited in that farmhouse, Kat knew exactly what would happen.

They'd both die.

***

He watched her walk away. Heard the soft creak of the floor beneath her feet and then the click of her bedroom door shutting. Rick pulled out his phone and called his boss—and good friend—Eric. Eric answered on the second ring.

"You're secure?" Eric's first question.

"The pampered princess is safe for the night. Are the other agents in place?" The eyes that would watch from a distance to make sure all threats were covered.

"They're guarding you right now."

Rick grunted. "Thanks."

"You're stocked with enough food and supplies to get you through the next week. Before you know it, she'll be out of your life."

Seven days. Hardly any time at all. "I think I'm gonna need a vacation after this one."

Eric laughed. "Trouble already?"

Trouble? He thought of her plump lips, the way she could make her voice go husky and trembly in a blink...and that truly world class ass of hers. "Kat is used to getting everything that she wants. She's going to find that I'm not the kind of guy she can just wrap around her finger because she smiles at me. It's wake up time for her."

Eric wasn't laughing any longer. "The danger around her is damn intense. If she's treating things like a game, she's going to wind up hurt."

"Not on my watch." The woman had been given two fucking teddy bears—the FBI agents—as protection. They'd let her get away with anything and everything. *Freaking brownie run?* But now she had a grizzly for protection.

No one would hurt her.

"Hmmm."

Rick didn't particularly like Eric's rumble. "What?"

"There's a whole lot about Kathleen O'Shaughnessy that's a mystery. The woman was kept out of the public eye for her entire life. Hell, a lot of folks didn't even know she existed, not until she ran out of that restaurant with her father's blood on her. She might look innocent—"

She didn't. Innocent was not a word that came to mind when Rick thought of her body, her lips, her eyes.

Sexy. Tempting.

Innocent? Not any day of the week.

"But I don't think she is," Eric added, voice gruff. "It's possible that her father was grooming her to take over the business. She could be every bit as dangerous as he was. For all we know, she's tricking the FBI. She *could* have been in on her father's murder, and when she vanished yesterday for that so-called bakery trip, she could've been checking in with her team."

And about that bakery run..."You trace the call she made yet?"

"We're having...a challenge."

"Bullshit." An immediate response. There was nothing that the Wilde tech team couldn't do.

"She called a burner. We were able to find the phone—its owner had ditched it. We're trying to figure out who purchased the phone and when, but turns out, the serial number on the thing matches a batch of burners that were reported stolen over a year ago. Considering her father's connections and the fact that she just called a phone, that, um, for all intents and purposes we'll just say 'fell off a delivery truck' somewhere...it's gonna take some time to figure out who she called."

"Shit." Rick hadn't wanted her to be evil. Why were the gorgeous, sexy ones always dangerous?

"Stay on guard with her. Don't believe anything she says."

Like he needed to be warned.

"Rick?" Eric seemed to be hesitating.

"What?"

"So, yes, this is going to sound, ah..."

He was stumbling. Very unlike Eric. "Just spit it out, man."

"I saw the way she looked at you, okay?"

Rick was lost. "And how was that?"

"Like a cat who'd just found a freaking delicious bowl of cream. The woman's eyes lit up, and she practically ran across the room to you."

No, she hadn't. Had she?

"Keep your guard up with her. She's..." Again, Eric hesitated.

Rick's jaw clenched. "You think she's gonna try and seduce me?"

Silence.

"I'm not a total dumbass. Don't worry. I've got this." He ran a hand over his jaw. "It's not amateur hour, here, buddy. I can keep my dick in my pants and my hands *off* her. I'm not about to fall prey to some—" He turned around and his words froze in his throat.

Because Kat was standing right there. Holy hell. She'd been behind him for *how* long? And why had the woman not made so much as a sound as she approached?

"Rick?" Tension sharpened Eric's voice. "What's wrong?"

"Nothing. Got to go, man. I'll check in with you tomorrow." He ended the call. Slapped the phone down on a nearby table. The cuff on his wrist bumped into the wood. Growling, he grabbed the key out of his pocket and practically ripped off the cuff before he shoved the handcuffs down near the phone. And all the while, Kat watched him with those deep, green eyes. "Is eavesdropping a hobby for you?" His gaze swept over her.

Her bare toes—the nails sporting a light blue polish—curled against the wood. "I didn't want to interrupt you while you were talking. That would have been poor manners. I was waiting patiently. Politely, if you will."

He lifted a brow. Crossed his arms over his chest.

"But I did learn some interesting things." Now her gaze dipped over his body. Lingered on his—

Hell, on his dick. The thing had shot up at the first sight of her.

"It's good to know that you can keep your dick in your pants," she told him, all prim and proper and earnest-like. "And that you can keep your hands off me."

His face burned. What in the hell? Since *when* did he blush about anything?

"But you stopped talking before you finished your last sentence." She stepped toward him. "You were saying you weren't going to fall prey to some...what? Some killer? Some cheap piece of ass?" Another step. "Some slut?"

His hands dropped. There had been pain in her words. He didn't like her pain. Not one bit. "No. That wasn't what I was going to say."

"Really? Because you wouldn't be the first to say any of those things. The media has been calling me a million names. And so have strangers. Everybody who reads my story on the web or in the papers—they all have opinions they love to share. Everyone thinks they know me. Criminal. Killer. Whore—"

"Stop it." He caught her hand. The urge to attack burned through him. But he didn't want to attack her. He wanted to attack anyone who'd said that shit. Anyone who'd hurt her. Anyone—

I hurt her. For just a moment, he could see the truth in her eyes. He'd hurt her.

He hadn't even thought that was possible.

He'd been wrong.

"I wasn't going to say any of those things." His hand swallowed hers. He looked down at her fingers. They looked so delicate, so elegant, while his were like frigging bear paws.

"Then what were you going to say?"

His gaze lifted. He gazed into her eyes and went with the truth. "I'm not going to fall prey to someone I am guarding. Even if she is the most beautiful woman I've ever seen."

Her lips parted, but she didn't speak.

He did. Rick found he had plenty to say. "The next time somebody calls you any name...you tell me. I'll kick the fool's ass."

"Why? Why would you care?"

"Protecting and defending. That's my job. That means no one hurts you in any way." *But I was the one who'd hurt her.* He'd be more careful.

"It's your job for seven days. After that, I'm someone else's problem."

He let go of her hand. Stepped back. Rubbed his chest. Why did it feel all funny? Probably because it had been one long-ass day and he needed to crash. "Why were you coming in here?" *Other than to eavesdrop?* Because he didn't buy that she hadn't wanted to listen to his conversation. He'd be more vigilant in the future.

"I was just coming to say thanks."

He waited.

"I am a pain in the ass. I get that. No big shocker. And I can be...hard to handle."

A quick laugh escaped him. The sound caught him off guard. He didn't laugh a lot.

"But I'll try not to drive you insane. You're doing your job. You don't deserve my anger when you're trying to help me." A ghost of a smile teased her lips. "I'll even try to play by your one hundred and one rules."

"I only gave you four rules."

Her head cocked. "Did you? It seemed like there were an awful lot more."

He was smiling. Eric had been so right. The woman was extremely dangerous.

"Good night, Rick," Kat said as she turned away.

He found himself rushing forward and curling his hand around her shoulder. "Wait."

She glanced back.

"Who'd you call?"

"I don't know what you—"

"No lies. Let's make that rule number five."

Her eyes narrowed.

"Tell me who you called when you vanished for that so-called brownie run. Because if you're working with someone, I need to know. Right now, you can't trust anyone but me, princess. Everyone from your old life wants you dead."

"Not everyone." She rolled her shoulders, and his hand fell back. "I called my old nanny, okay? I wanted to make sure she was all right. When all the craziness went down, I didn't exactly get a chance to check in with her."

"Your...nanny?" No way had he expected that response.

"Yes, Maria is seventy-three, and she doesn't need to get caught in this nightmare. I gave her the burner phone before the Feds dragged me away. I also gave her five thousand dollars and told her to get her ass on a plane back to Sicily. The phone call was to make sure she'd followed orders."

"Had she?"

"Yes. So I don't have to worry about Maria." Her long lashes swept down, concealing her gaze. "The last thing I wanted was for someone to try and hurt her...in order to get to me."

"Hurting your nanny would've hurt you?"

Her lashes flew up. "I am not a heartless bitch, thanks so much for asking. Maria raised me after my mother died. I was twelve when I buried my mother, and Maria was there for me after that. She was the closest person to me when I was a teen, so I wanted to make sure she was safe."

His gaze swept her face. "Huh."

"Huh? I'm kind of pouring my heart out to you, sharing all that I can, and you 'huh' me? Not cool." She marched for her bedroom.

He crossed his arms over his chest. "Wilde found the burner phone already. It wasn't in Sicily, so your *nanny* didn't take it there. You are lying to me, and it's important for me to know that you lie so well, you can do it without even a flicker of your expression. I'm impressed. You're world class."

Her shoulders stiffened. "You have no idea."

He was learning. Fast. "I'm guessing Maria never existed?"

She didn't look back. "My mother died when I was twelve. That part was absolutely true. I'm sure that's public record. Someone had to raise me after that."

"Your father."

A brittle laugh and a quick glance over her shoulder. "Like he had time. He was far too busy destroying the world to worry about me." A pause. "Good night, Rick."

"Good night, princess."

She spun toward him. "I'm *not—*"

"Good night, Kat." Softer.

She nodded.

"If you need me," Rick told her, "I'll be in the room right next to you."

"Why would I need you? How could anyone possibly find me here?" Her hand lifted and curled around the pearls she wore on her neck. "Besides, with big, bad you here, I'm sure that no one would dare try to get inside this place."

He stalked toward her. "You like mocking me?"

"No. But it's either that or burst into tears, and I've already cried plenty. I don't want to cry anymore. I just get headaches when I cry. And I'm an ugly crier. Really, really ugly."

He stiffened. Rick realized he didn't want to see her tears. Not because she was an ugly crier—he didn't think anything about her ever could be ugly—but because he didn't want to see her pain.

She reached for her doorknob. "The games can resume tomorrow. And maybe when we meet again, I'll have some rules for *you*."

"I look forward to hearing them."

She opened the door, but didn't go inside. Instead, Kat played with the pearls again. "You shouldn't. You shouldn't look forward to them at all."

CHAPTER FOUR

Kat held her breath as she flipped the lock on the front door. She'd already disengaged the security system—talk about a piece of cake. She'd watched Rick when he typed in the code, so now she had easy access to the control panel. She'd waited a few hours, giving herself a little while to sleep and recharge, but now she was on her way out of the farmhouse and out of the sexy bodyguard's life.

It was still an hour until dawn arrived. She'd sneak out under the cover of darkness and be long gone by the time Rick woke up.

After casting one quick glance over her shoulder, she opened the front door and stepped outside. The air was surprisingly brisk, and a shiver skated over her as the cold seemed to sink into her bones. She pulled the door shut, her gaze already darting toward the garage. She'd get the sports car, crank that baby up, and speed out of here before—

"Where do you think you're going?"

Jesus! She whirled. Her eyes locked on the big, shadowy form that was sprawled on one of the front porch chairs.

"Little early for a walk, don't you think?" Rick added, voice rasping.

Her heart was about to jump right out of her chest.

"But then, you're not going for a walk." He rose. Reached that towering, intimidating height and stalked toward her. "You actually thought you were going to sneak away on *my* watch."

The alarm had been set. He'd set it before going outside? Was this whole little scene a trap? Because it sure felt like one to her.

Rick stopped when he was less than a foot away from Kat. "What was the plan?"

Why waste time on a lie? "Get in the sports car. Get my ass out of here."

"You don't have keys."

"I don't need them." She'd learned to hotwire pretty much *any* ride out there when she'd just been a teen. No, some sweet, matronly nanny named Maria hadn't been looking out for her. Her father's guards had gotten her babysitting duty. They'd taught her lots of tricks she shouldn't know.

Hotwire a car in less than ten seconds? Check.

Break a man's arm in twelve different places with barely a flick of her hand? Check.

Shoot a target dead center from fifty yards away? Check again.

Use a knife to inflict maximum pain on your prey—

Unfortunately, check. The memories swirled around her, and she had to swallow back the lump in her throat.

"Hotwiring, hmm? I'll remember that you have hidden talents." He sighed. A long and frustrated sound. The same sound her soul was making. Then he said, "Kat, if you're going to run every time you think my back is turned, I'll have to haul out the cuffs again."

To be clear..."I didn't think your back was turned. I thought you were asleep." There was a distinct difference between the two things.

A rough laugh broke from him. The laugh made her shoulders stiffen. His laugh was all rusty and growly, and for some reason, she liked it.

Weird. Crazy.

"You need to get back inside," Rick told her, voice almost kind. Almost. For him, anyway. "Because you're not going anywhere without me."

He stared at her.

She glared at him. "You are going to make my life very difficult."

"I'm going to keep you alive. And you're welcome. Even though you quite obviously have some kind of death wish going on..."

"I don't."

"No? Leaving your only protection under the cover of darkness? Running out without a plan in place? Without a safe haven waiting? Yeah, that screams...*I don't take risks.*"

They faced off. Her hands were balled into fists on her hips.

His arms were crossed over that giant chest of his.

"You are pissing me off," she snapped.

"And you're going to drive me crazy. But I guess we have to learn to live with each other, hmm? So how about getting that sweet ass back inside. You're shivering, and I don't want you catching a cold."

He didn't want her catching a cold? Like *that* was what she was worried about. *Note to self. The new security guy likes lurking in the dark. Be aware.* "I don't want to have to hurt you."

"Princess...really? You think you can?"

She knew she could. "I'm getting out of here."

He laughed. "Nope. Not happening. It's not—"

She launched at him, moving fast, and her attack must have caught him by surprise because he stumbled back even as his hands came up and—

Whoosh. She felt the air pulse around her right before the wood on the side of the farmhouse exploded. For a moment, Kat froze. She tried to process what was happening. That sound...the wood...

Her head swiveled toward the wood. She looked at the angle. *A bullet.* It hadn't been an explosion. It had been a bullet slamming into the wood and sending fragments of the wooden wall splintering. *OhmyGod.* That spot...if she hadn't just shoved Rick back...that spot would have been...*the bullet would've gone through his head before it hit the house.*

While she was processing that very scary thought, Rick grabbed her. He scooped her into his arms, hunched his shoulders around her, and hauled ass back into the farmhouse. She didn't even have a chance to scream because in the next instant, they were inside. He kicked the door shut. Locked it. Ran toward the back of the place. Put her down in the kitchen, behind the big, wooden bar.

"Dammit to hell," Rick snarled. "Someone shot at us!"

He started to lunge up, but Kat grabbed his arm. "No, someone shot at *you!* That bullet lodged into the wood where *your* head would have been, not mine."

His dark eyes narrowed.

"So don't get any ideas about playing hero. Keep your butt in here with me! Stay covered. Stay low and—"

"I'm not the hero, princess. I'm just the guy who needs to kick some ass." He pulled away.

She grabbed for him again. "I know you have other agents out there! Let them handle this!" He was a target. What part of that was Rick not getting? The bullet had been meant for him! Him, not her.

He looked down at her hand. Looked back up at her. "Didn't realize you cared so much."

She...didn't. *Didn't*, of course.

"Don't worry, I'll be right back." His eyes were hard and so incredibly dark. "While I'm gone, you keep *your* sexy ass down, understand me? You stay here until I get back."

He leaned forward, and she thought he was going to kiss her. Thought he was going to put that gorgeous mouth of his on hers, and she tensed, scared and excited and a million other things.

But he turned away.

No.

She grabbed him right back. And Kat pressed her mouth to his.

She felt shock surge through him. Hard to miss it with the sudden stiffening of his body. So he was shocked. So what? His lips parted beneath hers. A growl broke from him, and the sound sent a shiver over her whole body. His tongue swept into her mouth, and desire exploded within her.

She'd initially grabbed him and kissed him to stop the crazy guy from running right back into gunfire. But now...

Now all she could think about was his mouth. The way his kiss made her feel. The way need surged through her whole body. A wild, reckless hunger that she hadn't experienced in so very long.

He pulled her against him, hauling her onto his lap as they crouched behind the counter, and her legs locked around his hips. His mouth was frantic on hers, and the man sure knew how to use his lips and tongue. No sloppy, slamming kiss. Just pure, white-hot perfection. Her legs curled around his hips as she straddled him, and there was no missing the hard, ever-growing length of his cock as it shoved against her. She rubbed against him, and this time, she was the one to growl. Or maybe it was more of a moan. Or—

"*Rick!*" A bellow that came from the front of the house. "Rick, are you hit?"

Um...

Rick tore his mouth from hers. He stared at her, breath panting, eyes even darker than before. His eyes blazed with a savage desire.

Her heart pounded in her chest. She licked her lips. Tasted him. And wanted more.

Problem. Big problem.

Footsteps raced toward them. She was still on top of Rick, and, yep, still straddling him. His hands were clamped around her hips, holding her in place.

"Rick, damn, man, tell me that you weren't shot!" The kitchen door flew open.

"He wasn't shot," Kat managed to say. Her voice was a wee bit high and breathy.

Her head turned. The footsteps were right beside them now, and so was the guy. Not quite as big as Rick. Tall, tattooed, and wearing an absolutely shocked expression, the man gaped at them. His dark brows climbed as he took in Kat, Rick, and their current position.

She needed to say something. "He was trying to run back into the line of fire." Her hands were on Rick's shoulders now. Such big, wide shoulders. *Yum.* She thought that so often around him. She had to get her shit together. The man was not an ice cream that she was going to eat. Kat cleared her throat. "So I distracted him."

The newcomer nodded. "Looks like you did one hell of a job."

She gave him a smile. She had thought that she'd done a pretty good job. *Go, me!*

"You *distracted* me?" Rick seemed to be choking.

Uh, oh. Her gaze darted back to him. Someone sure looked pissed. "I distracted you, but I really enjoyed it. Far more than I expected."

His gaze widened. "What?"

"You're an amazing kisser, Rick. Didn't expect that. Won't be forgetting it anytime soon."

He shook his head. Stared at her as if she was mad. "We're being shot at!"

The tattooed guy coughed. "The shooter is gone. High-tailed it out on an ATV. We've got agents tracking him, but he's got a big head start on us."

"He got away." Rick squeezed his eyes shut. His hold on Kat tightened. "He got away because I was making out with the princess."

He didn't need to sound so disgusted. "You can let go now," she told him, aware that a bite of frost had entered her tone.

He let go. She rose. So did he. He towered over her. Glared. The man loved his glares.

She gave him her sunniest smile in response. "You're welcome. I saved your ass from a lethal shot. Then I distracted you and kept you from running into a bullet. You owe me so much right now." Her heart was still double-timing it. Her fingers were also shaking, so she balled them into fists and propped them on her hips.

Rick's jaw locked. It took him a moment, but he gritted, "I'm not the target. *You* are. You didn't do anything but stop me from apprehending one of the many people who want you dead."

Yes, there was a rather long line of folks, but… "That bullet was aimed at you, not me." Why did she have to keep reminding him of that?

"You sure about that? Did you stop to consider that maybe the shooter just had shitty aim?"

"The mob doesn't usually hire shitty shooters. They hire professionals."

Tattooed and gorgeous cleared his throat.

Kat and Rick both looked at him.

"Ah, yeah, um, all signs are that it was a single shooter. He was waiting on the ridge."

"I was on the porch at least thirty minutes while I waited on her to come out," Rick snapped. "If I was the target, he could've hit me at any time. The guy was gunning for *her*."

Oh, Rick had just been waiting for her? Lurking so he could catch her? Because he knew her so well? For the moment, Kat ignored the fact that he had caught her. "You were in the chair, hidden in the dark. The sniper wouldn't have been able to take a kill shot from that angle. He waited on you to move, to come into his range, and then he fired." She knew her shots. A sniper had been one of her best buds back in the day. "Like I said before, if I hadn't miraculously saved your sorry butt, you'd have a bullet in the brain right now. I *still* haven't heard a thank you."

"You didn't save me! You attacked me! You thought you could knock me down and run away!"

Kat rolled one shoulder. "Call it what you will, the result is the same."

"Call it what I..." Rick shook his head. "No. For now, I'm done with this." He spun toward the other agent.

At least, Kat figured the other guy was an agent. Though with all of those dark, swirling tattoos, his tousled hair, and those bright eyes...he didn't *look* like the boring security type she'd seen before.

Kat gave him a little wave.

Without looking away from the other man, Rick reached out and grabbed her hand. He swallowed it in his bear claw. "You are not to flirt with Cole. You are not to do your routine of winding security personnel around your little finger."

"Are those rules six and seven?"

His hold tightened. She took that as a yes.

"Kathleen..." Rick snapped out her name. "This is Cole Vincent. He's my partner on your case."

"Hello, Cole Vincent."

His eyes gleamed for just a moment with humor. "Hello, Kathleen O'Shaughnessy."

"My friends call me Kat. You can call me—"

"He is not your friend," Rick interrupted. "He's an agent who is going to do his damn best to keep you alive."

Kat nodded. "Good to know."

Rick's body moved a little closer to hers. His attention remained fixed on Cole. "How the hell did the shooter find her?"

"No idea," Cole replied.

"How did he get past the agents?" Rick's frustration was obvious.

She knew how he'd gotten past them. "Because he's a professional," Kat muttered. "Because he gets paid to kill people for a living. This isn't his first time. He's a hired gun who knows how to do his job. Appear and disappear, just like a..." Oh, crap. "Ghost." She swallowed, twice. "*Ghost*. It could be him. He always did like the hard cases."

Rick and Cole were both staring at her. Waiting. What? Oh, right. Ghost was known in criminal circles. Most civilians didn't know about him. "Ghost is a hired gun who used to work for my father. Very much a rogue kind of fellow. I thought he'd quit the business, but for the right money, I guess anyone can come out of retirement." She shoved a lock of hair behind her ear. "He specialized in getting access to remote locations. The guy could sit still for hours before he took a shot and after he took the shot..." She snapped her fingers together. "Bam. He was gone. Vanished in a blink, and you did *not* see him again."

Cole whistled. "No wonder the Feds want you testifying in court. Just how much do you know about the East Coast crime families?"

Pretty much everything. She'd been extremely good at watching and listening. At staying quiet and out of the way. After a while, everyone had seemed to forget that she was there.

She'd never forget all the things she'd seen.

The screams still haunted her.

So, yes, there was a long line of people who wanted her dead. Rats died, after all. That was known in her world. But she had always hated that world, and she couldn't just let the guilty keep getting away with what they'd done.

"Does Ghost have a real name?" Rick's expression was thoughtful.

"I'm sure he does, but not one that I know. But maybe you can use those Wilde connections of yours to figure it out." She'd been more than helpful already.

"On it," Cole said as he yanked out his phone.

She tried to pull away from Rick. He didn't let her go.

"How did he find you?" Rick demanded.

"I have no idea." Her stomach twisted. She ignored the twist. "I guess the multiple SUV plan wasn't as fool-proof as you thought. I mean, he must have followed us from Wilde."

"No. We weren't followed." His gaze swept over her.

"Uh, well, we *must* have been followed. Not like I had a phone so that I could call and give away the location. And I didn't get to sneak off anywhere—"

She stopped. His expression had just darkened. Cole was in the corner, talking quietly into his phone. Rick edged toward her. Because she didn't particularly like the look in his eyes, she backed up. She kept backing up until her butt hit a drawer.

"You *were* sneaking off when I caught you on the porch. Was that the plan? Did you make arrangements to meet up with this Ghost person?"

"He was *shooting*. Not waiting to take me on a date. And, no, I didn't make any arrangements with him." *If* it had been Ghost.

"But you were trying to sneak away."

Guilty. "Because I thought I wasn't safe here with you. Obviously, I was right. The Feds can't be trusted. Wilde agents can't be trusted. Everywhere I go, people are selling me out." Didn't he get it? Frustration tore at her. "I can't trust anyone. There is too much money on my head. For the right price, most people would sell out their own families, much less a stranger. I'm a dead woman walking. If I'm going to survive this thing, I do it on my own. I do it—"

His hand rose and curled round her throat. What in the hell?

His fingers stroked lightly along the column of her throat. "Your pulse is racing like crazy."

"It does that when I'm scared as hell."

His touch was oddly soothing. "You keep getting tracked. The FBI changed your location multiple times, but you were still hunted..."

"Because agents were selling me out!"

"There are no FBI agents here. The shooter arrived too fast. There has to be something else..." His callused fingertips slid down her throat.

She shivered. Couldn't help it. Her throat had always been way too sensitive.

"You didn't bring anything with you but the clothes on your back," he murmured. His fingers were at the base of her throat. "I searched those while you showered."

What?

"But you also brought this necklace." He caught her pearl necklace with the edge of his index finger.

Cole wasn't talking on his phone any longer. He was edging closer to them.

Her hand rose and closed over Rick's. "It was my mother's necklace."

"And you got it...when?"

"When she died," Kat bit out. "My father gave it to me. It's the only thing of hers that I have."

His expression darkened. "Let me guess, you wear it all the time."

"Yes." She did.

"Princess, I'm sorry..." She could feel his hold tightening on the necklace.

Horror flooded through her. "No! Don't you *dare* do anything to my necklace! Don't—"

"Take it off."

"Get your hands *off* me!"

"Uh, Rick..." Cole cleared his throat. "How about we all settle down?"

Rick didn't even spare him a glance. His dark stare was locked fully on Kat. "Take the necklace off or I will take it off you."

How had she thought there was anything good or sexy about him? He was a straight-up monster. One bastard of a beast. "Are you *insane*? This was my mother's!" She'd told him that already. "My father wanted me to have it. He gave me one thing. *One good thing* to remember my mother, and this was it. It was the only time my dad ever got sentimental with me. The only time he seemed to *care*." She was saying too much. She needed to stop. Needed to pull the hell back.

But this was important. The necklace was the only link she had to her mother, and it was the only thing that let her believe her father had cared at all.

Rick's face could have been carved from stone. "Your father, by all accounts, was a sadistic psychopath."

She flinched. The truth freaking hurt.

"So for him to give you a sentimental necklace doesn't fit with what I know about him." His words were soft, yet they hit her with a brutal impact. "That doesn't fit, Kat, and I'm sorry. But you know what does make sense to me?"

She didn't want to know.

"He was a control freak, and I could see a man like him wanting to lojack his daughter. I could see someone like him wanting to have the ability to track his only child at every single moment. *That* goes along with the control freak that I think he was."

She couldn't breathe. "No."

"The shooter shouldn't have been at the farmhouse. You shouldn't have been traced this fast. I don't make mistakes like this. Wilde doesn't. The necklace is the common denominator between Wilde and the FBI agents." His jaw hardened even more before he gruffly ordered, "Take it off or I take it off you."

"You are such a dick!" Why had she kissed him? "I should've let you get shot!"

She shoved at his hand. Their fingers tangled. She felt the clasp of the necklace bite into the back of her neck. Then—

No!

The pressure at the back of her neck was gone. He'd pulled the necklace off her. Fury poured through Kat as she grabbed hard for his hand.

She saw the flash of remorse on his face. He should feel remorse. Their hands tangled again— and the pearls fell to the floor.

A slow motion, *please-God-no* fall to the floor.

They hit. The pearls rolled across the floor. She stared in horror and felt her eyes welling. The only thing she'd had from her mother. The *only* time her father had seemed to not be a cold-blooded monster.

"Kat," Rick's voice was even rougher. "I'm sorry."

She was going to make him sorry. "Not yet, but you will be."

He bent. Picked up a few pearls. Fisted his hand around them. "I can get the necklace back together, I can fix it. I can—*fuck*." He surged toward the kitchen counter. In a lightning-fast move, he put the pearls he'd just gathered on the marble surface and then slammed his hand on the pearls, crushing them.

"Stop!" Kat yelled. Hadn't he done enough? Damn him! She grabbed his arm and wrenched back. The pearls were a mess and...

"Lojacked," Rick muttered as he stared at the pearls he'd just crushed. "We have to get the hell out of here. *Now*."

There was something inside one of the pearls. It was small. So tiny, but it looked like...like a...*microchip?* Yes, some kind of computer chip. It was incredibly small. It was—

"A tracking chip," Cole spoke from behind her. "Looks like your father always knew where you were, Kat, every minute of the day and night, and now that he's out of the picture, someone is using his tech to hunt you down."

Their words beat at her. She couldn't look away from the chip. So small. It had been hidden in a fake pearl. When the necklace had broken, when the pearls had hit the kitchen tiles, the fake pearl had cracked, revealing the truth.

Not even that one moment with my father was real. He lied then, too.

"Has to be someone in his inner circle," Rick mused. "Someone who knew how he kept track of his daughter."

She backed away from them.

Rick's hand flew out and curled around her wrist. "I'm sorry."

"Screw you." Her only response. Pain was knifing through her. For some reason, his apologies made her hurt more. "Don't say you're sorry again. You were right, weren't you?"

His lips thinned before he said, "I'll fix the necklace, I promise. I'll send it to Wilde. I'll get them to make sure no more trackers are in any of the pearls. I'll get it back for you and then—"

"I don't want it." Didn't want another lie around her neck.

His fingers slid along her inner wrist. Moved over the faint bruise there with a careful caress. "I have to get you out of here, Kat. This location is compromised."

Everything in her life was compromised. Didn't he get that?

"The shooter could've seen the sports car. We can't take that ride." His gaze shot to Cole. "The bike ready to go?"

Bike? Her ears perked up a little.

Cole nodded. His expression seemed extra grim. "You need to haul ass. *Now*. I'll wait with a clean-up crew to see if anyone else shows for the target."

Then things happened fast. Very fast to her numb mind. They ran out of the farmhouse, with Cole beside them, his gun out. Other agents were there, too. She caught glimpses of them right before Rick shoved open the garage door. Once inside, he threw a tarp to the side and revealed a gleaming, black beast of a motorcycle.

Right. Ah... "I'm not riding that."

"You are because it will get us out of here hell fast. We can go off road, we can snake through the dark before dawn arrives, and I can keep you safe." He pushed a helmet at her. "Put this on and climb onto the bike."

"No 'please' from you?"

He looked at her in confusion.

"Right. Because you don't know how to ask. You just give cold orders. You are so charming. I can't believe women aren't beating down your door."

His brows lowered. "Would you *please* put on the helmet and *please* climb that hot ass of yours onto the motorcycle so we can get out of here before more people with guns come to try and kill you?"

"You have an obsession with my ass." She fiddled with the helmet. Couldn't think of any other way out of the situation except the bike. "Since you asked so nicely..." She climbed onto the bike.

"Scoot up."

Why? She'd left plenty of room for him in front of her.

"I'm your human shield, baby. You think I'm going to put you behind me? No way. I cover you." He patted the seat. "Scoot. Up." A pause. *"Please."*

She scooted up. Her hands curled around the handlebars.

He slid on behind her. Rick immediately covered her back, her side, her pretty much everything. "I'll drive. I can reach easily from here."

Yeah, because he was huge.

"You just sit back—" Rick began.

"If you say 'and relax' then I will have to hurt you." Her shoulders pressed back against him. "I'll be doing the driving. You just hold on."

"You can handle a motorcycle?"

She laughed at that question. "I can handle anything."

His hands moved to curl around her stomach. "I'll remember that."

She revved the bike, enjoyed that purring engine, and she nodded toward Cole.

"I'll tell you where to go," Rick said, voice rising over that purr. "And you don't stop until we get to the next safe house. No matter what, got me?"

"Just hold on," Kat replied. "Because this ride could get rough."

His hold tightened. "Tell me something I haven't already figured out."

CHAPTER FIVE

"Yeah, yeah, I want eyes on the farmhouse. Make sure the GPS is still transmitting, and let's see who the hell shows up. Make sure the FBI is invited to the party. They might want to welcome some of those visitors." Rick kept a tight grip on the phone as he stared out at the city and the rising sun. They'd double-timed it back to Atlanta and rushed into another of the Wilde safe houses before the city woke up. They were nestled in an old bar, one that had shut down last year. From the exterior, the building looked normal. A little ramshackle. Not much to see. But inside, Wilde had tech-blinged the hell out of the place.

He was currently on the second floor, staring out of one-way windows.

"So are we thinking that the FBI didn't sell her out?" Cole asked, his voice filling Rick's ear. "That she was just tracked by the necklace?"

"I'm not ready to say that. I don't trust the Feds, not completely."

"Neither do I." Cole's response wasn't surprising. The man was definitely anti-Fed most days.

"The shooter got away, and that pisses me off."

"Was he gunning for you—or her?"

I hate to say this but... "I think Kat was right. I think he was shooting at me."

"Why? She's the big game. The price on her head is supposed to be sky high. Why waste a bullet on her protection detail?"

A good question. One he wanted answered. In the meantime..."Let me know who gets caught in the net." Someone else would be showing up at the cabin, he was sure of it.

"Keep your eyes on her," Cole tossed back. "Eyes, hands...looked like you had all kinds of things on her earlier."

"Go fuck yourself."

Cole laughed before he hung up.

Rick tossed the phone onto the table. Then he glanced at the wall of security monitors to the right. Everything was quiet outside. Nothing unusual. Nothing suspicious. The motorcycle was parked downstairs, inside the building. Out of sight and ready to use if they needed to flee again.

He didn't want to run blindly. He wanted a plan.

He wanted—

Her. I fucking want her. Rick had a flash of being back in the kitchen with Kat. With her on his lap. His hands on her hips. His tongue in her mouth. He'd been ravenous for her. Blind to everything but the lust he felt. And she—had she felt the same way? Had she only been playing him? Hell, he didn't know what she'd been doing.

But it was time to find out.

He spun around and marched for her room. She'd gone in there shortly after they'd arrived, and he'd left her alone because he knew that he had to check in with the other Wilde agents. He'd needed to get a security detail on the bar. Rick wanted other agents watching the building. Not that other agents had done much good the last time they'd been attacked, but he still wanted those extra eyes on the exterior scene.

He reached her door, twisted the knob, and swung it open. "We need to talk, right the hell—"

Panties. Bra. That's all she wore. A black bra and matching panties. Her full breasts pushed against the silky cups, and the tiny panties that she had on barely covered her. She was all long limbs and curves and perfect temptation. And he was staring. Gaping.

Maybe drooling.

Get your shit together, man.

He spun away, turning his back on her. "I didn't know you were...changing."

"Well, I didn't know you were just going to barge in like you owned the place, so color us both surprised."

He swallowed. Three times. Flexed and fisted his hands. "I do."

"You do—what?"

"I own the place. Technically. I mean, I let Wilde use it for a safe house spot, and in return, Eric stocked it with tech, but the place is mine." He caught himself turning to look back at her. "Will you tell me when you're dressed?"

"I'm dressed."

His breath rushed out. "Thank Christ." He whirled toward her.

She was still in her panties and bra.

His eyes squeezed closed. His dick shoved toward her. "You are not dressed."

"I'm not naked. That means I'm dressed."

Rick shook his head. "You're playing a dangerous game."

"That's the only kind of game I know how to play."

"You're trying to seduce me."

"Yes. I thought that was obvious when I decided to keep standing in front of you just wearing my underwear."

His eyes flew open. "You like jerking me around?" Anger pulsed inside of him. So did desire. Damn. The things he wanted to do to her...*with* her...

It's a game. She doesn't want you. A woman like her wouldn't go for you in a million years.

"I'm not jerking you around." She made a mistake. She came closer.

Don't do it. If I reach out...I'll take. She didn't get that he wasn't the kind of guy who played. If he put his hands on her again, she was his. "Why are you doing this? Do you like to tempt every guy you—"

"Don't say insulting things that you will regret later."

His lips clamped together. He didn't want to think about her with any other guy. Not ever. He just wanted her. And that vanilla scent was all around him because she was right in front of him.

"I liked the kiss earlier," Kat told him softly.

I more than liked it. His chin lifted. "Bullshit. You kissed me to distract me. You wanted me to stay in the farmhouse with you." And so much for being Mr. Cool and In Control. Because he'd felt her mouth against his and he'd gone straight to blazing hot. *Burn, baby. Burn.*

"I did kiss you to distract you."

He could *not* have this talk with her while she was clad in those pieces of silk. He jerked his shirt off and tugged her forward.

"Uh, Rick, what are you—"

He pulled the shirt over her head, and the garment swallowed her. At least she was covered, though.

"This is...fabulous." She glanced down at the t-shirt that hung past her thighs.

"I can't talk to you when you're naked."

"I wasn't naked, for the second time, and you weren't supposed to talk. You were supposed to kiss me, and we were going to see if things became just as hot as they had before." Now her stare rose to pin his. "Except...I think you're afraid."

"Princess, I'm not afraid of anything."

She pulled up the t-shirt that he'd damn well just put on her and tossed it to the floor. Sonofabitch.

"I think you're afraid of wanting me."

He kept his eyes on hers. *Do not look down.* "I have a job to do. The job is to keep you safe. Not to fuck you."

"Why can't you do both?"

Why couldn't—"Seriously? Why the hell do you even want me?" Rick knew he wasn't handsome. He didn't look like some of the pretty-boy jerks he'd seen in bars. He was scary as hell. Too big, too rough, too dangerous. Too wild. And she was just going to stand there and offer her body to him? No. He didn't buy it. *She likes her games, and she's screwing with me.*

But her gaze didn't waver from his. "I want you because I like the way you make me feel." Her hand rose and pressed to her heart. "When we were kissing, I felt like my heart was about to race out of my chest. Heat filled me, and I ached. I wanted you, and I haven't wanted someone that much in a very, very long time."

Right. "That's not what the stories say." His hands had fisted again.

"You should know better than to believe everything you hear."

"I believe the intel that Wilde gives to me. You're a mob princess. Protected and pampered, and I'm sure you've had more lovers than—" No, screw that. He was *not* going to think of her with other lovers. Because when he thought of that, he wanted to fuck someone up.

"You don't know me. Wilde doesn't know me." She turned away. Grabbed a robe from the bed and pulled it on. Thank Christ. "And I think I was wrong about *you.*"

She was covered up, and he was extremely grateful that Wilde kept the place stocked with emergency clothes for men and women. Now that she wasn't only in her bra and panties, he could breathe again. Mostly. "I told you already, I'm not going to be another guy that you wrap around your finger. Maybe seduction is your game of choice, but it's not mine."

Her shoulders stiffened. Then she turned and faced him once more. Her face was completely without expression as she advanced toward him.

Her hand lifted, and her index finger stabbed into his chest. "Seduction isn't a game. None of this is a game." Another stab. "I'm running out of time. Is it so wrong to think that I wanted to live a little before I—" But she broke off. Her index finger stopped stabbing. Her hand fell back to her side. "Forget it. I want to get a little sleep, all right? Just leave me alone for a while."

He didn't move. "You wanted to live a little—before what?"

She stared at him.

And he knew. "You think you're gonna die."

"Well, I do have about a dozen targets on my back right now."

"You also have *me*. I'm not going to let anyone hurt you." His hand lifted. A lock of her hair had fallen over her cheek, and he brushed it back behind her ear. His hand lingered against her cheek. So smooth. So soft.

"That's why the first shot was aimed at you, Rick." Her eyes were such a deep green. He didn't know if he'd ever seen that particular shade of emerald with anyone else. "Because the people after me know that you have to be taken out. And they'll do it. They'll kill you so it will be easier to get me."

"I'm not dying."

"You could've died at the farmhouse. It's luck that you're standing in front of me right now. If I hadn't shoved you—"

Time to come clean. "I'd spotted the shooter right before you lunged at me. Saw the gleam of moonlight reflected off his gun. I was about to shove you down when you attacked first."

Her left eyebrow rose. She doubted him. Wasn't that cute?

Or insulting. He wasn't sure which yet.

"I thought it would be a shame," she whispered, "for you to die. For me to die...for us to go out without knowing just how amazing we would be together."

Okay. She was about to shred his control. If she kept saying sexy and sweet things like that, looking up at him with those eyes that promised so much...

Back away. She's pulling you into her web.

He didn't move. "Amazing, huh?"

"I'm fucking spectacular."

That matched up with his fantasies, check.

"And I'm betting you are, too. The heat we felt with that kiss—it was something special. I'm not going to pretend that I don't want you. I do. The only question is...Rick, do you want me?"

More than he could remember wanting anyone. "Be careful." A low, savage warning. "You are playing with fire."

"How many times do I have to tell you, I'm not playing?" Her hair slid over her shoulders. "It's just us here. You and me. What happens between us can stay between us. A secret that is never shared. You don't have to worry about your boss at Wilde finding out. If you think you're crossing some kind of line—forget it. No one ever needs to know." A ghost of a smile curved her lips even as sadness flashed in her eyes. "I've gotten very good at keeping secrets when it comes to lovers."

"Okay...what the hell does that mean?" And why did he get so freaking pissed anytime he thought of her with someone else?

"Forget it. This...it was a mistake. I should've known better." Now she turned away and put some distance between them. "I just...I thought you felt the same way."

He felt damn near *insane* around her.

"Then when you came in, and you saw me...I could have sworn...I swore I saw..." Her words trailed away.

"You did see it, baby."

Her gaze swung to meet his as she spun toward him once more.

"I want you. You saw lust. Plain and simple. You're gorgeous. Every man you meet probably wants you."

She flinched.

He didn't like that. "Kat?"

"I felt lust, too. And I didn't expect it. And I didn't expect you. But it won't be a problem again."

Yeah, it was pretty much going to be a constant problem because when he looked at her, he needed.

Her safety comes first. Priority one.

"It's probably for the best." Her voice was so husky. "Bad things tend to happen to men who want me."

"What in the hell does that mean?" He found himself asking that question too often with her.

"I'm really tired. Can we talk later?"

He wasn't moving. "Kat."

"Fine!" Her breath heaved out. "I had my first lover when I was seventeen. *Seventeen.* He wanted me, I wanted him, and after a lifetime of being locked away, it was just good to be *free.* Only we weren't free. Because you know what happened to him when my dad found out about our relationship?"

Rick's muscles locked down.

"My dad had the boy beat to hell and back. *Because he touched me.* Because my charming father had plans for me. My dad wasn't going to let anyone mess up those plans. He wasn't going to let anyone close to me. But he's gone now, and I thought—maybe, *maybe* with the time I have left...maybe I can take something for myself."

Rick could barely breathe. "You only had one lover?" Some lucky kid who'd touched her and then gotten the ever-loving-hell beat out of him?

"Two lovers. Thanks for asking. Not like I asked you for blow-by-blow details on your exes." Her lips curved down. "The second guy was when I was twenty-one. I thought he loved me. Realized later that *he* was playing games. He wanted to tell my dad that he'd fucked the big boss's daughter."

I want to tear the sonofabitch apart.

"He told my dad. They went to war. It was pretty much the nightmare you can imagine. There was no happy ending for anyone. Just blood and death. I never saw Gage again. I don't think anyone did."

Shit.

"Stop looking at me like that," Kat whispered.

Rick blinked. "Like what?"

"Like you pity me. You feel sorry for me. I don't want that." She shook her head. "I want a lover who *wants me.* I'm running out of time, and I thought that lover could be you. I was wrong. It won't happen again. So just—just get the hell out, okay?" Her eyes gleamed with tears. "While I still have a little damn pride left."

He hated those tears. *Hated* it when one lone tear leaked down her cheek. "No."

A part laugh, part sob escaped her. "I think you're the one who likes the mind games."

"I'm not scared of your dad beating the shit out of me."

"Good. Because he's dead."

"And I don't want to fuck you to screw one over on him."

"Again, good, *because he's—*"

"I wouldn't care if he was alive. My reaction to you would still be the same. You need to understand that. I look at you, and I want. I fucking crave. I want to strip you. Pick you up. Fuck you against the nearest wall."

Her lips parted.

"I want to sink so deeply into you that I freaking own part of you. My response to you isn't easy or civilized. It's savage. And you don't get that. You don't get exactly how dangerous it is for someone like me...to want someone like you."

She didn't get how hard it was to stand there when she'd been offering herself to him. How hard it was not to take and take until there was nothing left.

Until she was his.

Possession. A primitive response because he was a primitive kind of guy.

"I'm not scared of the mob. I'm not scared of the Feds. There is very little in this world that I fear. Know that. Fucking you wouldn't be about anything else but need for me. You're the sexiest woman I've ever seen." He exhaled on a rough sigh. "And if you want a freaking 'blow-by-blow' as you call it on my past lovers, I'll give it to you. Fair is fair. There weren't a lot of them. Most women don't take one look at me and think they've found the man of their dreams. I look more like a beast than Prince Charming."

"Prince Charming is an asshole. I met him years ago. Won't ever believe his lies again." Her head tilted. "And I don't think you're a beast."

He looked at his hands. Huge. Every part of him was. He was too strong and too rough. Had been as a kid, and as a man...he'd tried to hone his strength. But being at Wilde had just taught him how to use his strength and power in even more dangerous ways. "Some people are very good at lying." Rick thought of his best friend and the pain that would haunt him until he died. "I don't deal in lies. I don't have time for that shit. I say what I mean. I want you. I'm not going to pretend that I don't, but you don't know what you're going to get with me."

"Why don't you tell me?"

"Rough. Hard. Dirty. The kind of sex that will make you scream and claw. I'll want to drive you crazy because you'll sure as hell be driving me that way. But it isn't about emotion. It never is. I've never been in love, never will be. We only have a week together, and then you walk away. Hell, I think the federal government will probably make you into someone else and you'll vanish from my life. So think about all of that. Consider it long and hard before you decide that you really want *me*." Because if she made him an offer again, there was no way on God's green earth that he'd be strong enough to turn away. He swallowed down the lump in his throat. "Get your rest, Kat. The next few days and nights aren't going to be easy." Rick made himself head for the door.

"Stop."

If she told him that she still wanted him, if she—

"You came into my room for a reason. What was it?"

He'd been so caught up in her that he'd forgotten. Way to be a world class agent. "The shot fired at me..." He cleared his throat. "There are so many bounties on you, why would the shooter waste a bullet? Doesn't make sense."

"I told you...the shooter was trying to get rid of my protection. You were in the way." The floor squeaked beneath her feet. "I mean, I'm worth way more alive, so the shooter had to get you out of the way and then come after—"

He whirled around. "I thought there was a death order on you." Multiple kill orders, in fact.

"There is." She nodded, like it was the most normal thing in the world to have hits on her. "But certain individuals want me alive. They think I know information about my father's business that's important to them."

"Information, like what?" His temples were throbbing.

"Oh, I don't know..." Kat gave a little shrug. The right side of the robe dipped open and slid down one shoulder. She winced. "Maybe like...where my father's missing twenty million dollars may be hidden?"

Jesus.

CHAPTER SIX

He hadn't touched her all day long. He'd kept at least two feet between them. His voice had been almost painfully polite when he'd addressed her. Rick was playing by the rules, dammit. Yet every time he looked at her...

I want. I ache.

Rough. Hard. Dirty.

I want to sink so deeply into you that I fucking own part of you. My response to you isn't easy or civilized. It's savage. And you don't get that. You don't get just how dangerous it is for someone like me...to want someone like you.

Had he really told her all of that? What in the hell had happened to his control?

"Uh, Rick?"

He blinked.

Kat frowned at him. "You all right? You seemed to have zoned out there for a minute." Her elbow was on the countertop, her chin propped in her palm, and Kat had just caught him staring at her. All right? Not even close. His dick was so damn hard that he was pretty sure the zipper had left an impression on him. He *wanted* her, but he was not going to cross that line. Not.

Maybe.

Night had fallen in the city. They'd been cooped up all day long. Cabin fever had definitely set in. Rick felt as if he was about to jump out of his skin. Or maybe, jump her.

No, not happening.

"Cole will be here in a few moments," Rick told her as he continued using his polite voice. "He's coming to give us an update on the shooter."

A little furrow appeared between her brows. "Your agents didn't catch him?"

"He vanished into thin air." And no one else had showed up at the cabin, either. He'd been so certain someone else would follow her GPS signal and appear at the cabin, but, no dice.

"Unfortunately," Kat sighed, "disappearing is what Ghost does best. And if he's the one leading the pack after me, I'm screwed." She pushed away from the counter. Headed to the window and stared out at the city below. There were other bars on the block. Rick knew she could see people filling the street below.

If he strained, Rick could even hear the hum of music. Her body swayed just a little—as if to a beat—and he knew she heard the music, too. For a moment, her face reflected longing as she stared below.

"No, princess."

Her head whipped around.

"You are *not* going down there." He had to be the bad guy and break her heart, but it was for her protection. "The last thing we want is for someone with a camera to snap a pic of Antonio O'Shaughnessy's daughter as she parties in a club. This safe house is good for the moment. We don't want to have it burn down around us."

Her lips tightened. "What do you do for fun, Rick?"

"I handcuff myself to mob princesses."

Her eyes narrowed.

"Fine. I chase down bad guys. I kick some ass. Then I usually call it a night." His shoulders rose and fell, stretching the black t-shirt that he wore. "I'm not into the dance club scene." Hardly. He didn't know how to dance and would probably trip if he tried. "I don't tend to blend so well with the suits and the bullshitters." Understatement of the century. He lifted a brow. "But let me guess, you love that scene, huh? Your favorite thing?"

Her hand pressed to the cold window pane. "I have no idea. But I imagine it would be fun to find out."

Now she'd lost him. "What do you mean? I thought you partied it up on a regular basis—"

"*I* thought we'd covered that you had to stop believing the things you read. Why on earth would my dad let me go to clubs to party? For my entire life, I had guards close by. Especially after Jimmy."

"Jimmy?" The name seemed to burn in his throat.

"He was the boy I told you about, when I was seventeen..." Her voice trailed away. He hated the whisper of sadness that came into her voice. After a moment, she cleared her throat. "Clubbing wasn't allowed. Parties weren't allowed. I was a prisoner before my dad died..." Her shoulders lifted and fell. "Just like I'm a prisoner now."

"You're not a prisoner."

"Liar, liar."

"Kat."

"Tell it to the handcuffs, okay?"

He actually felt his cheeks burn. Rick shifted closer. About a foot separated them now. It was the closest he'd been to her all day long. "You're here for your protection."

"My dad used to say the same thing. That I couldn't go to a regular school for my protection. That I'd be targeted by his enemies out there. So I had to stay home. He had tutors brought to me. I couldn't go out to parties because his enemies would attack me. They'd use me against him. I had to stay locked away. I was trapped while everyone else was living."

There was so much pain in her words. He wanted to pull her into his arms and tell her that it was okay. But it wasn't okay. Nothing was okay for her. Killers were after her. Her life was on the line.

Her voice rose a little as she told him, "So, yeah, when you call me princess...maybe you're right, but not in the way you think. If anything, I'm like Rapunzel. I was trapped in a freaking tower all my life, and I've never really been free." Her hand still pressed to the glass but her gaze was totally on him.

"If you were locked away, how'd you learn to drive a motorcycle so well?" There were so many mysteries tied to Kat.

A smile tugged at her lips. "I learned because my guards got bored over the years. When you've got felons and killers dodging your steps, you learn the most interesting things."

"I'll bet." He'd never met another woman like her. She fascinated him.

"I learned how to hotwire any car out there. How to drive fast and hard—whether you're on a motorcycle, in the getaway vehicle that is a boring old sedan or anything else you can get your hands on. I know how to shoot. I know how to make a bomb." Her smile was gone. Her voice had turned brittle. "I know how to inflict maximum pain when I want to make someone suffer. I learned all the best things in life."

His hands flexed. He *wanted* to hold her. Just hold her.

"Stop it."

"Stop what?"

"Don't pity me."

He...he ached for her. He wanted to kick the ass of everyone who'd hurt her, and he wanted to wrap his arms around her and protect her from the whole friggin' world. Was that pity? Rick didn't think so. He was afraid to look too closely at just what he felt.

"You know what?" Kat muttered. "I think that's more than enough sharing for now. Because I'm standing here telling you everything about me, but I know pretty much nothing about you. Except that, you know, you like protecting and defending. It's your whole way of life."

His phone gave a little peal of sound. He turned away, snagged it from the table he'd put it on earlier, and read the text from Cole. He hurried toward the control panel and disabled the alarm. The alarm system covered both the first and second floors. "Cole's here," Rick said as he stared at the panel. "He'll be up in a few moments."

"Cole." She repeated the name. "He's the badass one with the tats."

Rick's jaw locked as he moved to face her again. "Yeah."

She gave a little nod. "I rather liked his ink."

"Don't," he growled.

"Don't—what? Sorry, but you'll have to be a little more specific if you're going to give me a new rule to memorize."

"Don't think about sleeping with him." Shit. Had he just said that? Yep, judging by her widening eyes, he had. *Fuck me.* If only he could snatch those words right back. He always said the wrong shit. Charming, he wasn't.

"Uh, I wasn't planning to sleep with Cole." She straightened. Her hand didn't press to the pane any longer. "What...is that supposed to be rule number eight? Don't sleep with your badass partner Cole?"

"It's...shit, yeah, it's a rule. *Don't sleep with him.*" Why was he so freaking jealous? What in the hell was happening to him?

"Someone sure got pissy awfully fast. And insulting."

She'd just called him pissy. Wonderful. He was obviously wowing her and making Kat realize what a catch he was. *How do I get this conversation back on track?* Though, had it ever really been on track?

She lifted her chin. "Is that what you think? That if I couldn't sleep with you, I would head on to the next guy on the list? Move right along until I found a willing participant?"

He didn't answer. No way was he answering that.

But she stalked toward him. Without her high heels, he towered over her even more.

"Listen up, sweet cheeks," she snapped at him. "I wasn't looking for just *anyone*. If *anyone* would've worked for me, I could've hooked up with one of the Feds. Trust me, they were willing. Especially Brisk."

Rick knew there had been a reason he didn't like that guy. Brisk had seemed to get way too close to Kat at that meeting in Wilde.

"I didn't want him," Kat continued doggedly. Angrily. "I wanted you. I reacted that way only to *you*. But thanks like hell for insulting me."

She spun away.

His hand flew out and curled around her wrist. He hadn't meant to insult her. He was just a damn dick. "I'm...jealous."

"No, you're a jackass."

"Guilty. I'm both." His hold tightened. "I don't want to think of you with other men."

She glanced at him and then rolled her eyes. "I thought you weren't going to lie to me. I liked that about you." A huff. "We're strangers. Strangers who kind of explode when we touch—"

He could feel the electricity surging between them again. *Again? Try always.*

"But you don't know me, Rick, not really, and I don't know you. So don't try to act like you're already jealous and—"

"If I told you I was thinking about sleeping with someone else right now, how would you feel?"

Her eyes blazed. "I'd feel like scratching that chick's eyes right out."

At least I'm not alone in this mess. He tugged her closer. "When I think about you and another man...that shit messes me up. I want to rip apart any asshole who gets too close to you and *not* because I'm supposed to be your bodyguard. Because I'm getting too possessive around you." Everything was moving too fast between them. Too fast. Too intense. Too consuming. He was trying to hold back, when, in truth, all he wanted to do was hold her and never let go.

"We just met," Kat murmured.

Yeah, but it didn't feel that way. Maybe because they only had a week together. Maybe because everything between them would always move fast. "I don't understand why we feel this way about each other," Rick continued as he fought to find the right words. With her, the right words mattered. "I've never reacted so strongly to another person." The intensity of his reaction to her floored him. "But when I think about you with anyone else—Cole or Brisk or even someone from your past—I see red. *I* want you. I want my hands on you. My mouth on you. But I know you aren't meant for me. I'm trying to play by the rules here, don't you see that?"

"You and your rules." Kat shook her head, sending her hair dancing over her shoulders. "Screw the rules." She leaned up toward him. Her mouth was so close. Her full lips tempted. "Maybe we should take what we want."

"I want you," he growled against her mouth. "Baby, I want—"

The door opened. A whistle filled the air. "Seriously, man?" Cole called out. "A second time? I mean, sure, I got that the first time might have been because of the adrenaline rush and all but...ah..."

Rick lifted his head. Locked eyes with Cole.

But Cole ignored Rick's *shut-the-hell-up* glare and kept right on talking as he exclaimed, "You have *never* been this handsy with anyone before. I mean, you're the rule follower. The one who is always telling everyone else you don't mix business and pleasure. You toe the line, you don't want what you can't have, you—"

"Stop oversharing, Cole," Rick snarled. He let go of Kat. Took a step back. Her scent followed him. The heat of her body seemed to still press to him. He took a breath and tasted her. Dammit. *Dammit.* He was losing control.

"Stop making out with the client," Cole tossed back as he turned and secured the lock. He reset the alarm. Not like it was his first time there. Cole always made himself at home when he came to Rick's place. He sauntered toward them, and his stare raked Kat. She'd wrapped her arms around her stomach and moved to stand closer to the counter.

She looked fragile. Beautiful. Sexy as hell.

Cole gave another whistle.

"Cole," Rick warned.

Cole's face turned hard as he kept staring at Kat. Well, harder than normal. He looked angry. Suspicious. Then Cole raked a hand over his face. "Rick, we need to talk. *Alone.*"

"It's my life you're talking about." Kat's voice was quiet but firm. "I think I deserve to hear whatever you've got to say."

Cole shook his head. "This is Wilde business. And I want to talk to Rick only."

She didn't move. "Did you find Ghost?"

"No. The shooter vanished. *If* it was Ghost, he got away."

She bit her lower lip. "Did anyone else show up at the cabin?"

"Not after you left. But one of the techs said your tracking device stopped transmitting after Rick smashed it to hell, so that was probably a tip-off to those hunting you. We got it up and running as fast as we could, but that brief transmission interruption could've been enough to alert the folks monitoring you." He rubbed a hand over his jaw. "They probably suspected the tracker had been found, and they watched from a distance, not wanting to expose themselves."

"If they were watching from a distance..." Her chest rose and fell too quickly. "What if you were followed here?"

"I wasn't." Cole was utterly confident.

"How do you know? Someone could've tailed you from the farmhouse. He's called *Ghost* for a reason, you know. He could've been on your trail the whole time, and you wouldn't know."

"I wasn't followed."

Kat didn't look convinced. "What if someone is tracking your car? Maybe the shooter tagged it before he fired that shot at Rick!"

"No. My ride was swept."

Standard procedure at Wilde. The vehicles were always checked for tracking devices. And explosives. But Rick didn't mention that particular detail. No sense alarming her more than was necessary.

"Besides," Cole told her, "I *changed* cars before I came here. This isn't my first rodeo. No one followed me. Your location is a secret. We're good."

Her gaze darted to the window. As Rick watched, her hand lifted to fiddle with her pearls. Only the pearls weren't there any longer. He knew that holding her pearls—touching them when she was nervous—was an old habit and his gut clenched. The memory of her crying as her pearls broke was etched into his mind. Talk about feeling like a grade A-asshole.

Her fingers touched the bare skin of her neck. He saw the flutter of her lashes. A quick flash of pain right before her hand dropped.

"I really need to talk with you, Rick," Cole groused. "Now."

"We can go downstairs." He pinned Kat with a hard glance. "You'll be fine up here. No one is going to get to you. Just—maybe grab something to eat. You can watch some TV. I'll be right back."

She didn't say anything as he and Cole hurriedly made their way downstairs. But leaving her caused a strange ache in Rick's chest.

On the first floor, the bar waited for them. Quiet and still. And it didn't take long for Cole to fire his first shot as he snapped, "Tell me you know how dangerous it is to fuck with a woman like her."

Rick rounded on him. "I'm not fucking her." *But I want to.*

"Not yet, maybe. But it would take a blind man to miss the tension between you two. When I found you at the farmhouse, you were locked tight to her and it looked like you never wanted to let go."

Yeah, well...*you try tasting a slice of paradise and just giving that shit up.*

"Then I go in tonight...hell, man, it would be obvious to anyone that you wanted to gobble her up."

Every muscle was tight with tension. "I can do my job."

Cole's gaze measured him. "Not like you'd be the first agent to fall for a client. Hell, it's a trend at Wilde. All the cool kids are doing it."

"I'm not *falling* for Kat. I'm doing my job."

Cole stared back at him. "You can't trust her."

"I'm *not* trusting her."

"The FBI knows about the tracker in her pearls. Eric talked to his buddy there. The agents who were guarding her—Bryan Brisk and Tom Wayne—are in some deep shit because they should've figured out about the tracker but they didn't."

Yeah, they should've figured it out. The fact that they hadn't made Rick suspicious. *Am I suspicious...or do I just not like Brisk?*

Cole blew out a hard breath. "Though now that the Feds understand how she was located, it looks like there wasn't a leak on their end, so they are wanting—"

"They are not getting her back." The low response rumbled from him and cut through Cole's words.

Cole blinked. "Uh...they don't want her back. They want *you* to get intel from her."

Rick wasn't sure he'd heard right.

"Eric got the order about an hour ago, though I have to wonder if the Feds didn't intend this shit the whole time."

"What shit? Explain yourself, man."

His lips thinned. "The idea is that Kat O'Shaughnessy is keeping secrets from the Feds, but she might just share those secrets with someone else...someone who is close to her."

He didn't like where this was going.

"Kat isn't the client," Cole muttered. He looked uncomfortable. "Look, don't shoot the messenger, I'm just passing along what I was told. The *Feds* are the clients here. And they want us— you—to work Kat. They dropped a bombshell to Eric that twenty million dollars is missing from her father's accounts. They think Kat knows where the money is hidden. They think that she knows plenty she isn't telling."

"She's scheduled to go to court and testify about a million damn things. From where I stand, the woman is cooperating." *I told her I wouldn't lie.*

"It's Agent Brisk that you need to talk with, okay? He's saying...the Feds *think* there is more going on. They don't want to be blindsided by her in a courtroom. They want someone to get close and make sure all of her secrets are out before she gets in front of a judge." The faint lines near Cole's mouth deepened. "And they want to make sure that Kat isn't sitting on twenty million, just waiting for the right moment to vanish *before* she ever gets to a courtroom."

What a cluster. "I'm supposed to keep her alive. My job is to keep her safe, not to learn the woman's secrets."

Cole's lips curled down. "Unfortunately, it looks like your job might be to do both."

***

There were certain things that Kat excelled at in this world. Like she'd told Rick, her babysitters had basically been hired thugs and killers. Her skills were on the super shady side.

Bake a cake? Oh, no, the thing would not rise. And it would taste like crap. Live life with a green thumb? Get a garden to grow and flowers to bloom? Nope, she killed what she touched. Anything on the softer side of life wasn't for her.

But...

She knew more than a few tricks to help her pass time.

Her father had wanted her locked away. Wanted to make sure that she lived in some kind of suffocating cage. She'd been fourteen the first time she learned how to sneak out of her room and get down the stairs without making a sound.

She'd wanted to be close to him. Wanted to see what her dad was doing.

So, unfortunately, she'd been fourteen the first time she saw him order a hit on someone.

The kind of memories that warped you for life, yes.

But she'd kept her sneaky skills. Rick wanted her to play nicely and just sit upstairs while he had a big chat with Cole? Not happening. She gave them a few moments to head down the stairs, then she tip-toed after them. She'd made a note of any squeaky steps when she'd first gone *up* the stairs with him, and now she was able to slip down without making even a whisper of sound.

She didn't like that Cole wanted to be alone with Rick. Like she'd told them, this was her life. She had a right to know what was happening. So she eased in close and she heard every single word.

"I'm supposed to keep her alive," Rick said. "My job is to keep her safe, not to learn the woman's secrets."

Yes, yes, that was Rick's job. She nodded. So Cole could just shove it. Agent Brisk could shove it. They could all—

"Unfortunately, it looks like your job might be to do both."

She wasn't even breathing as she waited for Rick's reply to Cole's not-so-charming statement. Rick needed to tell the other man to screw off. Needed to say that hell to the no, he wasn't going to try and use her for info.

But Rick didn't speak next. Cole did. Cole...who was increasingly getting on her bad side. And to think, she'd liked his tats at first.

"Come on, man," Cole urged in a wheedling way. "I saw the way she looked at you. She wants you. Use that. You can find out every secret she has."

"I'm not the type to seduce secrets out of women."

Kat inched closer. Her back flattened against the nearby wall. If she slid around that wall, they'd see her. So she stayed exactly where she was.

Rick still wasn't voicing the screaming denial that she wanted to hear. Would it *kill* the man to offer up a denial? Was that so much to ask?

"Okay, sure, buddy, you wouldn't be my number one Casanova choice, but I feel like you can rise to the occasion. Have some confidence, bro."

Her eyes narrowed. *Come on, Rick, say—*

"I'm not going to fuck her to get information."

Good to know. She moved a little bit more. Just a wee bit closer. Still not going around the wall though, just getting to its edge.

"Twenty million dollars has vanished." Cole sounded all big and dramatic. He should settle down. "According to the Feds, she took it. They think Kat is going to cut and run before she ever steps foot inside a courthouse. If she vanishes, their cases go down the drain."

She wasn't even breathing.

"Are you listening to me?" Cole demanded. "Twenty million dollars. The mob. This is all way above my pay grade."

It was above everyone's pay grade. The Feds were saying she had the money, huh? Interesting.

"You have less than a week with her. You'll be the one next to her twenty-four, seven. She might even spill secrets to you without you realizing it."

Rick hadn't spoken in a little while. He'd gone all dead silent on her. Did that mean he was actually considering Cole's words? Thinking about trying to seduce her for secrets? He probably thought her seduction wouldn't be hard. After all, she'd pretty much *thrown* herself at him earlier. Okay, there had been no pretty much to it. She *had* thrown herself at him. She'd paraded around in her underwear, and he'd still walked away. *Hello, pride crusher.* She also already *had* started spilling her secrets to him. She'd told him about her lovers. Why, why had she done that?

She'd kept those secrets for so long.

Rick was far more dangerous than she'd realized. He was—

"Hello, princess."

He was right in front of her.

CHAPTER SEVEN

"Eavesdropping again?" He cocked his head to the right and lifted one dark brow.

"Again?" She blinked. "You say that as if it's a habit I follow."

"Um, it is. You told me yourself, remember. You liked to listen when your father wasn't aware."

She was so screwed.

Cole rushed up behind him. "How the hell did you know she was there?"

Because she'd freaking *told* Rick her secrets. Kat would not be making that mistake again.

"I didn't hear her." Cole looked impressed. "Not so much as a rustle of sound." His gaze lit with admiration as he gaped at her. "What else can you do?"

"You have no idea."

Rick caught her hand and pulled her closer. "Don't worry about what she can do," he muttered to Cole.

Then they were heading toward the long bar counter. Rick motioned to one of the stools. "Sit."

She didn't. Did she *look* like a dog?

Rick caught himself. Or he caught the glare that she gave him. He cleared his throat. "Would you, um, please sit so we can talk?"

"Better." She hopped up onto the nearest bar stool and swung her bare foot.

His gaze locked on her foot.

She wiggled her toes at him. She hadn't paused to put on shoes. Sure, shoes had been waiting for her when they'd arrived. Shoes. Clothes. Everything. More Wilde magic. But she'd been in a hurry to get downstairs. And bare feet were quieter.

"What in the hell is going on between you two?" Cole demanded as he closed in. He got really close. A little too close as he frowned ever so suspiciously at her.

Cole was on her list now. The list of folks who pissed her off. "Well, I can tell you this much..." Her smile was cold. "Rick isn't going to be seducing secrets out of me, though thanks so much for offering us both that most awesome of times."

Cole opened his mouth, but couldn't seem to find the right words.

Or any words.

Her furious stare swung to Rick. "And way to offer up a denial there, Casanova."

He blinked.

"Just couldn't bring yourself to say, 'No, I'm not going to seduce that poor, fragile woman. She's been through enough. She needs a friend. She needs care. She doesn't need more betrayal in her life. I'm going to protect her and keep her safe and make sure that no one or nothing ever hurts her again.'"

Silence.

The uncomfortable kind. Maybe she'd gone overboard there. Whatever.

Kat waited.

Rick scraped a hand over his jaw and the beard that she would no longer think of as delectable. Finally, he rumbled, "I don't think of you as being particularly fragile."

That was his response?

"I think you might be kind of scary," Cole added. He sounded a little bemused. "You know, in a sexy, crazy way."

Her gaze flickered to him. "You're an asshole. And I don't like your tats any longer."

"What?"

She ignored him. Her stare swung back to Rick.

"Cole likes crazy women." Rick never looked away from her. "Crazy is his number one turn-on, so he meant that as a compliment."

She hadn't taken it that way.

"And I *am* here to keep you safe." He stepped closer. His dark eyes seemed to burn with intensity. "No one and nothing will harm you on my watch. But no, I don't think you're fragile. I think you're cunning, I think you're smart, and I think you might be one of the toughest people I've ever met."

Cole shifted a bit uncomfortably. "You should add sneaky to that list. Because I had no idea she was there listening."

Rick had known, though. Because he was starting to know her. *Big* problem.

"Time to go, Cole," Rick said as he inclined his head to his partner.

"But we still need to go over—"

"The shooter got away at the farmhouse. The Wilde agents outside of this place are in position. They'll watch us. They'll guard us, and we'll be clear for the next few days."

So wait, they *were* going to stay in that bar for the foreseeable future? No switching to another safe house?

"What about the twenty million?" Cole rasped.

Rick crossed his arms over that massive chest of his. "Kat, do you have the twenty million?"

Was he serious? "No. I don't have it stuffed in my bra."

His eyes narrowed.

She smiled. "I didn't take the money." Total honesty. Boom.

Rick glanced over at Cole. "There. She didn't take the money. Tell the Feds I managed to pry that secret out of her."

Cole took a step back. "You're just going to believe her?"

She shook her index finger at him, all disappointed-teacher-like. "Cole, you are insulting. What do you think...that I just lie for kicks?"

He knew better than to answer, she could see that truth on his face.

"You need to get going," Rick said. "Call me to check in tomorrow. If you get a hit on the shooter, I want to know."

Cole blew out a long breath and rolled back his shoulders. "You gonna be okay in here...with her?"

"Do I look uber dangerous?" Kat asked. "I promise not to hurt Rick. Does that help?"

Cole didn't crack a smile. "There are all kinds of hurt in this world."

That was certainly true. The other thing that was true? "I have no intention of hurting Rick. Unlike my father, I don't enjoy other people's pain."

Cole's gaze turned hard. Flat. "But you do enjoy lying, don't you? You think this is all some big game? We *know* you didn't call your ex-nanny. Don't try that bullshit. You connected with someone on that BS brownie run, but it wasn't her. If you're trying to touch base with some partner so that you can disappear, I don't want my friend getting caught in the crossfire."

He cared about Rick. Good to know. "I don't want anyone in the crossfire. And in case you forgot, I was the one who saved Rick at the farmhouse. I was the one who shoved him out of the way so that he wouldn't get shot. Frankly, I think I should get a thank you for that. But one hasn't been forthcoming."

"That was an accident," Cole fired back. "You were pissed. I saw you through my binoculars."

"Someone likes to watch," she murmured.

A muscle jerked in his jaw. "You shoved at Rick out of anger. You—" He stopped. His eyes widened, and he looked at her with brand new suspicion. "Unless you knew the shooter was there."

"What?"

"Unless you shoved Rick because you knew the shooter was there. Unless you planned it all."

She could practically see the wheels turning in his head. "You wanted Rick to be grateful to you. You wanted him to think you were good. The poor, misunderstood mob princess. You wanted—"

"I want you to stop talking," she snapped at him. "You don't know anything about me."

Cole surged forward.

Rick slammed a hand on his chest and shoved him right back. "I think I told you already..." His head turned so that he stared straight into Cole's eyes. "It's time for you to leave."

"But—but what if she—"

"Whether she's a killer, a con, or an innocent caught up in a nightmare, my job is the same. *Our* job is the same. She's got me until I walk her into the courthouse. She's got us both until then. We keep her alive, and we handle any BS that she throws our way."

Wow. His opinion of her was so overwhelmingly stellar. Not.

Cole turned away. Headed for the door. Was it her imagination or did he walk with a slight limp? Her gaze darted down his legs. Yes, that was a limp, barely noticeable.

Her stare lifted just as he glanced back at her. "You hurt my friend, and I'll make you regret it for the rest of your life."

"Duly noted." She waved her fingers in a shoo gesture. Did he notice that her fingers trembled? She hoped not.

He left. Silence reigned. She swiveled a little on the barstool. *Whether she's a killer, a con, or an innocent caught up in a nightmare, my job is the same.* Rick's words pounded at her head. He really didn't care what she was.

Who she was.

"Ignore Cole." Rick moved behind the bar. Grabbed for something under the counter and came back up with—was that vodka? Looked like it. "He's...he doesn't get close to a lot of people, and when he does, Cole tends to go all in."

"He's your own personal pit bull. Got it."

Rick shook his head. "You want a drink?"

"Uh, yes, please." Though a big part of her wondered...was he just trying to get her drunk so that he could go after her secrets? Ha. Nice try. Little did he know that she'd drink him under the table any day of the week.

Rick splashed some vodka in a glass and pushed it across the bar top.

Her fingers curled around the glass. "What about you?"

"Vodka is my kryptonite." He saluted her with the bottle. "Since I'm working on keeping the bad guys off you...and my own hands *off* you, too...seems like a good idea to stay sober."

She lifted the shot glass and downed the vodka in one gulp. She barely felt the burn before she slammed the glass back on the counter.

He studied her. "You're good at lying."

"Thank you for noticing." She batted her lashes at him. Kept up the act. "Some people never recognize your skills."

He poured more vodka into the glass.

She grabbed the shot glass. Drained it. Slapped it on the bar top. *I could do this all night.*

"Did you know the shooter was there?"

Ohmygoodness. She pushed up, leaned across the bar, and put her hand on his cheek. "You are so adorable."

He stiffened.

"Do you think you can get me drunk and then grill me?"

"I think I can ask you questions and you'll answer me in a nice, civilized manner."

"Being civilized is boring. The FBI suits were civilized. They were boring me to tears." Her fingers slid over the edge of his beard. "Then I saw you. You looked infinitely more interesting."

He growled.

"That is so hot. You have this whole rough, untamed thing going on. It's a real turn-on." Another stroke/pat of her fingers.

His hand flew up and his fingers clamped around her wrist. "Stop trying to play me."

Anger beat inside of her. "Why? Weren't *you* thinking about playing me? Because I sure didn't hear a big denial when your good buddy Cole was telling you to seduce me and get me to whisper all my secrets to you during pillow talk."

His hold tightened. "That what you want? My denial. Fine. You've got it. I won't seduce you to learn your secrets."

His touch scorched her.

"If we're ever in bed together," he continued in that deep, rumbly voice that made her toes curl, "it won't be because I'm trying to get intel. It's gonna be because you've driven me straight past the point of control. All I'll want is you. To be in you as deep as I can go."

Maybe the drinks were making her a little lightheaded. Or maybe he was.

"How about I get the same promise from you?" He was still holding her wrist.

Same promise? "Sure. I won't seduce you to learn your secrets."

Did his lips twitch? "How about you don't seduce me because you're trying to use me?"

She tugged. He let her go. Cocking her head, Kat reminded him, "We covered this already. I was *trying* to seduce you because I wanted you. Nothing more."

"Women like you don't want men like me."

"I have zero idea what that statement means but I'm sure it's insulting."

"It means...you're fucking gorgeous."

She smiled at him. "See. You can be charming. In a grim, growling way."

"I look like someone's worst nightmare."

More like my best dream. "Darling, who *have* you been hanging out with?"

"I tend to say the wrong shit to women."

Okay, now she could nod. "I have noticed that. But it's kind of cute in its way."

"Cute?" Rick choked on the word.

She fought a smile.

"I told you before, I'm too rough. Too hard."

She flattened both of her hands on the bar top. "And I think I told you that I like both of those things. It's like you are making a turn on list for me."

His lips parted. She wanted his mouth on hers. She leaned forward. He did, too. He—

"Who were you going to meet, Kat?"

He had just killed her mood. "Way to not score, Rick. I think we can add this moment to your 'I tend to say the wrong shit to women' list. And this time, it's really not cute."

"You left the farmhouse and you were going to meet someone. Two seconds later, a bullet fires. Maybe Cole was right. Maybe you were going to meet the shooter. Maybe you knew he was there all along."

She searched his gaze. "Ah. There it is." A few things clicked into place for her. "That's why you're being all..." She mimicked his deep voice, and said, *"We can't have sex. No, no."*

"Kat..."

"It's because you had the same suspicion. Even before Cole came in, spouting his ideas, you had already gotten it into your head that I was guilty." So disappointing. She leaned back on the stool.

"Who were you going to meet?"

"Um, I was going to meet up with your fancy little sports car. We had a hot date planned. I was going to hotwire her, and then I was going to get the heck out of there."

"You were running?"

Bingo. "It's what I do."

"Why?"

"Why?" Fine. Hard truth time. "Because I don't want to die. Because I didn't trust those FBI agents for a moment, and I knew I was a dead woman with them. Because I didn't know you—I still don't know you—and trust isn't real big and easy for me. So running and protecting myself seemed like the best option."

They stared at each other.

"You still planning to run?" Rick finally asked her.

She didn't answer. *Absolutely.*

"Hell, I'll take that as a yes." He reached under the bar again. Was he bringing out more alcohol? She could use more.

"Take it any way you want," she told him, angry and just so very soul tired. "But it's my life. The Feds think they've taken my life away, and I have to do something to stay—"

She caught the glint of metal as his hand lifted. "*No.*"

"Yes."

"You are *not* cuffing me again."

"If you're running, I am, and you just told me that you might be planning to run. It's a chance I can't take." He looked at the cuffs, then at her. "Sorry, princess."

"You know, you keep saying sorry when you make jackass moves." Her heart thundered in her chest. "And here I thought you weren't going to lie to me."

"Kat..."

"I warned you before...one day, I will make sure that you really *are* sorry." Did he understand that she was making him a promise?

"Fair enough." His voice was rough and rasping. "But at least when that day comes, you'll still be alive. Because, see, that's all that can matter to me. It's not about whether you like me—"

She *didn't.*

"Whether you trust me—"

Not going to happen.

"It's about you staying alive. I'm going to keep you alive. Count on that."

CHAPTER EIGHT

He was already sorry. Oh, damn, but Rick was *sorry*. Because while he was cuffed to Kat, he had to stay right beside her. Beside her as in...in the same bed with her. He'd taken her upstairs to his room and even though the bed was king-sized, it seemed a million times too small to him.

She was on one side. He was as far on the other side as it was possible to be. She'd rolled away from him, and his arm extended toward her because of the handcuffs. Darkness surrounded them. Her breathing was light and easy, but he knew she wasn't asleep.

Neither was he.

"Well, this isn't quite what I imagined," Kat finally announced. "If you'd told me that I'd be spending the night cuffed in bed with a sexy guy, I would've called you crazy. Though I have to admit, the reality of bondage time with you is just not living up to the fantasy. Very disappointed."

He stared straight up.

"We can ditch the cuffs. I'm not running tonight."

Oh, yeah, he wanted to believe that. He just couldn't.

"Are you pretending to be asleep?" The covers rustled. He felt her turn toward him. "Because I know you're wide awake. Your body is as stiff as a board and you haven't so much as twitched for the last five minutes."

He'd been attempting to stay still so that she would go to sleep.

"Rick." A sigh. "What am I going to do with you?"

Anything you want. No, that wasn't the answer he was supposed to give. He could *not* give that answer.

She rolled closer.

His phone rang. The shrill tone had him jerking in the darkness as his free hand flew out toward the nightstand and grabbed the phone. His gaze narrowed on the number that he didn't recognize. It wasn't like *his* private number was easy to get. Telemarketers didn't call him so—

The phone rang again.

He swiped his finger over the screen and shoved the phone to his ear. "Who the hell is this?"

"You have five minutes to get her out of there. Her location is compromised." The voice was flat and hard, and one that he didn't recognize.

"What?" Rick surged upright.

"You heard me. Stop wasting time and *get her out.*"

"Listen, asshole, I'm not going to believe anything that you say to me, okay? Obviously, this is a trick, and I'm hanging up the phone." Because the guy could be trying to triangulate the cell signal and *find* them.

"You're at the damn bar. I already have your location. So do they. Move her out now or she's dead."

The caller hung up on *him*.

"Rick?" Kat sat up next to him in the bed. "What's happening?"

He was already dialing again. Putting in a call to Cole.

"Yo." Cole answered on the second ring. "Trouble with the princess already—"

"Is this location compromised?" He climbed out of bed.

Kat yelped as their linked hands had her being pulled across the mattress.

"No. No, it shouldn't be," Cole assured him.

"Just got some mystery call saying it was." He rattled off the caller's number. "Trace it. Now. He said I have five minutes before unwelcome visitors are here." Rick ended the call. Turned toward Kat. "We're moving."

She shoved up on the mattress. "What's going on?"

"The caller didn't just guess that we were at the bar."

"I have no idea what you're talking about. You need to slow things down. I didn't *hear* your phone call. Okay, I mean, I heard what you were saying, but not what the person on the other end of the line was telling you. Explain things to me. Slowly."

"No time for slow. If the guy is right, then in five minutes, this place is going to be crawling with bastards looking for you." And if the guy wasn't right, the location was still compromised. They had to move, right then.

She jumped out of the bed. "Where are my shoes?" She was wearing jeans and a t-shirt.

Uncomfortable clothes for bed, but after he'd cuffed her, she'd refused to change. Since she'd worn her jeans and t-shirt, he'd kept his on, too. Rick had figured the more clothes they wore in bed together, the better. Or, rather, the less temptation.

"Get the cuffs off!" Kat cried out when they both tried to surge into two different directions—each of them looking for shoes.

He hesitated. If they got out in the open and this was a trick—one that she and a mystery partner were working—Kat would be in the wind. She could vanish on him.

And if it wasn't a trick, then he needed to be as close as possible to her. Close enough to come between her and a bullet. "Not yet."

"Not yet? Not *yet?*" She gave a frustrated scream.

Yeah. His soul pretty much felt the same way. They'd deal.

She got her shoes. He got his shoes and his gun. Then he dropped the phone he'd used moments before. The line was compromised. He paused to grab a burner from his stash, and then they were rushing down the stairs. He got them out the back door, down the alley, around the corner...

And shoved her against the side of the building when he saw the two dark vans rushing down the street.

He pinned her between the building and his body, holding her there.

"Why didn't we take the motorcycle?" Kat whispered.

"Because it's easier to disappear in a crowd." The crowd that was right across the street. Heading in and out of the bars. They just had to get into the mix of people, and they could slip away.

The vans braked near the curb. Their headlights cut into the darkness. When the men got out of the vehicles, they were wearing ski masks.

Shit.

They ran for Rick's bar. He waited until the masked men were inside and then... "Come on." He and Kat made a break for it. They shot across the street. Left the dark and empty corner behind and headed for the packed bars. They rushed forward, hurtling through the throng, and Rick shoved a hundred at the first bouncer he saw so that they could get in the front door of the nearest club.

Music blared. Bodies gyrated. Drinks poured.

"Oh, wow," Kat said, gazing around with a smile on her face. "This place is awesome."

The place was a perfect hiding spot. Crammed with people. Dimly lit.

"Can we dance? Let's dance," Kat urged him.

"A hit team just came for you," he gritted as he yanked her closer to him. "This isn't a party night. This is me trying to keep you alive."

She looked up at him. "And we stick out more when we just stand here." Her voice was low. Husky. "Everyone else is dancing. If we want to blend in, we have to dance, too." He heard a faint click. Her hand lifted, revealing the cuffs—the unlocked cuffs—that dangled from her fingertips.

"And part one of blending in is that we ditch these."

She'd picked the cuffs. *What* had she even used to pick them?

Growling, he grabbed the cuffs and shoved them into his back pocket. Then he put both hands on her and hauled her closer. They moved onto the dance floor because she was right. They were sticking out, and they needed to blend.

They needed to look like every other couple there.

"When they search your place and I'm not there..." Her body swayed against his. "What will they do next?"

"Hunt." Rick's mind was spinning as he tried to figure out what to do. He needed backup. The other Wilde agents were close by, but he'd been careful when they left the safe house. The Wilde agents might not have even seen them.

He could call in his backup. Have a new car waiting in moments.

But he didn't.

How did the hit team learn her location?

Kat didn't have a tracker on her any longer. So did that mean that someone else had given the location away? But the Feds didn't know where she was.

Only Wilde agents knew.

Fuck, fuck, fuck.

He leaned over her. His mouth brushed against her ear. "I have to talk with Cole." He trusted his partner. And he trusted Eric Wilde. Those were the two people he needed right then.

She shivered.

Had he touched the delicate shell of her ear with his mouth? Maybe. Had it been deliberate? Maybe.

His head lifted, and he glanced around. He needed a quiet space, but going outside wasn't an option for him at that moment. He was trying to think through this shit. It was hard to think with blaring music and gyrating bodies that kept bumping into him.

As his gaze drifted, he saw the other men staring. Not at him—their avid gazes were on Kat.

One tall, blond asshole was staring at her like he'd just found a four-course meal.

Rick moved his body, turning so that he was in the blond's line of sight. Then he mouthed, "Fuck off." Very clearly.

The guy fucked off and hurried away.

A few others had their eyes on her. Her ass was shaking, her body was swaying, and Kat sure seemed to be having the time of her life. They were *running* for her life, and she was acting like it was the best clubbing experience ever.

She was also attracting too much attention. So much for blending. Kat wasn't the blending type. She wore jeans and a tight t-shirt. Other women were in designer dresses and short skirts, but it was Kat who caught the attention of the eager jerks in the club.

The movements of her body were sexy as fuck. She was smiling, her eyes were lit up, her hair was tousled.

And the other men there wanted to fuck her. They saw her, they wanted...and Rick wanted to kick their asses.

His head lowered toward hers.

"Rick?"

His mouth *took* hers. A hot, deep kiss of possession. He wanted anyone who saw them to see a man obsessed with the woman before him. A man who wanted her more than anything.

She kissed him back. Kat gave a little moan and returned the kiss with wild abandon. Her lips were soft and silken, and her tongue slid against his in the purest temptation. Desire exploded inside of Rick. It pulsed and churned, and he wanted her. Right the hell then.

With a supreme, freaking effort, he tore away from her lips. He locked his arm around her, and they made their way toward the spiral staircase that led upstairs. A guy with bulging biceps stepped into his path.

"Need a room," Rick snarled at him, keeping a tight hold on Kat. His fingers were curled around her hips. "Need it *now*."

The fellow's knowing gaze went from Rick to Kat. "You'll have to pay for a VIP space."

"Tell me some shit I don't know." With his left hand, he dragged a wad of cash from his wallet. His right stayed locked to Kat.

The bouncer took the cash and motioned upward. "Second room on the right is free."

Rick dragged Kat against him. Kissed her again. Wild. Fierce. Then he pushed her in front of him.

She turned back, staring at him with slightly dazed eyes. "Rick. What are we—"

"Upstairs, baby. *Now*."

She blinked at him and didn't start climbing the stairs. And he got the terrible feeling in the pit of his stomach that she was about to say something wrong. The kind of wrong that would give away the ruse he was trying to create.

So he scooped her up. Tossed her over his shoulder. Made sure he was holding her carefully as he hauled ass up to the second floor. He went straight to the second room. Kicked the door closed. Locked it. *Flimsy-ass lock.* Then slid Kat down his body until her feet touched the floor.

She stared at him with her wide, incredible eyes. "I...I don't know what's happening. Are we here to—"

"Make a call," he finished, voice rumbling and low. "I needed a quiet space. Had to get us one."

She shook her head. "What?"

"I had to make sure everyone downstairs remembered a couple." He yanked out the burner phone. "Not a bodyguard and his target."

Kat sucked in a breath.

He dialed Cole, his eyes drifting to the door to make sure that no one had followed them.

The phone rang. Rang—

"Hello?"

"Cole, we had visitors. The kind in freaking ski masks."

Kat kicked Rick's shin.

He frowned at her. The kick hadn't hurt. He'd barely felt a thing. But why was she kicking him?

She pulled back her foot to kick again.

He rushed forward, pinning her against the wall and his body. "*Don't.*" He had a lot of shit to deal with at the moment. Getting kicked by Kat wasn't something else he wanted on his list.

"Don't what?" Cole asked.

Rick growled. "Who called me? Did you trace the number?"

"Yeah...yeah, but you're not going to like it."

What did he like about the night?

"It came from Wilde Protection and Securities. That's the number for some assistant on the seventh floor. It looks like—shit, Eric is going over the security footage right now, but it looks like someone broke into our building. They called you from inside Wilde. Do you know what kind of skill it would take to pull off something like that?"

He had a clue.

Cole added quickly, "The agents watching your bar called in the arrival of the black vans and they swarmed fast, but not fast enough to stop the bad guys."

"Seriously? What the fuck?"

"Your unexpected visitors blasted their way inside, and, when they saw the place was empty, they raced away. Our agents tailed them for blocks, but then got held up when one of the perps shot out the tires on a Wilde car."

"Wonderful. This shit is insane." Shots flying on the streets? When civilians were around? The Atlanta PD would freak.

"Listen, Rick, we have boots on the ground. They're searching the streets and more backup is on the way. Just tell me where you want the Wilde agents to pick you up."

How had the mystery caller gotten into Wilde? It wasn't that easy. You didn't just waltz inside the place. It would take some serious skills to pull off a move like that.

Kat glared at him. "You're an asshole."

"Tell me something I don't know," he muttered right back.

"Uh...I thought I just *had* told you something," Cole responded, sounding confused. "The call came from inside our own agency. If that doesn't set off a million alarms for you, I don't know what does. So let's get you hooked up with the agents who are close by and then we can—"

"No."

"No?" Cole's voice rose.

Kat kept glaring at Rick. Probably because he was trapping her with his body. "Don't kick me."

"I'm not kicking you," Cole snapped. "Though I'm wondering what the hell you are thinking." A long breath. "What do you mean, 'no'?" Cole asked.

"I mean I don't know who the hell to trust right now. The night is going to shit, and I have to get Kat away from this scene. I'll call you—only you—when I have her secure."

"But, Rick—"

He smashed the phone against the wall. Then he whirled away. Tossed the remains into a garbage can and looked back at Kat.

Kat watched him with huge eyes and then said, "Okay, Hulk, how about you take a breath and settle down?"

His jaw clenched as he gritted, "Princess, you're the one kicking."

"Because you're jerking me around! You're using me! You're kissing me and making me think you want me when really you were just doing some kind of cover crap and—"

Dammit. He marched right back to her. Locked his hands around her shoulders and hauled her close.

She stopped talking.

"I'm not jerking you around. Let's be clear. I want you so badly my whole body aches right now."

"But...What? You do?"

"Move your hips two inches closer, and you'll know the fucking truth on that."

Her body stiffened.

"I kissed you down there because I pretty much always want to kiss you."

Her lips parted.

"But I did also need a cover. You were attracting too much attention."

"I wasn't doing anything!"

"Yeah, you didn't need to do much more. Men noticed you. They were remembering you. I had to get you covered."

"And you thought you'd cover me with your mouth? Interesting."

Had she inched closer? One inch?

"If the people down there are questioned, they'll remember two lovers who couldn't keep their hands off each other." His hands were very much on her, and he didn't want to let go. "Like I said before, they won't remember a bodyguard and his target. They'll remember a hot and heavy couple. Maybe a jealous asshole guy who wanted his woman more than anything else."

She bit her lower lip.

"Right now, I only trust Cole and my boss, Eric. I can't put my faith in anyone else because your life is on the line. So we aren't turning to the other agents. I'm getting you away. I'm getting you off everyone's radar, and then we'll figure out our next move."

She moved closer. Last freaking inch.

He saw her pupils expand.

A shudder worked the length of his body. She didn't get it. The woman was playing with fire. They were both about to go up in flames. "Kat."

"Tell me how I can help."

Oh, the things she could do...No, no, he had to *focus*. "Stay close to me. We're going back downstairs. We're getting out of this club." *Out of the city*. "We're going to need a new phone and transportation."

She nodded. "Okay. Got it."

"You don't leave my side even for a moment, understand?" For all he knew, the people after her could already be in the club. He was starting to think the bad guys were everywhere.

"I'll stay close."

He kissed her. Lowered his head and pressed his lips to hers in another frantic, hungry kiss. He shouldn't be touching her, Rick knew it, but...screw that. He *wanted* her. The more he was with her, the wilder he seemed to become. He'd been so careful over the last few years. Ever since his best friend—a damn psychopath—had gone down in a hail of flames and fury, Rick had been careful. He'd done his job. He'd gone through the motions of living. He'd done everything the *right* way. The boring, safe way.

But things were different with Kat. He was different with her.

She pulled back. Licked her lower lip.

A rumble built in his chest.

"No one is watching us now," Kat whispered. "Why the kiss?"

"Because I want your mouth." *Get moving. No time now.* "Because I want you."

His hand twined with hers. No handcuffs. Just them. "Let's go."

Moments later, they were rushing back down the stairs. If anything, the crowd seemed even thicker. The music was louder. He pulled Kat closer as they weaved through the throng. The blond asshole who had been watching her earlier looked up, as if on cue, and his gaze settled on Kat.

Someone can't take a message.

The asshole hurried toward Kat. "Hey! Hey!"

Kat stilled. Crap. "Let's go," Rick growled in her ear.

She didn't go. Her head turned until she was staring at the blond.

He straightened. Puffed out his chest. Sauntered toward her.

Obviously, the woman could not take a direction to save her life. Hadn't he just said they had to move? That they weren't trying to attract attention? What game was she playing?

The blond smiled as he approached Kat. All toothy and extra-white grin. "Has anyone ever told you that you are absolutely gorgeous?"

"No." She tilted her head. Stared at him. Kept her left hand twined with Rick's.

"Hmm. Then, baby, you've been with the wrong men." A dismissive glance toward Rick.

If I punch him, I make a scene. I'm trying to not make a scene.

But the fool was way too close to Kat.

And getting closer every moment.

"Why the hell are you with a guy like him? You need someone like me, someone who can appreciate all that you are." His gaze dipped down her figure.

The blond's body swayed a bit.

Yeah, drunk courage. Otherwise, that dumbass would know better than to come toward Rick. "You want to get your ass kicked?" Rick asked, genuinely curious.

The blond blinked. "No, I want...her."

"*You're not getting her.*" One fast punch would take the blond down. One punch wouldn't attract too much attention.

Before Rick could swing, the blond stumbled toward Kat. He put his arms around her. *Oh, hell, no.*

Rick reacted in a flash. He yanked her back, put Kat behind him, and drove one fist into the blond's jaw. The asshole went down as the music kept blaring.

None of the other dancers even paused to glance at the fallen man.

Kat grabbed Rick's arm. "Did you just knock him out?"

"Let's go."

"One punch, that was pretty—"

"Let's *go*." He was two seconds away from carrying her out of there. He'd told the woman not to stop, and what had she done? Decided to have a slow-as-you-please chat with an asshole.

Luckily, Rick didn't have to carry her out because she was finally moving, and at a really good clip, too. Moments later, they were outside, and his gaze immediately swept the area as he searched for threats. He kept to the side of the building, holding her close. "We'll need transportation out of here." Staying on the streets wasn't ideal. They needed a car. Maybe a taxi or an Uber, but if they went that route, then they ran the risk that the driver might remember them.

"Got us covered." She lifted her hand. Keys dangled from her fingers.

"Where in the hell did you get those?"

"The same place I got...this." And just like she was doing some magic show sleight-of-hand trick, a phone danced next to the keys. He almost expected her to say *Abracadabra*.

Rick shook his head. "When? Where?"

"The blond. He looked drunk enough that he wouldn't notice a bump and grab, and then he did me the solid of bumping into *me* first. Made everything easier."

No way. "You're a pickpocket?"

"I told you I had skills."

Yes, she had. "I told you we needed to leave the club! Not attract attention." He caught her elbow and guided her down the street. He kept looking for threats—and options.

"I didn't attract attention," Kat grumbled. "I was just doing what you asked."

He stumbled. "I didn't ask you to steal the guy's ride."

Lights flashed from a nearby parked car. A red Benz. He realized Kat had just pushed the unlock button on the keys.

"Look, his car is right here. Perfect." She sounded particularly pleased with herself. *She's a pickpocket and a car thief.* "What are we waiting for?"

The flashing lights were attracting attention. Jeez. His hand fisted over hers. He leaned in close. "Stop."

"Why? And why are you so grumpy? I helped!"

Grumpy? Did he look like one of the seven freaking dwarves?

"You said we needed a phone and transportation. I got us both. You are welcome." She shook off his hand and headed for the Benz.

Uh, no. "We aren't stealing a car!"

She looked over her shoulder. "Why not?"

He glanced around again. They couldn't stay out in the open like this. "Because it's illegal, that's why." He kept his voice low. "I'm not going to be busted for stealing that dick's ride."

"I won't be busted. The Feds will pretty much forgive anything I do as long as I testify for them. I'll say I stole the car and made you get in. So...*come on.*"

They needed to get off the street. They needed to get the hell out of there.

She came back to him and brushed her body against his. "We can leave an apology note, okay? Will that work for you? We'll take the ride to our new, hopefully super safe location and leave an *I'm sorry* note for the jerk."

"The car probably has GPS tracking. We take it, he reports it as stolen, and then we're busted. By the bad guys, and the good ones." Rick grabbed the keys from her in a lightning-fast move.

"Hey!"

He tossed the keys near the car. The asshole could find them later.

"I've got a plan." He could hear his plan in the distance. "And *leave* the phone, too. We don't want to be tracked by it. He wakes up, and who do you think he'll believe stole from him?"

The same guy who cold-cocked his ass.

She grumbled, "Maybe he'll just think it was someone in the packed club? Like, those whole two hundred folks in there?" But she put the phone down. Grudgingly.

He didn't have any more time to waste. No one seemed to be paying them much attention. He didn't see the black vans or any Wilde agents. No sense pushing their luck, though.

"We're not running." He wrapped an arm around her shoulders and pulled her close. "We're taking our time," he rumbled as they started down the street. "Anyone who sees us will see two lovers." He nuzzled her. "That's all. We go down three blocks, we take a right, and then we'll hop on the bus."

Her head pressed against him. "Are you serious? I give you a Benz and you give me a bus?"

His lips twitched. "We'll take the bus until we get to the streetcar pick-up area. We'll get on there, and we'll be long gone before anyone starts hunting." A lie, he knew people were already hunting her. "The streetcar runs until one a.m. on the weekend. We got this. Trust me."

***

Eric Wilde stormed into his office. He tossed his coat aside, and his hands clenched into fists. Someone had broken into *his* place? His? Oh, the hell, no. "I want every security feed we've got," he snapped to his assistant Dennis. "I want every shot, every signal. I want to know why in the *hell* I wasn't alerted to a break-in here."

"Uh, uh, yes, Eric, I'll—"

A knock at the door. The open door. Eric glared when he saw Agent Bryan Brisk. He'd known the fellow would be showing up. Hell, he was actually surprised that he'd beaten Brisk to Wilde.

"We need to talk," Bryan told him flatly. There was no sign of the other agent, Tom Wayne. Was he downstairs?

Eric pointed at Dennis. "Get me what I need."

Dennis rushed out. Bryan shut the door behind him.

The agent was still wearing one of his Bureau suits, but his collar was undone. His hair was rumpled, and a five o'clock shadow covered his jaw. "She's compromised."

"No, she's not. Rick is still with her. She's *safe*."

"The problem wasn't with the FBI. My boss doesn't believe so, either. We misinterpreted the situation before."

He didn't need this crap right now. "Agent, look, I don't have any intel to give you yet, but I will. So just get your ass back to your hotel room or wherever you were staying. When I know more, I'll update you on the—"

"The FBI is taking over again. Wilde was breached. You and your agents are done with Kat for now."

Eric crossed his arms over his chest. "Excuse me?"

"I've been told that I should take over Kat's security detail again, immediately."

"Oh, really? Because I wasn't informed of this change. Didn't get a phone call from your boss telling me that my team was out."

The agent squared his shoulders. "I'm here. Thought that would be notification enough."

"It's not. I'll talk to your boss myself. And, in the meantime, you should know...Kat is currently off grid."

Bryan's nostrils flared. "What the hell does that mean?"

"What the hell do you *think* it means?"

The agent's face reddened.

"It's a typical security response in situations like this," Eric said as he struggled to keep his voice flat. *Someone broke into my building. Someone will pay.* There actually wasn't a typical security response because shit like this had never happened before. No one should have gotten past Eric's security, and he was pretty much losing his shit right then. But he kept up his calm front as he added, "Rick understands that Kat's security has been compromised, so he'll be going dark until they are at a safe location. He will be moving her, and fast, and he'll make certain that she stays alive."

"How long until he contacts you?" Bryan gritted out.

Eric smiled at him. "I don't know. Why don't we just wait and see?"

"Bullshit! You are *lying* to me. You're lying to a federal agent. I could have your ass thrown in jail."

Well, the agent had some anger issues. Good to know. "Why don't you try?" Eric invited.

Bryan glared at him. "The leak was in *your* building. Isn't it obvious what happened? A Wilde agent was bought off. One agent...hell, could be a dozen of them."

"No," Eric replied flatly.

"The big, high and mighty Wilde business is burning down around you. Your agents have sold out Kathleen O'Shaughnessy. You're compromised. She needs to be brought to me. Now."

Eric tried to think of a tactful way to say...*Go fuck yourself.* But, he'd never been big on tact. "Go fuck yourself."

"You're telling the FBI—"

"I'm telling *you*...get out of my office. I deal directly with your supervisor, no one else. Until I hear from him that Wilde is no longer in charge of Kathleen's security, nothing will change." He fought his growing rage. "But you're not going to stand in my office and accuse *my* agents of being on the take. Everyone here has passed a thorough background check, and I've never doubted anyone on my team."

"You were never dealing with a situation like this one, either. Twenty million dollars—that money will tempt anyone."

"Good-bye, Agent Brisk. We're done here."

"No, you *will* be seeing me again." Bryan turned on his heel and stormed out.

Eric stared after him, frowning. Eric had a bad feeling in the pit of his stomach. The twisting, churning feeling that told him that things were about to get even worse.

Dennis poked his head inside Eric's office. "Working on the security footage, boss."

Eric nodded, but his mind was elsewhere. He reached for his phone and called his FBI contact. The line rang and rang. No answer.

Not a good sign.

What in the hell was going on?

CHAPTER NINE

The streetcar was deserted. Kat sat on the hard seat, her hands twisting in front of her. Rick glowered from the seat across from her. The guy probably had no clue how sexy she found his glower. She wasn't going to tell him. Instead, she cleared her throat and said, "So you're a Boy Scout."

His brows lifted. "Hardly."

"You wouldn't let me steal a car. You wouldn't let me steal a phone."

"You *did* steal the phone."

Yes, she had. It had been ridiculously easy. "Just what would it take to make you break some rules?"

The streetcar hurtled forward.

Rick didn't answer.

Fine. Whatever. She glanced out of the window and stared at the darkness.

"I'd need a pretty good fucking reason to break the law."

"My family never really worried about reasons. They just did it."

"And you're like your family? Like your dad?"

No. I never want to be like him. "Desperate times call for desperate measures. Isn't that a saying? I don't know how much more desperate I can get."

"I'm not going to let you get hurt."

"But what if you get hurt trying to protect me?" Her gaze flew back to him. "You think I enjoy having blood on my hands? Was that some sort of little trivia detail that was in my bio? Kat likes blood. She doesn't mind innocent people dying. And her turn-ons include men who can cook."

She surged out of the seat. Took four steps forward. Realized there was no place for her to go. They were trapped on the empty streetcar. She knew being alone there was deliberate. He'd waited to make sure no one else was getting on the car before he'd urged her inside.

Being alone with him was making her twitchy.

"Kat..." He rose. Seemed to swallow all of the space in the streetcar. "I don't think you like having blood on your hands." He caught her hand in his. "And I know you're not like your dad."

"Well, most people aren't psychotic killers so it's good to know you think I'm not like him." She pulled her hand away and took a step back. "How about this? How about you stop with the touching and the hot looks and the whole simmering sexuality thing you have going on? Because I'm not in the mood to play." She was at the end of her rope. "You say you want me. You know I want you. So don't touch me again unless you're following through, big guy. Touch me if you mean it. Touch me because that precious control of yours is shot." The way hers was. Adrenaline crashed through her body. Her fingers were shaking. Her whole body was too tight and too strained and she was barely holding everything together.

She backed away from him.

Then he stalked forward. "I told you already, I'm not playing."

Her back hit the side of the car.

"I warned you before, too, about what would happen if I took you."

Like she'd ever been the type to heed warnings. *That* part should have been in her bio.

He kept coming forward. He stopped right in front of her, the heat of his body surrounding her. Churning up her emotions and her need even more.

His hand rose and his fingers caressed her neck. She knew he had to feel her racing pulse beneath his touch.

"I wasn't supposed to want you," he said.

She hadn't counted on him, either. "Maybe it's the adrenaline." Or maybe it was just the appeal of the forbidden. They were supposed to stay apart, so she wanted nothing more than to get closer to him.

"But I..." A furrow dug between his brows. "I can't remember ever needing someone so much."

"What are you going to do about that?"

His hand rose. Sank into the thickness of her hair as he tipped back her head. "I think I'm going to make you scream."

Promises, promises.

"Scream with so much pleasure that for a while, we both forget everything else." He kissed her. Deep and hard and with that wild need that she craved. Her hands flew up and locked around him. His left hand dropped to her ass and in the next instant, he'd lifted her up. He held her with that fierce strength of his, caging her between him and the metal wall. The wall vibrated as the streetcar hurtled forward, and the vibration shook through her whole body. Or maybe he was the one shaking her. The lust she felt for him *shook* her.

She'd long since kissed any hope of future happiness good-bye. When you were the daughter of a mob boss, you didn't get some sweet, fairy tale, happily ever after BS ending. And with her father's death, with the bounties on her head, she'd known that she was already living on borrowed time as it was.

But to have Rick...to have *this*. To feel this much need and lust for someone...to be able to let go even in the midst of chaos and just feel...it was worth everything.

"When I get you alone, you're mine." His rough promise.

Um, they were alone.

"Not here, sweetheart. Even as much as I want you, not here. Because the first time, I want to savor every single inch of your body," Rick growled the words as he kissed his way down her throat.

Sounded like a great plan to her. But she got to savor him, too.

The streetcar slowed. His head lifted. "This is our stop."

She sucked in a breath.

He stared at her. "Trust me."

She didn't exactly have a choice on that one. Other options at this point? None.

"Don't run from me. Don't lie to me."

"I want the same from you." She wet her lips. Saw the flash of his pupils as they expanded. "Don't lie to me. Don't run from what I am."

"Baby, I'd never run from you."

Easy for him to say now. Harder when he learned all of her secrets. *If* he learned them.

With a screech, the car stopped. A moment later, the doors surged open. They rushed into the night.

***

The motel was obviously not the Ritz, but it was mostly clean and safe. Rick shut the door behind him. Secured all the locks and swept his gaze over Kat. She was walking around the room, her steps a little hesitant. They'd stopped at a nearby store—one that ran twenty-four, seven—to pick up some needed supplies. A new phone. Burner phones were so cheap these days.

Condoms.

A *very* much needed supply item. Because there was no way he was sleeping in that bed with her all night and not having her. Or, rather, for what was left of the night.

He opened the bag he carried. Tossed the burner onto the dresser that waited under the TV. And he put the box of condoms on the wobbly nightstand.

Kat's gaze immediately went to the condoms. Then to him.

The air in the little room got very, very thick.

She clasped her hands together. "I know sex won't change anything between us."

His head cocked.

"It's not...I mean, I don't expect anything to change. You'll take me to the courthouse. I'll go inside and do my part, and we'll never see each other again after that."

He advanced toward her. Right then, he didn't want to think about life after Kat. He only wanted to think about...*Kat*.

"I'm not looking for some crazy, emotional declaration. I get that isn't who we are."

He grabbed the hem of his shirt and yanked it over his head. The shirt dropped behind him.

Her lips parted. Her gaze darted over him. Then... "Um, so, I know it's just sex. Just need. And I'm good with that."

He kicked off his shoes. Ditched his socks. He straightened and his hands went to the snap of his jeans.

She stared. "I'm...good with really hot, really awesome sex with you."

A smile tugged at his lips. "You're so sure it will be awesome, huh?"

"I have high expectations based on what happens to me when you kiss me."

His heart gave a little jerk at the response he hadn't expected. "And what happens when I kiss you?"

"My whole body heats up. I go from zero to wanting you pretty much instantly. I want to get closer to you. I crave you. I haven't ever felt that way about someone before. Not that intently. Not that fast."

Good to know. Something else that was good to know...His hand reached out and curled around the hem of her shirt. He tugged her forward. "I'll make damn sure sex with me is *awesome* for you. I won't stop until you're screaming my name."

But her gaze slid to the left. Then to the right. "Walls here are real thin. Don't know if that's such a good idea. What with us keeping a low profile and all."

"Good point," he told her, not letting any hint of humor slip into his voice. "I'll take care of the screams. No one else will hear you but me." He pulled her a little closer. "You know, you were the one naked last time. Now I'm standing in front of you with only half my clothes on."

"I wasn't naked. I was in my underwear. There's a difference." Her words were husky and rushed.

He studied her with a sharpening gaze. "Have you changed your mind?" *God, please don't have—*

"No, but I think I'm nervous."

Nervous he could handle. He could handle anything she wanted to throw at him.

"My track record with lovers isn't the greatest. Bad things tend to happen to men who want me. And I just realized I don't want anything bad to ever happen to you."

That was sweet. She was sweet. Nothing like what he'd thought. He pulled her forward those last few inches, using his hold on her shirt. Her head tipped back as she stared up at him. "Nothing bad will happen," he swore. "Not to either of us." Rick kissed her. He started the kiss slow. Savoring. Sampling. Because as he'd told her before, when he got her, he intended to enjoy every inch of her. *And I've got you, princess.* Right or wrong, he had her.

Her lips parted beneath his. He thrust his tongue into her mouth even as his fingers slid under her shirt to touch warm, smooth skin. Up, up, his hands went as he enjoyed her body. He felt the edge of her bra, wanted it out of the way. Wanted her breasts out so that he could lick and taste.

But he had to get her ready. Her body was still tense. She'd been talking about need and desire, but with the big moment actually there, she was hesitating. He didn't want any fear in her mind when they were together. He only wanted desire. He didn't want her worrying about the past or the future.

The past didn't matter. The future—who the hell knew what would happen? All that mattered was this moment.

He pulled his mouth from hers. Began to kiss a hot path down her neck. He knew she was sensitive along the delicate column of her throat. He'd made a mental note of that spot earlier. Now he sucked her neck lightly. Licked. Allowed the most sensual of bites.

Her body shuddered against him. Her nails bit into his shoulders. "Rick!"

He knew that she was with him. Hell, yes. "The clothes need to go."

"Absolutely," she agreed in her sultry, husky voice. Only she didn't move to strip off her own clothes. Her hands dropped between them and reached for the snap of his jeans. A second later, the zipper was hissing down, and his eager cock shoved toward her.

"Not the underwear type, huh? I'll remember that." Her fingers curled around him. Stroked. Had his eyes rolling back in his head—

"Kat."

"Oh, God, I love it when you growl my name like that. It's all wild and hot and like you don't care about anything but me."

He lifted her into his arms. Carried her to the bed. In a flash, he had her on the bed while he stretched on top of her, careful not to crush her. He'd *always* have to be careful with her. "Right at this moment, there is nothing I care about more than you."

Her lips curved. Her smile was gorgeous.

He kissed her. He *loved* her mouth.

He also loved having her without clothes. So when he tore his mouth from hers a few moments later, he edged back long enough to lift up her shirt. To toss it aside, then his hands went for her bra and he fumbled and—

There. The bra fell away. Her round breasts thrust toward him, the nipples tight and dark, and he took one into his mouth.

Fuck, yes.

She arched beneath him and gasped out his name.

His hand slid down her body. His fingers moved between her legs, and he stroked her through the jeans. Stroked her as he licked and sucked and wanted to *devour* her.

Her hips surged up toward him. "The jeans have got to go!"

His thought exactly.

He pulled back, moving to his knees beside her. Kat kicked away her shoes, and when he jerked down her jeans, he took her socks with them. She was left clad in silky, sexy panties, and for a moment, he just stared at her.

All of the moisture dried from his mouth.

"Are you going to look?" Kat asked him. "Or are you going to touch?"

"How about I do one better?" His voice was savage with need. "How about I taste?" He moved between her legs, pushed her thighs farther apart, and put his mouth on her. The silk was between him and her hot core, for the moment. She gave a sharp cry and pushed toward him.

He used his mouth on her. Licked against the silk. Enjoyed the way her body shuddered and the way she gasped his name. Lust built higher, darker, and rougher inside of him. He reached for the panties and wasn't the least bit surprised when they ripped beneath his fingers. Not like he'd ever been able to handle delicate things.

But I will handle her.

He looked up at her. Her cheeks were flushed, her lips red and plump, and her eyes were shining. He swallowed and managed to say, "If I'm too rough, *stop* me. Tell me to back the hell off, and I will."

"I don't want you backing off. I want you *in* me."

He felt his control shatter at her hot, dark words. His mouth went back to her. Nothing between his lips and her flesh this time. She tasted so good. He could make a meal of her. He licked and sucked and thrust his tongue over her clit. Stroking, rubbing, loving the way she—

"*Rick!*"

She was coming already. He could taste her pleasure, and it made him even wilder. Her voice was close to a scream, and he had to be careful. He'd made a promise to her.

He rose up her body.

Her lips parted and he knew—

She's going to scream. Can't let anyone else hear her.

Rick kissed her. His fingers thrust into her as he helped her to ride out her orgasm, and her inner muscles clamped tightly around him. So tight.

She was going to feel *insane* around his dick.

He kept working her, stroking her until the trembles eased. His mouth lifted.

Her breath panted out.

He grabbed for the condoms. Tore the box open. Ripped into one of the foil packets. He had the condom on in record time as he pushed his eager cock toward the entrance to her body. She looked so small compared to him. Fragile. Breakable.

"What in the world are you *waiting* for?" Her nails scraped down his arms. "I'm going crazy. Get inside. *Now!*"

Maybe not so fragile. Maybe—maybe just fucking perfect.

He surged into her. The bed rocked beneath them. Her breath choked out and her nails bit even deeper into his arms.

"Kat?"

"One minute...no, one second...just give me...a second..." Her breath sawed out. "There's an awful lot of you."

He kissed her. *Get control. Keep it.* His hand slid between their bodies and caressed her.

"I'm good. Better than good." She caught his lower lip. Nipped it. "Don't hold back with me. I want everything you've got."

But he had his control, for the moment, and he was holding onto it with a death grip. He needed more care with her. He *would* show her care.

"Rick!"

He withdrew, thrust deep, but it was a restrained thrust. Not wild. Not so desperate.

"No." Another nip on his lower lip from Kat. "That's not you. I want the real you. Give me everything!" Her legs locked around his hips as her sex clamped greedily around him. "Fuck me hard, like you super mean it."

Fuck her like...he was torn between laughing with an odd joy and fucking her like he was a man possessed. Option two won. He withdrew again, then slammed deep. Control? Gone. Need? Consuming. He withdrew and thrust. Their bodies grew slick with sweat. He wanted in deeper, more, and he grabbed her legs and heaved them over his shoulders. Her body twisted and surged against his, and her hands fell to fist around the sheets. Her body went bow tight, and he knew a scream was coming from her.

"Kat," he tried to caution.

One of her hands flew up and covered her own mouth. Her eyes grew wide behind her hand and he felt the contractions of her climax squeeze him.

He grabbed her hand, pulled it away, and slid his own fingers over her pretty lips.

She caught his index finger and sucked it into her mouth. Her tongue licked, dipping around the finger and driving him mad.

He rolled on the bed, dragging her on top of him and sealing them together even harder. "Ride me," he snarled.

She did. Her knees slammed into the bed. Up and down. He cupped her breasts, stroked her nipples and shoved his cock in her so hard that she arched up.

And she came again. He felt her whole body quake right before Rick's own release hit him. An eruption of pleasure so intense that he was the one who opened his mouth to bellow.

She leaned forward and put her hand over his mouth. He bit her palm and she moaned with pleasure. He loved the way she moaned. Loved the way she looked when she came. Loved—*Get it together, man. It's just sex. Just. Sex.*

Her hand slid away from his mouth. His dick was hard and thick inside of her, even though he'd just come. He was hard again—still?—because he already wanted more.

"That..." She paused to lick her lips. "Okay, that definitely qualified as awesome."

Rick thought it qualified as one hell of a lot more.

He rolled her over again, moving her onto her side, and he carefully withdrew from her. She still flinched though. Hell. "I'm...sorry."

"For what? Three super orgasms?" She closed her eyes and yawned. "You are not forgiven."

His lips curved. "And you're not forgiven for the best—"

He broke off. Her eyes had cracked opened and locked on him.

"The best what?" Kat asked as she stretched, seeming not to be bothered at all by the fact that she was completely naked. No shyness, and he loved that. He could look at her body all day and night.

Her fingers fluttered in the air. "The best what, Rick?"

The best sex of my life. Was a guy just supposed to blurt shit out like that?

Before he could answer, her gaze had dropped down his body. "You're...still up?"

Up? "Hell, yeah," he rasped. "I'm pretty much always that way around you."

The pink in her cheeks deepened.

"But you're probably sore. You need rest." He could be a gentleman, dammit. He *could* do this. "I'll keep my hands off you."

She slid from the bed. Rolled back her shoulders as she stood and stared at him. "Keep your hands away? How incredibly boring that sounds."

His chest warmed. "Well, I don't want you to be bored."

"I am sore. I should probably take a hot shower to see if that helps." She batted her lashes

at him. *She's flirting with me. And it's cute as hell.*
"Want to join me?"

I'd like to see someone try and stop me.
"Yeah, princess, I sure do." He swallowed because
his voice sounded barely human. "Why don't you
go in the bathroom and get the water going? I'll be
right there."

Her smile was like a knife to his chest and he
had no freaking idea why.

She slipped into the bathroom. Shut the door
behind her. A moment later, he heard the shower
turn on.

He tossed the condom into the garbage and
ripped the burner phone from the plastic pack. He
dialed fast a moment later.

Cole answered immediately. He'd figured his
friend would be standing by.

"She's safe," Rick growled. That was all he was
going to say. That was all—

"We've got a major freaking problem."

CHAPTER TEN

Kat stared into the mirror. It fogged up fast because the hot water sent steam into every corner of the small room. Her hand swiped over the glass. Her eyes—too dazed and too big—stared back at her.

She'd tried to handle the whole bedroom scene with confidence. Tried to act like wild, insane sex was just—you know. A thing.

My whole body is shaking. Her knees were trembling. Her hands flew down and clamped around the edge of the sink's countertop. It was either clamp on or fall down.

Sex at seventeen had been a quick, messy fumble. Then poor Jimmy had gotten the hell beat out of him. She'd had to throw herself between him and her father's men. One of those guys hadn't pulled his fist back fast enough.

The blow had crashed into her face.

For a moment, everyone had been stunned. Blood had dripped down her chin. She'd been shaking, and she'd known that if she didn't do *something,* Jimmy would die that night.

So she'd fought like hell for him. She'd punched and hit at the others who'd swarmed. She'd yelled at her father. Stood her ground in the face of his rage and demanded that Jimmy be let go. He hadn't done anything wrong. His crime was that he was a seventeen-year-old boy who'd thought that he loved her.

Jimmy had been dropped off at the nearest hospital. She'd promised her father she'd never see him again.

She had never looked for Jimmy.

As far as her last lover...the sex had been good. Sure, Gage had been a lying pile of crap, but the sex had been fine. *Fine.*

She'd found out later that he'd been using her. Typical, in her world—a place full of liars, users, and killers.

Was it any wonder she was ready to escape?

Sex with Rick hadn't been fine. Sex with him had been mind-blowing. Insane. *And I want it again.*

She ached, and Kat didn't care. One day, she'd look back on her time with him, if she was lucky, if she *lived* long enough to look back—one day when she was passing her time in some pretend, Witness Protection existence in the middle of nowhere—she'd look back and she'd smile when she thought of sex with Rick.

Smile and fantasize a bit.

She shoved open the glass shower door and slid inside.

***

"We've got a shit ton of problems right now," Rick retorted, keeping his voice low, "so you'll need to be more specific."

"Agent Brisk walked into Eric's office tonight and said Wilde is off the case. The Feds want to take over again, and they want Kat returned to them right away."

"No, no, the last time we talked, you said the Feds were still out. That *we* were watching her—"

"Status has changed. Brisk says the leak wasn't on their end. They must figure she was tracked via the necklace while in their custody. As to how someone found her tonight, well, now the Feds don't seem to be trusting *us*."

"You're shitting me."

"If only. Our security system went *down*. Do you hear me? Do you know how impossible that is? Our state-of-the-art security, in our own building, went dark for five minutes. Someone got in. Someone got access to files—to our safe houses, to our agents' private numbers—someone got access to *her*. And Bryan Brisk is saying that a Wilde agent was bought off. That it had to be an inside job."

"Screw him."

"He...may not be wrong."

Rick's gaze shot to the closed bathroom door.

"Hell, man, you said yourself...you couldn't trust anyone but me and Eric. Maybe someone in Wilde did roll. An awful lot of money is up for grabs when it comes to Kathleen O'Shaughnessy."

"Tell me something I don't know."

"All right...Eric is trying to contact his buddy at the FBI. You know, the one who *actually* hired us? Brisk's boss? Only the guy seems to have fallen off the radar."

Not good.

"So until Eric makes contact with the FBI Brass who actually hired us, Eric wants you to keep staying close to Kat. He says we're not turning her over to anyone until he finds out exactly what is happening. Don't bring her in. Keep her hidden, until you hear otherwise from either me or Eric."

Hell, yes. He'd known he could count on Eric. "I can do that."

"I figured staying close wouldn't be a problem. Not with the way you were looking at her."

"Fuck off."

"*Rick.*"

The intensity in his friend's voice stopped Rick right before he would've hung up the phone.

"Be careful. Like I said, I *saw* how you looked at her."

"I've got this."

"Just make sure she doesn't get *you*. Because this is going to end, one way or another. She'll be out of your life, and you'll be out of hers."

He knew that. They'd agreed, hadn't they? No emotions. Just sex. Sex and protection. That was his new package—protect her from the bad guys and give her more pleasure than she could stand.

Yeah, I've gone freaking insane.

"This isn't like you," Cole continued carefully, as if he was searching for the right words. "We both know it. You never get involved. Not on any of your cases."

Because he didn't get close to anyone. He usually kept everyone out. It was just safer that way. Hell, when you screw up so badly that you missed the fact that your best fucking friend was a psychopath who got off on setting fires...you tended to be a little gun shy with people.

Cole knew about Rick's past. Not many people knew. Even fewer understood. There were some secrets he hadn't been able to share at all.

Like the fact that he'd ignored his suspicions about Daniel Morgan. Ignored his instincts. Back when he'd been a firefighter, he'd been so close to Daniel. The guy had been more like a brother than a friend. But then a few things had started to nag at Rick. He'd just brushed the nagging aside.

And people had died. All because he'd been blinded by his friendship. Blinded by trust that he'd put in the wrong person.

"Be careful," Cole urged again.

"I've got this." He ended the call. Tossed the phone onto the bed—the tangled covers. Clothes littered the floor, and the scrap of silk that *had* been Kat's panties—before Rick had torn them off her—waited near his foot.

Emotions could blind a man. With Kat, he *wasn't* letting emotions get in the way. This was physical, that was all. Lust. His judgment wouldn't be clouded.

He'd do the job.

He strode toward the bathroom door. When he yanked it open, steam immediately drifted out and surrounded him. The pounding of the water filled his ears. He could see the curvy outline of her body behind the steamed-up glass of the shower door.

For a moment, he didn't move.

Just physical. Lust. A savage hunger.

She turned toward him. Opened the shower door. Her wet hair slid over her shoulders and droplets of water trailed over her skin. "I was starting to think you weren't joining me."

Did he look like a dumbass? Maybe. In two steps, he was in that shower. The water poured on him, hot and hard, and his mouth took hers. The water was on her lips, her body slid against his, and he realized how easy it would be to get lost in her.

He picked her up and pushed her back against the tiled wall. He didn't take his mouth from hers. He *couldn't* stop kissing her. Her mouth was heaven, and she tasted like the sweetest sin.

Her legs wrapped around his hips as the water pounded down on them. His eager dick shoved at the entrance of her body. It would be so simple to thrust into her. To drive deep and hard. To feel the hot paradise of her body clinging tightly to him.

But...

Shit. The condoms are in the other room.

Her hips arched against him. Her mouth tore from his as she moaned his name. Her head tipped back, and his mouth went straight for the curve of her throat. His beard was probably too damn rough. He should be careful, he should—

"I want you to fuck me," she whispered.

Yeah, that was absolutely on his to-do list. His dick was rock hard, and he wanted nothing more than to plunge deep into her. But he'd said he'd protect her. And that meant he took care of her in every way.

His lips pressed to her throat, and his hand slid between their bodies. He pushed a finger into her, and Kat hissed out a breath. "You're so tight, princess." He worked another finger into her. Her delicate inner muscles squeezed him. Fucking perfection.

He worked her with his fingers, sliding them in and out, and making damn sure that his thumb pushed to her clit. Over and over. He stroked. He worked her into a frenzy. He could feel the tightening of her body. The wild tremors right before—

She came. She choked out his name and her head jerked down fast as she bit his shoulder.

Sexiest thing in the world.

Her sex was squeezing his fingers, her whole body was trembling, and if he didn't get inside of her—in the next sixty seconds—he'd go crazy.

He carried her out of the shower. Left the water pounding. Got her to the bed. Grabbed for the condoms and yanked one on—

"Rick?"

He drove into her. They both gasped. Her hands came up and his fingers twined with hers before he pinned her hands to the bed. He couldn't hold back. He thrust hard and fast and he stared into her eyes. Her breath heaved faster. Her hips arched to meet him. She wasn't just taking his thrusts, she was driving right back at him. Holding him as tightly as she could. Arching against him. Squeezing him hard with her inner muscles. Making him even wilder.

They came together. He'd never come at the same time as a lover before. He erupted in her and felt the contractions of her release at the same time. This climax was even more powerful than the first one had been. It ripped through him. Seemed to explode in every cell of his body. His mouth crashed on hers and he kissed her as they came.

His heart thundered in his ears. Reality came back—very, very slowly. He lifted his head. She stared up at him and—

Was she blinking away tears? His heart didn't thunder. It seemed to skip a beat. "Baby?"

She smiled at him. "I think you left the water running."

He'd—

Shit.

Muttering a curse, he withdrew from her. She gave a quick wince. Crap. "I'm sorry."

Kat caught his hand. "You didn't hurt me. Not even a little bit."

He swallowed. Hurried into the bathroom and turned off the shower. He ditched the condom and—

Rick caught his reflection in the mirror. *Hello, Scary-As-Hell.* Kat had just taken him into her body? Offered herself to him?

He couldn't believe that she wasn't running for the hills. That she wasn't—

Running?

He shot out of that bathroom, lunging fast, and his gaze immediately went for the bed as frantic fear filled him.

But Kat wasn't running. She hadn't slipped out while his back was turned. *Of course,* she hadn't slipped out. He'd barely been gone two minutes. Maybe a minute. Why was he freaking out?

"What's wrong?" Kat propped up on one elbow as she stared at him.

He stalked toward her. Her hair was tousled, her cheeks flushed, her lips swollen from his mouth. His hand reached out to her, and his fingers trailed over the column of her throat. "I left marks on you. I should shave."

"Do *not* even think of shaving that beard. I love it in a million different ways." She smiled at him. "And I don't mind the marks on my neck...or my thighs."

His dick twitched. Always eager. For her. He pressed the button on the wall to turn out the lights. Darkness filled the room.

"The marks will fade in no time. They'll probably be gone by morning. They won't last." She yawned. "Can we sleep together?"

His lips curved. "I thought we just did."

"No, that was our *awesome* sex. And I told you it would be that good." She settled down in the bed. "I mean actually sleep together. Me and you, in this bed. I don't want you pulling some of your crazy BS where you invent some rule about how you can't actually sleep in the same bed with a client."

That probably was a Wilde rule. But he wouldn't be the first agent to ignore that rule. Rick climbed into the bed with her.

Immediately, she rolled closer. "Now just put your arm around my shoulders."

His arm lifted and, tentatively, he curled his arm around her shoulders as she burrowed closer to him.

Kat gave a light laugh. "The way you're acting, I'd think you never actually slept with a lover before."

He hadn't. Had sex, yes, but stuck around for the morning after? No, his lovers had been ready to walk after the fun was done.

His hand slid over her shoulder, smoothing her hair. Rick realized that he liked having her that close. Her scent was all around him, and he liked it.

I like her.

"I'm not supposed to tell you my secrets." Her voice had turned husky, sleepy. "Since you're just going to sell me out to the FBI."

"I'm *not*."

"But this secret doesn't matter. I've never actually slept in the same bed with a man before. Didn't exactly have the opportunity with poor Jimmy, and as for Gage, we were meeting in secret, and when you're meeting a lover in secret, it's not like there's a whole lot of cuddle time."

His muscles tightened.

"It's nicer than I expected. I like being with you, this way."

His mouth brushed over her temple. "I like it, too." A truth for a truth. "But, baby, got to say, I *don't* like hearing about you meeting in secret with another lover. Think we covered it before, but just in case you missed it, I'm possessive and jealous as hell when it comes to you."

Her head tilted back. "Gage didn't care about me."

"That makes me want to kick his ass all the more."

"Because...you're jealous."

"Because the fucker hurt you." Another truth that pushed out of him under the cover of the darkness. Hell, it looked like he was the one over sharing. Rick cleared his throat. "You should get some sleep."

"I don't usually sleep well. Too many sins on my soul. But I think it might be different this time." She snuggled closer.

Holy hell, she was *snuggling* with him.

"Rick, have you ever trusted the wrong person?" Her voice was even softer. A little slurred.

"Yeah, baby, I have."

"What happened...when you realized what you'd done?"

He thought of the fire. The smoke. The death. "I left him to die in a fucking inferno that he'd set."

She stiffened. "Uh, what?" Now she didn't sound so sleepy.

Why was he sharing this with her? But his lips parted and Rick heard himself say, "I was a firefighter, way back before Wilde. I worked with my best friend. Daniel Morgan was the kind of guy everyone loved. Charming and easy going, the guy was a hero. Or at least, that was what people thought."

She was silent.

"I grew suspicious about him. We started having some big fires. Damn big blazes, and

Daniel knew too much about them. He reacted too quickly. He'd be able to analyze the scene too fast. Hell, I know I'm not making sense, but things just seemed *off* to me. I had a knot in my gut that I couldn't shake, only I didn't say anything about it. I was suspicious, but...he was my best friend."

Her hand pressed over his heart.

"Then one day...one fire...I found him with his fiancée. God, Julia. I can't forget her face in those flames. Daniel was going to kill her because she'd found out that he was setting fires. Setting them just so he could be the first on scene and put them out. People *died* in those fires. Daniel didn't care. He just wanted the glory. He was going to kill Julia so that he could keep right on being the hero in the world's eyes." He sucked in a breath and, for a moment, Rick could taste ash.

"What happened to Julia?"

"I dragged her out of the fire." He swallowed. "There wasn't enough time to save them both. The building was falling down around us. I got hit by a beam. Shit, I was just trying to hold onto Julia and..." *And Daniel was screaming. Telling me to leave her. That I was his friend. That I should save him.*

He didn't think Julia even remembered those final cries. He'd never mentioned them to her. He hadn't wanted her to realize that he'd had to make a choice that day. He'd chosen her.

"Julia is one of the best people I've ever met," he said, voice gruff in the darkness. "I wasn't going to let her die in that fire. We both got out. Daniel didn't. Then we made sure the world knew the truth about him." He swallowed the taste of ash. "Julia is the one who got me to start working with Wilde. She became an agent and she dragged *me* with her. We worked together as partners for a while. She's absolutely amazing."

"I think I'm jealous now," Kat whispered. "She sounds great."

She was. "She'll always be one of my best friends, but I promise, you don't need to be jealous of a damn thing. We are only friends. And the guy who owns her heart now—if I so much as looked sideways at Julia, he'd attack. I mean, I'd kick his ass, but he'd still attack."

She gave a soft laugh.

"She thinks I saved her," he added as his fingers trailed over Kat's shoulder. "But after Daniel died, the guilt was eating me alive. I ignored my suspicions about him, I trusted the wrong person, and people died." The guilt would never go away completely. "She made me keep living. Got my ass focused on something else. Got me to help others again."

"Where is she now?"

"Finally living her happily ever after with her rock star."

"What?"

A rusty laugh came from him. "Let's just say that Julia settled down with a guy I never expected her to like. She's happy now, and she deserves that happiness."

"Good. I like it when people get happy endings."

He stared at her in the darkness. "You deserve to be happy, too."

"You shouldn't be too sure about that." A soft whisper.

"You're not your father. You haven't hurt anyone—"

"I guess we both had psychopaths in our lives, huh? The wrong people who were far too close to us." Now she sounded sad. "You stopped your monster, though. I didn't. Many people would say I don't deserve anything but a prison cell."

"Kat…" He hated the pain he could feel pulsing from her.

"I tried to go to the cops. No one knows that. I had evidence. I had a video of him that I took after everything with Gage blew up. I had a video of my dad ordering a hit. I went to the cops. I—" She stopped. "How did you do it?"

He didn't understand. "Do what?"

She pulled away.

He didn't like that. He'd been enjoying having her in his arms.

She sat up in bed. "You just talked to me. You were *kind* to me. That's how you did it." She drew her knees up. Wrapped her arms around them.

"Baby, I don't understand what's happening right now."

"I'm telling you secrets, not even trying to stop, and all you had to do was be *kind*. Does that tell you how messed up I am?"

"You're not messed up."

"But I am." She rose from the bed and wrapped a sheet around her body. "I'm telling you secrets that no one should know."

He wanted her back in the bed. Back in his arms.

"I had evidence. I'm not the cold-blooded bitch everyone thinks. I had video. I was *so* careful. I was going to bring him down. I was going to stop him." Her words tumbled out in rapid fire succession. "I went to the cops, and do you know what happened?"

Rick's hand fisted around the covers.

"The cops were working for my father. They destroyed the evidence in front of me. They called him. He came to get me. On the ride home, he just said one thing to me. Only one. Do you want to know what he said? Do you want that secret, too?"

No. "Kat, you don't have to tell me—"

"He said... 'The next time you betray me, you're dead. Daughter or not, you're dead.'"

Fuck, fuck, *fuck*.

She turned away. The exterior light fell through the blinds and he saw the sheet trailing behind her like a wedding gown. Kat opened the bathroom door and stepped inside. A moment later, the door closed with a soft click.

His hand was still fisted around the covers, and his heart—the damn thing *hurt*.

***

She came out of the bathroom twenty minutes later. Kat kept the light off when she slipped into the motel room. Her eyes were puffy and her chest ached. She *hated* crying. There was no point in it. Crying always made her head ache and turned her eyes red. Some people felt better after they cried. She was not one of those people.

She was an ugly crier, too. So things just sucked all around.

She glanced in the general direction of the chair she'd seen earlier. Her eyes adjusted to the dimness of the room as she found the chair. She'd curl up in the chair and—

"You don't have to talk to me. You don't have to do anything but curl up in my arms and sleep."

His voice was low and rough and ever so tempting.

"I don't want your secrets. Don't tell me a fucking thing. I just want you in my arms because I like the way you feel when you're against me."

She still had the sheet wrapped around her body. She tugged it with her as she crept across the floor.

"I'm not trying to be kind so I can learn your secrets. Hell, I don't think I have been particularly *kind* to you, and I want to fix that. I think you deserve kind. I think you deserve a whole lot more than that."

She didn't speak. She was afraid if she started speaking, she just might cry. She couldn't remember the last time she'd felt truly safe or truly happy. Fear was pretty much her constant companion. She kept her mask in place, made jokes all the time, seemed confident because the truth was that she didn't want anyone to see how terrified and screwed up she was.

"Will you sleep in my arms?" Rick asked her. He reached out a hand toward her. "I think I'd sleep better with you near me."

She took a step toward him. Made herself stop. "Because you think I'll run?" Her voice was too husky.

"No. Because I feel better when you're close to me. I like having you close, Kat."

Her lip was trembling. "It doesn't make sense to sleep in the lumpy chair." She walked around the bed. Perched on the side opposite him. Slowly lowered her body down until she was flat on the mattress. "Not when there is room for us both here."

He turned toward her. She felt the mattress dip. "I'm not trying to learn your secrets for the FBI. As far as I'm concerned, the FBI can fuck off."

"I don't have the twenty million. That's what everyone really cares about. I've already told the FBI everything I saw my father do. Yes, I still have to testify in court. Over and over. But the people pushing—they want the money."

He reached for her hand.

She flinched.

His hold tightened. "I don't give a fuck about the money."

What was she supposed to believe? That he cared about her? No. They'd already covered that it was only sex between them. Sex that would change nothing. Emotions weren't involved. He was doing his job. Unfortunately, his job wasn't just protecting her. It was exposing her secrets.

She tried to concentrate on breathing. In and out. In and out.

"I don't tell a lot of people about how I screwed up with Daniel. Hell, I only told Cole because the guy got me drunk with vodka. I understand all about not wanting to share your past or your pain with anyone else."

In and out. She just kept breathing. But her fingers had curled around his. Traitorous fingers. What was up with them?

"Your father hurt you. You deserved someone who would love you and take care of you, but instead, hell, baby, we both know you got—"

"A monster." For some reason, it was easier for her to say it than to hear others call him that.

"I thought I had a best friend I could trust. He was closer to me than any brother would've been. Hell, we *were* brothers. That's what firefighting was. A brotherhood. Brothers, sisters—we were a family. And when you realized your family member—the one closest to you—is a murderer, it changes everything."

Try realizing that truth when you're fourteen. Until then, she'd thought her father was just a businessman.

"You aren't alone. I'm here with you, and I will stay with you."

Until their time was up. Until she walked into the courtroom. Wasn't even seven days now. Time was sliding away.

The mattress dipped again. His lips brushed over her temple. "I'm sorry I hurt you. That wasn't my intention. Hurting you is the last thing I want."

She wet her lips. "Why?" A strangled whisper. She was nothing to him. A great sex partner, okay, sure, but—

"Because when you cry, I want to fucking destroy things. I want to make sure you never know a moment's pain. And since *I'm* the one who hurt you...hell, I can't—"

"You haven't hurt me," she cut through his words softly. "You've actually been kinder than most."

"No, baby, I—"

"I'm really tired, Rick. Let's go to sleep."

Silence. Then... "Okay, baby. Okay." His fingers were still twined with hers. "But..."

She waited.

Nothing else came.

"But what?" Kat finally asked.

"But I really liked it when we cuddled." He sounded all growly and uncomfortable and...cute.

She found herself smiling. She didn't mean to smile. She just did. Eventually, her eyes closed. Her breathing became easier. Sleep took her.

She slid toward him. Cuddled. And didn't dream of monsters.

***

Rick's hold tightened on Kat. She'd rolled toward him. Put her head on his chest. Her hand curled over his side. She'd only moved toward him when she slept. When she was vulnerable and the wall around her had fallen down.

He *had* hurt her. He hadn't meant to. Making her cry was the last thing he wanted. He'd just started telling her about his past, and he hadn't hesitated. He'd never told another lover, but opening up with her had been so easy.

Sex. Just sex.

Who the fuck am I kidding?

His arm curled around her, and he pulled her even closer.

Kat was more than sex, and he was in deep trouble.

CHAPTER ELEVEN

The bed was empty. Rick's hand had reached for Kat, but when he just touched the cool sheet, his eyes immediately flew open. Alarm had his heart racing as he surged upright and his gaze raked the motel room. The *empty* motel room.

Shit. He jumped from the bed. Grabbed for his jeans and tried to hop into them. He'd slept like the dead. What was wrong with him? He usually woke at the lightest of sounds. But Kat would be good at staying quiet while she slipped away. He had one leg in his jeans. He hopped to get in the next leg and turned to see—

Kat, with her left shoulder propped against the bathroom doorframe. She watched him, a faint smile on her lips and her brows raised.

He yanked the jeans up to his hips. Zipped and buttoned in a flash.

"Is this your normal morning routine?" Kat asked. Damn, she looked good. Her face had been scrubbed clean and her wet hair slid over her shoulders. A towel curled around her body. *She was only wearing a towel.* Sexy as fuck and his dick immediately jumped to full and happy attention even as he realized...

She'd taken a shower and he hadn't heard the thunder of the water?

I am so losing my edge.

She was staring expectantly at him. She'd asked him a question, only he had zero clue what that question had been. Rick rolled back his shoulders. "Say again?" What in the hell had she said?

Her smile stretched as she motioned toward him. Down him. "The jumping routine when you get out of bed. Do you hop into your clothes every day?"

"I thought you were gone." The words came from him before he could think better of them. As soon as they were out—

Her smile faded. "Oh. I see. You thought I'd run from you."

Why do I always say the wrong shit? "I...didn't see you in the bathroom."

"I opened the door just as you started hopping, so, no, you wouldn't have seen me. Your back was turned at the time." A pause. "You thought I had sex with you and then ran away the next day? Is that what your lovers usually do?"

"They don't stay the night."

"Their choice? Or yours?"

"Both." He took a step toward her. Then stopped. "I'm not big on...having someone that close. It's too intimate."

She seemed to consider that. "Sleeping together is intimate, but sex isn't?"

Yes. No. Dammit.

Her gaze held his. "You said you wanted me close last night."

"You're different." He took a few more steps toward her. Slowly, the way a hunter would approach prey.

"Why am I different? Because you thought that if you had me in your arms, you'd wake up when I tried to slip away?" Kat shook her head.

"Obviously, that didn't happen," he muttered.

"You were sleeping hard, and, to tell you the truth, I thought you were cute. You didn't want to let me go when I was ready to get out of bed. I had to pry your hands loose."

"Cute?" Rick repeated as he stood before her. Cute was insulting. Teddy bears were cute. He didn't want her to think of him as *cute*. Dangerous. Sexy. Why couldn't she call him those things? Cute was a straight-up insult.

Her head angled back. "Yeah, cute. You even whispered my name when I slid out of bed."

He had not, had he? Oh, jeez. Rick could feel his cheeks heat. Good thing the beard covered so much of his face.

Her eyes twinkled as her hand rose and patted his cheek. "Actually, I think what you said was Kat, dear Kat, I love—"

Gunfire. Bullets exploded through the door of the motel room. Kat screamed and Rick lunged forward and tackled her, driving her back into the bathroom. They hit the tiled floor too hard, even though he was trying to twist and shield her. She was still on the bottom and took the brunt of the impact.

"Kat?"

Wood splintered behind him. He twisted around and saw that some jackass was kicking in the front door. The bullets had been aimed at the secondary lock Rick had secured the night before—that stupid piece of metal that would stop

someone from accessing the room even if the
intruder had a key to the main lock. That little side
piece that most motel guests never used but he
always put in place.

"Stay down!" Rick ordered as he leapt to his
feet. He rushed for his own gun and when the
intruder succeeded in kicking in the door—took
the guy four attempts, Rick could hear his
struggle—Rick attacked.

He grabbed the intruder and slammed the
fellow's wrist back against the wooden doorframe.
The intruder screamed, and his gun hit the floor.
Barely pausing, Rick kicked the bastard's gun out
of way before he shoved the jerk against the
nearest wall. Rick's breath sawed hard out of his
lungs as he jammed the muzzle of his own weapon
under the soon-to-be-dead man's chin.

"Rick! Don't! He's a kid!"

Kat's voice barely registered over the
pounding of his heartbeat.

She grabbed Rick's arm. Held tight. "*Don't.
He's a kid!*"

A kid with a death wish. But Rick finally
stopped seeing red and realized he was staring
down at bleached blond hair. Stringy, bleached
blond hair. *Familiar* hair. A flushed face, and
wild, blood-shot blue eyes. "Step back, Kat. *Now.*"
A lethal order.

She let him go. Stepped back. "Don't kill him.
Please."

Rick's stare raked the pimply face and weak
jaw. It was the kid from the motel's check-in desk.
"Seriously?" Rick snarled. "I have to deal with
wannabe hit men in training?"

"Please, God, don't kill me!" Tears trailed down the fool's face. His voice broke during the plea, cracking all over the place. "I was just—*don't kill me!*"

First...the guy wasn't a kid, despite what Kat had just claimed. He might look young, but Rick figured the attacker before him was probably close to twenty-one.

Second... "You're the dumbass who came in with a gun blazing, and now you want *me* to hold back?" Unbelievable.

The desk clerk's watery eyes were about to bulge out of his head. "Yes—*please!*"

Sonofabitch.

Those watery eyes whipped to Kat. Widened even more.

Rick's back teeth locked. "Kat, are you still wearing the towel?" If it had fallen when they flew onto that bathroom floor...

"Uh, yeah, I'm still wearing it."

Okay, so the punk before him wasn't getting a full-on view of Kat. Rick didn't have to drive his fist at the guy...yet. "Go get dressed, Kat."

"Only if you promise *not* to kill him."

The punk nodded eagerly. "Yes, yes, please, man, promise *not* to kill me! Promise it to the pretty lady!"

Rick glared at the fool. "Why would I make a promise that I might not keep?"

All of the frantic color immediately bled from the jerk's face. Rick kept his weapon in place, jabbing it under that weak, trembling chin. "Get dressed, Kat. The other motel guests would've heard the shots. We have to leave, now."

The desk clerk shook his head. "Th-there's no one else!"

Rick heard the rustle of clothing behind him. He didn't dare look at Kat. "You'd better be planning to dress in the bathroom," he snapped back at her.

"I'm afraid if I leave you alone with him, you'll kill the kid!"

Do not strip in front of him, or I will shoot him. "He's not a fucking kid. And he just tried to kill us."

"No, no!" The punk's eyes were so huge. Those wide eyes swung over Rick's shoulder toward—

"You look at her right now, and my finger might squeeze the trigger. Trust me, I'm feeling real twitchy."

The fellow's eyes flew back to Rick.

"Good. Very good." If Kat wasn't leaving the room, he'd make sure the sonofabitch wasn't watching her. "What did you mean when you said no one else was here?"

"I..." His Adam's apple bobbed. "This place is a shithole. H-hardly anyone ever stays here."

All right. Fine. It was a shithole. He could agree on that point.

"The other guests—it was only two truckers. They left right after dawn."

So no one would be rushing to call the cops. Fair enough. "Want to tell me why you were trying to kill me?"

Sweat beaded the guy's forehead and cheeks and mixed with the tears still on his face. "I wasn't. I swear. I was only—I was only gonna make sure you stayed put."

Footsteps hurried behind him. "I'm dressed, okay? Can we all take a breath?"

"No." He kept his glare on the desk clerk. "What's your name?"

"J-Joey."

"Joey, *why* did you want us to stay put?"

He gulped. Didn't answer.

Kat answered. With a sigh, she said, "He wanted us to stay put because he figured out who we are. He probably called someone and that someone told him that we weren't to leave the motel."

He wanted to pound Joey. "You didn't even see her face." He'd made sure of it the night before.

"I-I saw yours, man. And I got a tip...my cousin Quincy said some big ballers were looking for you. That you'd have a pretty lady with you and she would be worth so much money..."

Kat cleared her throat. "Did he just say 'big ballers'?"

Rick's fury was boiling out of control. "You called your cousin. You told him we were here. Then you came in with a gun. I think I should shoot you right now."

"*I wasn't going to kill anyone!* I shot the door because you had that stupid second lock in place! I was only going to use my gun to scare you so that you and the woman would stay here until my payment arrived!"

Rick leaned in closer to Joey. "Do I look scared?"

"N-no..."

"Joey," Kat sighed his name. "You've made a terrible mistake."

He gulped. "I-I see that now. If you'll just get your b-boyfriend to let me go..."

Rick shook his head.

"Oh, God," Joey whimpered. "*God.*"

"You're not going to get the *payment* you want," Rick told him flatly. "Your cousin called people higher up the food chain, and soon they will all be racing over here." He paused. "What do you think they'll do when they find you...but the lady and I are both long gone?"

Joey shuddered. "Man, man, I am so *screwed!*"

"Yeah, you are. Night, night, asshole." He yanked back the gun and slammed his left fist into Joey's face. Joey crumpled like a rag doll and fell to the floor.

Kat moved closer to Rick and stared down at the prone desk clerk.

"I used my left hand," Rick muttered. "Didn't hit as hard as I could have."

Her gaze darted up to lock with his. He couldn't read the emotion in her eyes.

"I'm *not* your father, dammit. I wasn't going to kill the sonofabitch." *Not unless killing him had been necessary.* "But I couldn't have him rushing after us so I knocked his ass out." His gaze swept over her. She was in jeans and her t-shirt again. Her shoes were on. Okay, fine, now he had to get his ass fully dressed so they could get out of there. Rick spun away and finished dressing in a blink. He grabbed the burner phone and caught Kat's hand in his. "Let's get the hell out of here."

She hurried to keep up with him.

He put the burner to his ear. Called Cole as they ran through what was a completely deserted parking lot. If they left the motel on foot, the bad guys coming after them would have the advantage. They'd be tracked down too fast. And if they left in a car...hell, the only car was a piece of shit sedan near the motel's office. Rick was betting it was Joey's ride.

The team coming after them would know to look for Joey's vehicle. It was a lose/lose situation.

"Yo," Cole answered, voice tense. "What can I do?"

Rick rattled off the address of the motel. "Get Wilde agents and the cops out here. There's an unconscious idiot in room seven, and he's about to be swarmed by his buddies—folks who were looking for *me* because it looks like I've made my way onto the mob's most wanted list, too."

Cole swore. "I'll get them there ASAP."

"We're clearing out. I'll call you again when we're secure." But with eyes everywhere, just how secure could they be?

He glared at the sedan. Such a piece of shit.

Keys jingled near him. His head whipped toward Kat. She held car keys in her hand. "I took these off Joey while you were getting dressed."

Of *course,* she had.

"I know you have that rule about stealing cars. Probably like rule eight or something from that list you were spouting at me, but this *is* a desperate situation."

Damn desperate.

Her head inclined toward the car. "There is no way that car has GPS tracking on it."

They'd be lucky if the dented, rusty heap even cranked.

"And he *did* shoot into our motel room. Doesn't he deserve a little payback for that move?" She jiggled the keys one more time.

They had to get out of there, fast. No other ride was around.

"I'll steal it. You can just come along for the ride." She rushed toward the POS car.

A moment later, Kat jumped in and had the engine—well, not purring, but sputtering to life. With no other option coming to him, Rick climbed into the passenger side.

He was stealing a car.

No, he was stealing a POS.

"Buckle up," Kat told him, voice oddly cheery. "I like to go fast."

In that thing? Good luck—

She shot forward. Turned out, the POS could haul ass.

***

"Wake up, dumbass." Something hit Joey.

He groaned.

Something hit him again. Right in the face.

His eyes fluttered open.

And he saw the guy crouched before him. The guy *slapped* Joey.

"Hey, hey, stop!" Joey cried out.

The fellow whipped out a gun.

Joey froze. Why was everyone shoving guns into his face? *Hold up...is that my gun?*

"They aren't here," the stranger snarled at him. "I was told that Kat and her bodyguard were *here*."

Joey's gaze flew around the room. Empty. "H-how long was I out?"

"Where the fuck did they go?"

"Do I look like I know?" Joey shouted back, then he wished he could take those words back because the man in front of him looked so enraged. "Oh, damn, mister, just settle down. Just—"

"No cars are in the parking lot. Did you have a car here? Did they take it?"

He had no idea if they'd taken it. "Y-yeah, yeah, I-I had a car here. My baby was—"

"What does your car look like?"

"She's...a little rusty. Dark blue. Sedan from the 90s, but that engine can purr—"

The gun fired. Joey didn't even scream. The bullet slammed into his chest and it felt like a ball of fire hit him. The pain was instant and consuming and his body slumped.

"That's what you get," the man rose. Shook his head. Dropped the gun.

Wait...that is my gun. He shot me with my own gun.

The shooter's gloved hand caught Joey's chin. "You're gonna die. So if you believe in God, this is when you should start praying."

Joey didn't have time to pray. He didn't even have time to beg.

CHAPTER TWELVE

"Where the hell did you learn to drive like that?"

Kat's hands tightened around the steering wheel. She'd gotten them away from the rundown motel and *far, far* away as fast as she could. She'd stayed on back roads. She'd pushed the old sedan and stroked her like a rock star, and now they were safe. For the moment, anyway. They were hidden on a dirt road in what she figured had to be the middle of nowhere.

She turned and gave Rick a slow smile. "The man who taught me how to drive used to be my dad's best getaway guy."

"Fuck. Of course, he was."

"I've always thought I'd be a great race car driver." She considered it. "Any chance Witness Protection can set me up with something like that? What do you think those odds are?"

"Right now, I just want you to *live* long enough to get to the courthouse."

His curt response had her heart squeezing in her chest. "Are you sure this is a safe place to stop?" While she'd been driving like Vin Diesel, he'd been barking out directions to her. She'd followed his orders because trusting him was the only option.

And...she did trust him. When had that happened?

"Yeah. It's safe. For the moment. We can't keep running blind. I need to check in with Cole and figure out what's happening."

She knew what was happening. Kat was being hunted.

"Come on. Let's get out. Stretch our legs." He shoved open his door.

Kat followed suit. The sunlight hit her hard, and she blinked a few times. "We should get another car. Switch it out." Switch cars, get new plates. Keep moving. Always keep moving.

Her gaze cut to Rick. He had the burner phone up to his ear. *Checking in with Cole.* The one who wanted Rick to learn all of her secrets. She didn't exactly get the warm and fuzzies whenever she thought of Cole.

Her gaze slid around the area. Trees surrounded her. Birds were chirping. Everything looked so incredibly normal.

But she was terrified.

***

Cole put the phone to his ear and turned away from the Feds—and the Atlanta PD. "Mom," he said loudly as he spoke into the phone, "I'm at work. No, I can't talk right now. I don't care what's wrong with your computer..." He walked toward the motel room door, but his gaze darted back to the body.

Jesus.

The kid's shirt was covered with blood. A typical result when you were shot in the chest at point blank range.

"Mom, give me a minute. Give me just…" He hurried outside. "A minute." Cole's breath heaved out. Okay, it was still not safe to talk freely because there were a few uniform cops around, but he casually strode away from them and jumped into his car. He slammed the door shut. Once Cole was certain that he wouldn't be overheard, he snapped, "Man, we have a fucking huge problem."

"Yeah, we're being hunted down like animals. That *is* a problem."

"Tell me you didn't kill him."

"What?"

"The guy at the motel. I saw the marks on the door. I know he shot his way inside your room, and if you shot him back, if you had to return fire, then it's self-defense. I get that. Just tell me what went down." He pulled in a breath and tried to think through the situation. "We can fix this. Hell, right after I found the body, I called Eric and he's already getting that criminal defense buddy of his—Kendrick Shaw—on standby for you. We've got this—"

"Cole, what in the hell are you talking about?"

Cole's fingers tapped over the top of the steering wheel. "I'm talking about the dead body in room seven at the no-tell motel. The guy soaked in blood because he took a gun blast straight to the chest. The fellow sporting a busted lip and swollen face. Fuck, the cops have their crime scene team here." A pause. "Tell me that they won't find your DNA on him—"

"They're gonna find my DNA on him. If that's Joey you're talking about..." Rick's voice was thick. "My DNA will be on him."

Joey? "*Shit*. Okay, you need to come in." Exactly what Eric had said to Cole less than ten minutes before. *Get Rick's ass in.* "We need to clear this up." He glanced back at the motel. "At least Detective Layla Lopez is here. We've got a friendly cop who can help to make sure you don't get your ass immediately tossed into a cell." Hopefully.

"Listen to me, Cole. I didn't kill that guy. When I left him, Joey was unconscious in the motel room. Unconscious, not dead. Kat saw everything. She can back up my story."

This was bad. So bad. "What in the hell happened?"

"The motel desk clerk—Joey—he shot up our door and rushed inside. He'd called some cousin of his because the bastards hunting Kat have spread word to look for me. Joey was planning to hold us there until the people with money came to take me off his hands. I didn't feel like staying, so I knocked his ass out." A sigh. "I'm guessing whoever shot Joey didn't like it when he arrived and found that Kat and I were gone."

Didn't like it? "Serious understatement." Cole's temples were throbbing. "You have to come in, man. Dammit, you left *condoms* here. I saw a crime scene tech bagging them."

"Fuck."

"Yeah, obviously, you fucked and got fucked because your DNA is going to link you to the room, to the dead guy, to all kinds of shit. Come in. Eric will get Kendrick Shaw to go with you to the station. We'll talk all of this out, and hopefully, keep you out of jail."

Silence.

Cole's gaze darted to motel room number seven. A woman with dark hair and wearing a stylish white shirt and elegant black pants stood close to the door. A badge was clipped to her hip, and a holster rested under her arm. Detective Layla Lopez searched the parking lot. It didn't take long for her attention to land on him.

Wonderful. His windows weren't tinted so Cole knew she could see him as he huddled on his phone. He tried for a casual wave.

Layla immediately headed for him.

"Fuck, fuck, *fuck* me to hell and back."

"Cole. Calm your ass down."

"I *am* calm! Layla is stalking toward me right now. A dead body is in your motel room, and you are about to go down in flames." He blew out a breath. "Go to the Wilde building. Eric wants you to meet him there."

"What about Kat?"

"We'll deal with her when you get there!" Layla was closing in fast.

"She's in danger. Her enemies have already gotten inside Wilde once before. If I bring her back, hell, I could be handing her to them on a silver platter."

"And if you don't come back, you're screwed. You'll be a wanted man, and I'm not just talking wanted by the mob. The cops will be after you, too. *Everyone* will be after you. She's not worth it, buddy. That woman is not worth your life."

Layla's knuckles tapped on his window.

"Get to Wilde," Cole rasped. "As fast as you can. Eric and I will make sure you're taken care of." He ended the call. Shoved the phone under his seat and opened his car door.

Layla stepped back.

"Detective Lopez!" He tried going the formal route since he wanted to get on her good side. Now didn't feel like the moment to press the friend/good acquaintance angle. "I stepped out of the motel room because I didn't want to get in the way of your fine team's work. I have to say, I am so glad you were the one assigned to investigate this—"

"Drop the BS. You requested my presence when you called in the dead body." Her head cocked as her hands went to her hips. "What's going on?"

His lips parted. *Okay, what can I tell her?*

"Don't bother bullshitting me. I know Kat O'Shaughnessy is involved."

"You do? How do you know that?"

"Because I'm good at my job. Because I know the mob is looking for her and I also know..." She pointed to the left, toward a uniform who paced near a crying, red-faced man. "I know the vic's cousin is spilling his guts because Quincy over there has never actually seen a dead body until this morning. He's a young punk playing in a league that is way, way over his head. Quincy thought he and his cuz Joey were going to get some fast cash and gain some street cred. Quincy didn't realize that in the new game he's trying to play, people will die."

The vic in the motel room had looked so young...

"Someone roughed up Joey Lucas. Joey's the dead guy, by the way. Joey has a busted lip, maybe a broken nose, and swelling on his face. He was obviously punched before he was killed, so someone was probably torturing him for information. My techs are searching for evidence, getting DNA, and I'm hoping for a hit in the system."

She might get a hit, all right. Cole slammed the car door shut. "About that..."

Layla's eyes narrowed. "My day is already shit. Do not tell me—"

"It is about Kat O' Shaughnessy. You were right on that score."

She waited. He was pretty sure she started tapping her foot. He didn't look down, though.

He held her gaze. "Rick Williams is with her." She knew Rick. He was hoping that familiarity would help everyone. "He's keeping her safe."

"If Rick and Kathleen O'Shaughnessy witnessed the murder, I need to talk to them. *Now.*"

Working on that. He winced. "Things are a little tricky..."

Layla took a step toward him.

And a silver SUV pulled up at the scene. Her head turned as she stared at the vehicle, and when two guys in suits stepped out—

"Feds." Layla shook her head in disgust. "Coming to try and take over *my* scene?"

He recognized the two agents. Bryan Brisk and Tom Wayne. He'd first seen them at Wilde because he'd been the agent to escort them out of the building the night they'd come to drop off Kat. Bryan Brisk's face was shadowed by stubble, and his jaw was clenched as he approached.

"Someone is a little late to the party," Cole muttered.

Bryan and Tom glared at him. Then Bryan demanded to know, "Where in the hell is Kat O'Shaughnessy?"

***

"If you don't come back, you're screwed. You'll be a wanted man, and I'm not just talking wanted by the mob. The cops will be after you, too. Everyone will be after you. She's not worth it, buddy. That woman is not worth your life."

Cole's words replayed in Rick's head as his fingers tightened around the phone. He breathed slow and easy as he tried to figure out a way to escape this nightmare. Turning Kat in wasn't an option for him. If he turned her in...

She's dead.

"What did your partner say?" Kat crept toward him. She bit her lower lip as her gaze darted over his face. After studying his expression, she winced. "It was bad. I can tell. Really bad."

Understatement. "Joey is dead."

She didn't react.

"The kid who came into our motel room, gun blazing?" Rick prompted. "Joey. He's dead, he's—"

"How?"

"Blast to the chest. Cole said the cops are at the scene now, and shit, both of our DNA is gonna be everywhere." Especially his DNA. He'd driven his bare fist into the guy's face and had felt Joey's lip bust beneath the impact. "The cops will link us to him."

"But we didn't kill him! We left him alive." Kat shook her head. "He was supposed to live."

"Yeah, well, I'm guessing the people looking for you didn't appreciate arriving to find that we'd gotten away again."

Her eyes closed. "He's dead because of me."

"No." Rick surged forward. His hands circled around her wrists. "No, Kat. Dammit, look at me."

Her eyes opened.

"He's dead because he was playing a game with the mob. Because he was ready to sell you out and sell me out. He wasn't some innocent—Joey came in with a gun and he was shooting."

"He didn't know the people he was tangling with," she whispered. "I know them. I'm the reason for all of this, I'm the—"

"Joey died because he was greedy. He wanted money. He died because of his choices, not yours."

She yanked her hands from him and stepped back. "My choices led to all of this, don't you see that? I'm the one who went to the Feds when my dad died. I could've just kept my mouth shut. I'm the rat, I'm the one who—"

"You are not!" Fury exploded from him. "You're trying to do what's right. You're trying to shut those bastards down. I get that you grew up in a life where you didn't talk, where you kept the mob's secrets, but baby, you know they are monsters. You know this has to end. You are doing what's right and good because *you* are good." Once more, he reached for her. He kept his hold easy, gentle, because she deserved that. "God, princess, you are so good. You're the one who was begging me not to kill the jerk at the motel even though he was more than ready to kill us. And don't buy the BS he spouted about only trying to hold us there. He rushed in—*shooting a gun.* He waited until the other motel guests were gone so there would be no witnesses. He was ready to kill you, and you were still fighting for his life." Rick shook his head. "You do that, don't you? You fight for other people. Over and over again." He could see it now. He could see her. "Who fights for you?"

Her lips parted. "Rick—"

A twig snapped.

Every muscle in his body clamped down.

It could have just been an animal. A squirrel. A raccoon. They were surrounded by the woods on that old dirt road. When they'd been driving, he'd been giving Kat directions because he had a final destination in mind—a place that *had* to be safe. A place no one else would know about.

But...

Her body pressed closer to his. She'd gone quiet at the snap, too.

Everything seemed to have gone quiet. Even the birds weren't chirping.

We were followed. Somehow, they'd been tracked. He'd looked back as they'd driven to make sure no cars shadowed them. He'd given her twists and turns to take, just to make sure they weren't tailed. But someone out there was very, very good.

He motioned to the car. *"Get in,"* Rick told her.

She nodded.

He pulled out his gun. He'd had it shoved in the waistband of his jeans, so it was close and ready. Rick put his mouth to her ear. "If I'm not back in five minutes, leave."

Kat began to shake her head.

Keeping his voice a whisper, he told her, "If anyone comes out of those woods but me, *leave.*"

He needed her to follow his order.

Kat gave a grudging nod.

You'd better follow that order, sweetheart. He held tight to his weapon. He was a big freaking guy, so most people thought he probably made a lot of noise when he moved around. But he'd been trained by the best. Rick knew how to move without making a sound. Someone was in those woods. Watching. Hunting.

Rick was going after the bastard.

***

Kat slid into the car and locked the doors. Shit, *shit!* Her heart raced in her chest as her breath heaved out in frantic puffs.

It was just a twig snapping. Just a twig. There's probably some squirrel out there laughing his ass off because he was going about his business and grabbing some nuts and two humans freaked out.

Only...she was more than freaked out. She was terrified. The guy at the motel was dead. How many people were going to have to die before this nightmare ended?

Rick can't die.

The idea of anything happening to Rick had pain shooting through her. She needed to help him. He thought that she'd simply drive away and leave him? No. Not going down. But if things got bad out there, she'd need some kind of weapon.

She reached for the glove box. Rick had searched it earlier while she was driving, and Kat remembered seeing—*yes*! A screwdriver. Her fingers curled around the base of the screwdriver as she yanked it from the glove box. In a pinch, this thing would work wonderfully. Now, to help Rick.

She turned toward the driver side door—

And she opened her mouth to scream when she saw the man standing there.

CHAPTER THIRTEEN

He tapped his gun against the glass of the window. Just tapped it. All casual-like. Kat knew that if he wanted to shoot her, he could.

He wasn't shooting, not yet.

Then he pointed to the lock. Tapped again with his gun.

Oh, right. Kat knew how this worked. She was supposed to be brought in alive. So the man with the gun was probably going to try and avoid shooting her in the head right then and there.

Her right hand slid the screwdriver down low in an attempt to keep it hidden. Kat didn't think he'd seen it yet. That was good. Her left hand unlocked the door and pushed it open. The door groaned.

"Where's the bodyguard?"

Kat blinked innocently before widening her eyes. "What bodyguard?"

His lips thinned. "Cute." He motioned with the gun. "Move it, Kat."

She climbed from the car and made sure the screwdriver stayed behind her right leg. Her gaze locked on the man. He was tall, not as big in height or in the shoulders as Rick was, but still fit. Still outweighing her by at least fifty pounds. Though she knew that when it came to taking down an opponent, size didn't matter.

The bigger they are, the harder I'll make them fall.

His eyes were shielded by a pair of aviator sunglasses. His jaw was hard, clean shaven, his forehead high and his dark hair shoved back in a haphazard style. He was a handsome man. *A handsome hit man.* And something about him nagged at her.

"You come with me right now, and I won't hurt the bodyguard." His voice was low, barely a whisper, and the odd sense of familiarity hit her again.

For the moment, she ignored that flare of familiarity. She had to focus on staying alive. On keeping *Rick* alive. If the fellow was offering not to hurt Rick...

"Sure, I'll come with you." Kat gave him a smile. "I've been trying to get away from that other guy for days, anyway." Such a lie, but whatever. The jerk was probably the type who'd believe her lies and tricks. She just wanted to get him away from Rick. Then she was going to shove her screwdriver into his side at the first opportunity.

Jesus. I am my father's daughter.

She choked down the knowledge and kept the stupid smile on her face.

The hit man cocked his head. "You've been trying to get away from him?"

He was awfully chatty.

"Didn't look that way back at the farmhouse," he added, eyes squinting with suspicion.

Her heart stopped. In that instant, things went from being bad—okay, *very* bad—to complete nightmare land. *Farmhouse.* He'd been the one firing at Rick back at the farmhouse. She licked her lower lip and managed to ask, "Are you Ghost?"

He smiled. Dimples winked at her. "You've heard of me."

Oh, God. Oh, God. Her whole body shut down as she stared at those dimples. Dimples that she knew, and, hell, yes, she was staring straight at a ghost. Her body swayed.

He inclined his head toward her. "Hold the thought, would you? I need to take care of something." Then he whirled.

Kat saw that Rick had been creeping up behind him. Rick had his gun aimed and ready to fire.

Rick was going to shoot.

Ghost was going to shoot.

Hell, they'd both probably *die* right in front of her. This was never going to end. More blood. More violence.

But...

Not Rick! Not him! An inhuman scream tore from Kat as she yanked up her screwdriver.

Ghost glanced back at her. She didn't hesitate. She drove that screwdriver at him as hard as she could. In that split second, she could see her own reflection in his sun glasses. Kat figured Ghost had two choices.

He could shoot her. The gun was in his hand. He could fire and stop her. This close, a bullet would probably kill her, though, and Kat knew she was worth a whole lot alive.

Or, if Ghost didn't shoot her, he could try to wrest the screwdriver from her. He'd have to drop his gun to do it.

Those thoughts pummeled through her in that instant. That one instant that seemed to last forever.

Then the gun fell from Ghost's fingers. He grabbed for her. His fingers closed around her wrist and he twisted her hand. Kat didn't cry out at the flash of pain. Not then. She kicked him as hard as she could and then locked her leg behind his. They both went down, crashing hard, but he rolled quickly, trapping her beneath his body and whipping the screwdriver from her right hand before he shoved the sharp tip—it was an X-head—into her side.

Everything happened so fast. So incredibly fast.

As the screwdriver pushed against her, Kat sucked in a breath and smiled.

"Are you crazy?" Ghost snarled at her.

Rick's gun pressed to his temple. "I'd be real, *real* careful in the next few moments. My finger is twitchy, and it gets even more so whenever people insult Kat."

Ghost's sunglasses were still in place. Her smiling reflection stared back at her. Ghost definitely wasn't smiling. His lips had pressed into a thin line. His nostrils flared before he told Rick, "I've got a screwdriver shoved to her ribs. Push me, and I'll have to hurt her."

"If you don't drop the screwdriver right now, I'll blow your brains out. Push me," Rick fired right back, voice low and lethal, "and see if I'm fucking bluffing."

"He's not bluffing," Kat assured the man above her. "I don't think he ever bluffs."

Ghost's jaw clenched. "You knew he was circling back around the whole time, didn't you? Putting you in the car—that made you bait. You're okay with your lover doing that shit to you?"

A growl escaped Rick. "Maybe I should just blow your brains out for shits and giggles."

Before Rick could fire, Ghost dropped the screwdriver. Laughed. "Hardly your gig, *hero*. You don't shoot. You don't kill."

"I do when there's a reason. Now stand your ass up. I don't want you *touching* her."

Slowly, Ghost rose. He smirked, and, oh, God, she knew he was going to say—

"Hate to break it to you, hero, but I've done a whole lot more than just *touch* her."

Before Rick could react, Kat did. Still on the ground, she shoved her sneakered foot up and slammed it right into Ghost's balls. He groaned, all of the color drained from his face, and his knees buckled as he slumped against the old car.

Savage satisfaction filled her. Kat scrambled up. "*That's* for shooting at Rick back at the farmhouse." She got ready to attack again. "And *this* is for vanishing—"

Rick grabbed her. He locked one arm around her midriff and hauled her back against him. He kept that arm around her waist while his other hand aimed his gun. "Kat...God, you are sexy as fuck. Remind me not to piss you off in the future."

Ghost was still groaning.

Kat snaked away from Rick and grabbed Ghost's discarded gun. She joined Rick again, both of them pointing their weapons at the man who was finally straightening up.

"I expected so much more," Rick drawled, "from the guy who was supposed to be this great hit man. I mean, getting the drop on you wasn't that hard."

Ghost smirked. "I could say the same thing about you."

"But I'm the one with the gun."

"So am I," Kat added as she glared at the man who should not be there. Not, a million times *not*. Ghost's sunglasses were on the ground, and now she could see his golden eyes—*his eyes haven't changed*. No, they had. They were hard and cold when, long ago, they'd always been warm.

"I want answers." Rick's voice was flat. "You give them to me, or I shoot. Clear enough?"

Ghost didn't lose his smirk.

"First, who the fuck are you? And I don't want to hear some BS answer with a code name like Ghost. I want to know who I'm staring at."

Ghost inclined his head toward Kat. "She knows. Ask her."

"I'm asking *you*."

Silence. Well, a few birds had started to chirp again. That was something. Kat couldn't look away from the man before her.

"You implied that you knew Kat well," Rick's voice was even rougher.

"It wasn't an implication," Ghost replied, all smug. "I *do* know her well. Intimately so. Long time, no see, huh, Kat?"

"You are such a bastard." To think, she'd once tried to—

"My friends call me James," Ghost announced. "Though, back in the day, a number of select people called me Jimmy."

She heard Rick suck in a sharp breath. Her head turned to stare at him. Oh, yes, he was pissed. *Raging.*

Without looking at Kat, Rick snapped, "He's the jackass you saved when you were seventeen?"

She had spared a glance back toward Ghost—*crap, Jimmy!*—when Rick asked the question, so she saw the flash of surprise on the other man's face.

"You told him about me?" Jimmy—James—Ghost—*whoever* the hell he was—asked.

Kat nodded. Her hand tightened on the gun she held. It felt oddly heavy in her hand.

"But he's nobody," he groused. "Just a hired guard to you. Someone you fucked to pass the time. Why would you—"

Rick sighed. "Yeah, my turn." He lunged forward and rammed his fist into Jimmy's face. Jimmy's head snapped back and he cried out—

"Fuck!"

Right before he tried to take a swing at Rick.

The swung froze when he realized Rick had his gun pointed right at Jimmy's face.

"No, you don't get to hit back," Rick told him flatly. "You're not the one with the gun."

Blood dripped from Jimmy's lip. "You don't know Kat."

Her stomach was twisting and churning.

"If you knew her, you'd realize...her number one turn-off? Physical violence. She hates that shit because she saw her bastard of a father order it her whole life." Jimmy laughed and spit some blood on the ground. "So you think you're being all badass and protective of her? Throwing punches at me and at the jerk back at the motel? You're not. You're just driving her away from you. Making her see that the so-called hero is just as much of a monster as her old man."

Kat took a step back. "H-how did you know Rick had hit the guy at the motel?"

Jimmy's lips pressed together.

"*How did you know?*" Oh, God. He was Ghost. Ghost was a killer. A hit man. "You killed him?" The Jimmy she'd known—what felt like a lifetime ago—had been a fun-loving boy. He'd smiled often. He'd had big dreams. He'd—

Become a killer.

"I didn't kill him, Kat. He wasn't a target for me. *Kat*. Dammit, *look* at me."

She didn't want to look at him. She didn't know him. She never had. "Can we tie him up?" Kat said to Rick. "Then get the hell out of here? You can call your partner and he can bring the cops to pick him up. I'm sure there are lots of cases that can be tied to him." She edged closer to Rick. "Let's *go*."

Rick backed up a few steps with her, but then he stopped. His body went rock hard and she knew he wasn't budging again.

"*Kat!*" Her name seemed torn from Jimmy. "I didn't kill the jerk at the motel. I was there, yes, but that's because I've been after you." His eyes

FIGHTING FOR HER   197

widened when Rick's body rocked forward. "Shit, don't swing at me again, hoss. I'm just—*I was at the motel. I was watching Kat, okay?* Just watching!"

She was afraid she'd be sick. All she wanted to do was run.

Wasn't that always what she wanted to do? Run, run, and never look back.

Because behind her, everything was a dumpster fire straight from hell.

"Listen to me!" Ghost nearly shouted. "I saw you two rush out of that motel room, and when you left, I poked my head in. The guy was unconscious, but his face was already swelling from your punch. Didn't take a genius to figure out what had gone down in there. I didn't have time to wait for him to wake up. I figured company was already on the way. I got out of there and got back to hunting Kat." He winced after he said that last part. "Sorry, but it's my job."

"Killing Kat is your job?" Rick's voice had turned absolutely savage. For a moment, she thought he was going to pull the trigger. She could see the intent on his face. So much rage.

The same kind of rage she'd often seen on her father's face.

"Don't," Kat whispered.

Rick didn't lower his gun. His finger was too ready to fire.

So she squared her shoulders, and she moved between Rick's gun and Jimmy. Not like it was the first time she'd stood between him and a bullet. Only this time, she wasn't doing it to save Jimmy.

She was doing it to save Rick. He didn't need to go down this path. Sure as hell not for her. He *was* the hero. He was the good guy. She wouldn't bring him into her nightmare.

"Kat." Rick's eyes blazed at her. "What in the hell are you doing? Get away from him."

"Don't shoot him. Just—let's go. Let's leave. Please, Rick. I don't want more blood on me. I'm drowning in it as it is."

Rick gave a rough nod. "Okay, princess. I won't kill the sonofabitch...right now."

Right now?

He offered his left hand to her. "Come back to my side."

She took a step toward him.

"Kat..." Jimmy breathed her name.

She looked back at him.

His expression showed his confusion. "Why in the hell would you still be trying to save me?"

"That's my problem. I'm trying to save everyone. And maybe what's left of my own soul." She shook her head. "You're alive. I thought..." Her words trailed away. It took her a moment, but she managed, "God, you became one of them? That's what you did with your life?"

"Kat—"

Rick pulled her to his side. His stare stayed on Ghost. "I told Kat I wouldn't kill you right now. I won't. But I'll have your ass locked in jail before you know it."

Jimmy laughed. "A cell won't hold me. Trying to put me in one will be a major mistake on your part." He swiped his hand over his face, brushing away the blood that kept blooming on his lip. "You need me free, buddy."

"I'm *not* your buddy."

"No, you're not. You're an asshole who has something that's very important to me."

Ghost didn't mean her. He was trying to *kill* her or take her to some high mob bidder. She wasn't important. He'd been out of her life for so many years. And during those years, the sweet Jimmy she'd known had become...this?

"You're a hit man," she accused him.

"Guilty." The smirk was back.

"You're called Ghost. And you—you worked for my father."

The smirk faded. "I've worked for plenty of people. You'd be surprised at who all has blood on their hands."

She still held Ghost's gun in her right hand. How many people had he killed with that gun? "Rick, we need to move. He could be keeping us out here deliberately, making us wait while his boss has a chance to show up. Just like Joey tried to do at the motel." Her knees were shaking. "Let's *go*." She wanted to get away from the very real *ghost* from her past.

Rick's lips brushed over her temple. "It's okay, baby."

No, nothing was okay. "We need to get him secured. Do you still have those cuffs?" She hoped they weren't back in the motel room. She honestly had no clue where they might be. He'd just kept producing them like a manic magician before, and she was sure hoping he could make them appear again.

"I don't have the cuffs, but we can just knock his ass out," Rick said, sounding way too pleased with that prospect. "I'll lock him in the trunk."

Jimmy shook his head. "That shit is not necessary."

"Oh, but I think it is," Rick assured him.

Jimmy's chin jutted into the air. "You're jealous and pissed because you realized I had her before you—"

"I'm pissed because you're a piece of shit who wants to hurt Kat. There is no jealousy. You never deserved her. You won't ever have her again. Simple." Rick turned to Kat. "You don't have to watch me knock him out."

Jimmy laughed. "You're not saying that to protect her! You're saying it because you know I told you the truth a few minutes ago. The more violent you are, the less Kat will want you. So *you* don't want her to watch." His gaze blazed at Kat as he continued, "I figured it out long ago, and now he understands, too. You turn from men who are violent. You hate them because they remind you too much of your dear old dad. So the more you see your hero in all his unheroic glory, the more you'll turn from him, too."

"Stop talking," Kat snapped at him.

"Why?" Jimmy tossed right back. "I thought you both wanted to hear about me. I thought you wanted to know who I was working for." More laughter. "Here's the big joke—no damn way will my boss ever show up. Because the dead don't just crawl out of their graves and make an appearance." He made that announcement and then lunged forward. His hand whipped up—whipped up holding a knife.

Oh, God, where had Jimmy gotten the knife from?

He was rushing straight at Rick. He was either going to stab Rick or Rick would be forced to kill Ghost. *No. I won't let this happen!* Without hesitation, her hand flew up. She fired and the bullet blasted into Jimmy's shoulder.

The knife fell as his body jerked back.

Her body jerked, too. Her whole arm seemed to shake and throb.

Blood covered Jimmy's shoulder. "What the fuck?" He gaped at her.

"Graze," she managed. "I *grazed* you because that's what I was trying to do." She licked bone-dry lips. "The next shot will be to your heart, and you know I mean what I say. So understand me...You won't hurt, Rick. You *won't*."

He stared at her, looking oddly...pleased for someone who'd just gotten shot. *Grazed.*

"How did you find me?" Kat demanded.

"I'm a good tracker. The best there is. Getting to the motel was easy..." He threw a glare at Rick. "Just thought like old hero over there. Once I got in his head, it was easy."

"You're not in my head."

"Oh, I bet I am. You're thinking about me and Kat and all the things we've done together. Bet all of that is playing through your head over and over again."

"I will rip you apart." Rick's voice...it was *terrifying*.

"I'm in your head, and you're off your game. But then, you got off your game the minute you fucked her."

Rick...*smiled*. Oh, damn. Since when was a smile so scary?

"I was back there, trailing you the whole way while you were driving this fucking sedan. You didn't spot *me* because you are too caught up in her."

Rick's smile stretched a little more. The smile didn't touch his eyes. He stepped forward and Ghost's sunglasses crunched beneath his feet. "Go open the trunk, Kat."

She grabbed the keys from inside the vehicle and hurried around to the trunk. She heard the thud of flesh hitting flesh and Kat flinched. "Rick!"

She looked up.

In the next second, Rick was leading Ghost to the rear of the vehicle. Ghost's face appeared even more battered. *He sent me to open the trunk so he could drive his fist into Ghost's face, and I wouldn't see him do it.*

Rick had his gun trained on the hit man.

"Get in the trunk," Rick ordered him.

"No fucking way, I am not—"

Rick slammed the gun into the side of the hit man's head. When Ghost staggered, Rick grabbed him and tossed the guy inside. Rick slammed the trunk closed. One hand gripped his gun and the other fisted on top of the trunk's lid.

Kat stood there, her whole body tight with tension. Jimmy—damn him—he was right. She hated violence. Hated the sight of it. Hated everything about it.

Even though I just shot a man.

"The car is so old, it won't have the easy open latch mechanism that the new models have in their trunks." Rick heaved out a breath. "Jackass will have to work his way through the back seat. That buys us some time." He tucked his gun into the waistband of his jeans and whipped out his phone. "I'll get Cole to send cops to this location. Cops, Feds, whoever is closest—they can drag this asshole away."

"Rick..."

"We're leaving now." He put the phone to his ear. He rattled off a location—some highway number and something about the third dirt road, gave a quick rundown on Ghost, and hung up. He curled his arm around her. "You can hotwire anything, right?"

"Y-yes."

"Good. Because I'm pretty sure that bastard's keys are in the trunk with him." He paused and stared down at her. "He was here to kill me and take you."

She swayed. Steadied herself.

"I want to beat the hell out of him. I want to *kill* him."

Kat shook her head. "That's not you. It's not what you do."

"Baby, I don't think you understand the real me."

Kat took a step back.

"I will never hurt you," he promised her. His eyes were dark and intense. "I swear it. But, baby, I can't let threats to you stand."

Something banged into the back of the trunk. Probably either Jimmy's hand or foot. It banged again. Harder.

"If he is Ghost, he's probably the number one threat to you. We have to make sure he's in custody. He can't come at you again."

She knew that. She knew—

"I'd thought that I would take you to a cabin in the mountains. An old property that belonged to a friend." Sadly, Rick shook his head. "I can't. I realize that now. My only choice is to take you in."

Take her in? Oh, no, she did not like the sound of that. "Rick?"

"We've got a dead body in our wake. We've got a hit man in the trunk. I'm not sure what the hell is coming next, but I can't risk you. I'm taking you in, and I'm making sure you have a full team around you."

Jimmy was still slamming into the trunk, but that old sedan was holding steady.

"You'll hotwire his ride—I saw it when I was in the woods. We'll take it back to Wilde. We aren't going to sit here and wait. You have to get out of the line of fire. You need a freaking barricade of agents around you, and that's what I'm going to make sure you have."

He was taking her in. Turning her over to someone else? *Leaving* her?

Of course, he is. Because being with her was dangerous. Because Rick had an infamous hit man locked in the trunk—a hit man who happened to be one of her ex-lovers. This whole scene was probably a million times more than what Rick had bargained for when he'd first taken the job.

Simple fact...Rick wanted out. He wanted away from her.

So suck it up. Tell him you understand. He's bailing on you, the same way plenty of others have. No big deal. Story of your life.

Only...it was a big deal. Because this time, it hurt about a thousand times worse than all the other abandonments. But Kat stiffened her spine. Pasted a smile on her face. "Right. Of course. Let's get moving. We've already been in the open too long."

She hurried forward, moving blindly toward the trees. Ghost's car had to be out there somewhere.

Rick caught her arm and swung her around to face him. "Kat?" A furrow appeared between his brows. "What's wrong?"

"What isn't wrong?' She shook her head. Pulled away. "Let's go." Go...before she started crying. No, she would *not* cry. She wouldn't.

They had to *go*.

Rick had to leave her. And she had to figure out how to survive on her own.

The memories will be nice. At least I got to make those. At least I got to pretend, for just a little while...

"The vehicle is this way." He directed her toward the right. They walked a while, and bam, there it was. A sleek beauty just waiting. Kat slipped inside and hotwired it. Had the engine purring even as Rick went toward the back of the trunk.

"I'll be damned."

She twisted around and then poked her head out the driver's side window. "What is it?"

"A gun store. A knife store." He moved to the side, holding handcuffs and rope. "And everything you need for bondage."

Her heart *hurt*. "He was going to tie me up and take me to his boss." That BS about Jimmy's boss being a dead man? No, she hadn't bought it for a second. Jimmy was a liar, straight to his core.

Rick's face hardened.

"He could've already called his boss." Her body turned icy. "Come on, Rick, *now*."

He slammed the trunk and was in the passenger seat a moment later. She shoved the gas pedal into the floorboard and hauled ass out of there.

***

James Smith kicked at the trunk again. Sonofafuckingbitch...*of course,* he would be in a car that had been built before 2002. Before easy to find trunk release levers were required to be in all cars. He was in an ancient pile of crap, he couldn't find the release lever, he couldn't find the old school trunk release *cable,* and there was nothing in that tight, closed-in space that he could use to even try prying open the trunk's latch.

As freaking embarrassing as it was to admit, he'd even lost his damn keys. He'd dropped them when he yanked out his knife and made a swipe at Rick. *Right before Kat shot me.*

He was so screwed.

He tried to maneuver his body around, but the tiny trunk was sure as hell not meant for a guy with his size. The big, asshole bruiser Rick had shoved him in there tight, and now James was about to lose everything that mattered.

"I am going to *kill* him," James snarled. He didn't have a phone on him. There was no one he could call for help. Not like he *would* call anyone. Because being locked in the trunk of a piece of shit car was *not* the way he wanted anyone in the business to find him. How the hell would he ever live that one down? Bad enough that he'd gotten overpowered by the grizzly bear, but to be left in a trunk for cops to find?

His head lifted and slammed down—over and over—against the bottom of the trunk. It was *not* his day. And if twenty million hadn't been up for grabs, there was no way he would be in this mess. Twenty million was making *everyone* crazy.

How long did he have before the cops came storming up? Or the FBI? Or whoever the hell Rick was calling?

He could get out of his mess. If he could just position his body the right way, maybe he could kick through the back seat. *If I weren't already wedged in here like a trapped sardine!*

But going through the back seat was his only option. He had to kick or punch until he could break through. The only question was...would he be able to get out before Rick's cavalry party arrived? James sure as shit hoped so.

***

Rick was nearly crushing the phone in his hand. He'd made his calls—a call to Cole. Another call to Eric.

Wilde agents would be rushing to the scene to handle Ghost. The authorities would be with him. They were running in hot because everyone wanted to get the hit man in custody.

His head turned. Kat was staring dead ahead. Her whole body was tense, but she seemed so incredibly fragile to him. "Kat..." He cleared his throat because he still sounded too furious. He *was* furious. Not with her. With the bastard who'd tried to hurt her. "I'm guessing you had no idea Ghost was your ex?" *I want to punch the sonofabitch again.*

"Not until I saw his smile. Everything else had changed about him. Those dimples were the same." Her voice was wrong. Too flat. All the emotion gone. Her hold tightened on the wheel. "I once offered my life in place of his."

Rick rubbed his chest. "'Cause you loved him that much?"

"Because I didn't want anyone dying for me. And now, he's the one who's leading the pack to get my head. He wants to tie me up and deliver me to the mob. To the highest bidder." A bitter laugh. "Maybe I should have let my father kill him when I had the chance."

He reached out and touched her wrist. "Kat—"

She flinched. "Don't, okay?"

"Don't what?"

"Don't touch me. I kind of...I'm kind of barely holding everything together right now. I get that we need to return to the Wilde office as fast as we can. Things are too crazy. But I knew they *would* get crazy. Everything in my life always does, and you're not the first one who couldn't handle it." A pause. "Handle *me*."

His hand pulled away from her. If she didn't want him touching her, he wouldn't. But she needed to understand... "I can handle anything you throw at me."

She shook her head.

"I can handle it, baby."

"We'll get to Wilde. You'll turn me over to someone else. They'll either keep me safe or I'll die. It is what it is."

"What the hell? I'm not turning you over to anyone! You're staying with me!"

She slanted him a quick glance. Was that...hope? It had damn well better be.

"Listen to me," Rick gritted out. "No one is taking you from me. I am *not* giving you up! You are mine. *Mine*. Got it?" He would never forget when she'd shot Ghost because the guy had lunged at Rick. She hadn't hesitated. Just fired.

Incredible. Brave. She'd kicked the jerk in the balls. She'd fought with a fury. She'd *fired* that gun. She was strong and brave and wild, and he was so crazy in love with—

Stop the thought. Stop it.

"I'm not giving you up," he said again, his voice still rough. "You're mine, Kat."

"Until I walk in the courthouse? You promise me?"

Rick nodded. "Yeah, baby, until you walk in that courthouse. I promise." But the truth was...he didn't just want her until she headed into court. He wanted her...always.

He didn't want to let her go, not at all.

He just wanted her.

But how in the hell was he going to keep his princess with him?

CHAPTER FOURTEEN

Finally. James drove his fist through the opening he'd made in the back seat. He'd been pounding at that thing forever. Maybe cars made from the freaking nineties were just sturdy as hell, but it had taken all of his strength to get through. Of course, the fact that his right arm had been bleeding like crazy the whole time hadn't helped. He was weak. He was drenched in sweat. And he was pissed.

How long had it taken him? James had no clue. He needed to haul ass out of there. Or maybe...hell, maybe instead of walking out of those woods, he'd take the sedan. Kat wasn't the only one who knew how to hotwire a vehicle.

But Rick probably told his buddies to be on the lookout for this car. There's probably an APB out for it now.

It was a chance he'd have to take. Running on foot would be too slow.

The freaking sedan. James had bullshitted about *how* he'd tailed them to the woods. He *had* thought like Rick. And he'd figured that if the man had to flee from the motel, he'd take the sedan. Not like there were other choices. So James had tagged the vehicle. A small tracking device under the bumper. Then, when Rick and Kat had fled, chasing after them had been easy.

But he wanted Rick to think he'd been distracted. Getting into your enemy's head? Always a good plan.

James dragged his body through the opening he'd made in the back seat. His breath sawed in and out, and his right arm burned with pain. Graze, his ass. That wound was no graze. Kat had taken off a chunk of his arm. Really given him something to remember her by. As if he'd ever be able to forget Kat.

He shoved open the right, rear door and hauled himself out. He—

"Freeze."

A woman stood there, legs shoulder width apart, a gun held competently in her grip. She had the gun pointed at him. Her dark hair was swept up into a twist, exposing the long column of her throat. She was beautiful. Really gorgeous. A lady with a gun...totally his type. Or she would have been, if she also hadn't been sporting a badge on her hip.

The badge kind of ruined things.

"Put your hands up," she ordered in a flat, I'll-kick-your-ass voice. "Now."

He lifted his hands. Or, made a show of *trying* to lift them. "I'm shot," he whimpered. "Someone shot me...shoved me in the trunk and—"

"Do I look stupid? I know who you are, Ghost." She inclined her head, and suddenly, there were a whole lot of uniformed cops coming out of the trees.

Jeez. Had they all just been waiting for him to finally drag his ass out of the sedan?

Only, they weren't *all* cops. Because he recognized the dark-haired, tattooed fellow who stayed behind the uniforms. Cole Vincent. Cole had been at the farmhouse. The guy was thick with Rick. Figured a Wilde agent would be there. "What do you guys do?" James demanded as he glared at Cole. "Smell blood in the water like sharks?"

Cole smiled at him.

"I *told* you," the gorgeous lady with the gun and badge called out, "put your hands up!"

He lifted his hands. "You're making a mistake. I'm the *victim* here. You need to be rounding up Rick Williams. That guy has gone off the deep end. He's crazy obsessed with Kathleen O'Shaughnessy. He found out that I was her ex, and man, he went *insane*."

She took a step toward him. "The fact that you're a hit man after the client he's protecting—that had nothing to do with his sudden bout of insanity?"

"A hit man?" James smiled. "I think you're got me confused with someone else."

She held his gaze. "I don't think I do."

"Look, I need medical attention. I need a trip to the hospital." There would be so many ways that he could escape a hospital. "I feel weak. I-I think I'm gonna pass out—" His hands began to lower.

"Cuff him," she barked. "And, dammit, someone get an EMT!"

He smiled. Handcuffs? A breeze. Hell, he'd been the one to first teach Kat how to sneak out of them.

***

Kat wasn't talking. They'd made it back to Wilde, and as soon as they'd arrived, Eric had met them—Eric and a small army of Wilde agents. Eric's "inner circle"—so to speak. All of the agents had worked with Eric since he'd first opened Wilde, and Rick was very glad to see those familiar faces.

But no one spoke as they rode the elevator up to Eric's office. And when it came time to actually *enter* his office...only Eric, Kat, and Rick stepped inside.

Once they crossed the threshold—*surprise, surprise*—Eric's brother Ben was waiting inside. The younger Wilde wasn't in the security business. He was a lawyer and also one of Rick's closest friends. And at Ben's side, another familiar figure waited—an African American male with a completely shaved head and wearing both a perfectly cut suit and a clear *What-Have-You-Done-Now* expression on his face. Defense attorney Kendrick Shaw was obviously not pleased.

"Uh, oh," Rick said when he caught sight of Kendrick. "You brought in the big guns."

Eric shut the door behind Rick. "No one will get in this office without my permission. I have an army of agents right outside this door."

Yeah, they'd all just seen them.

Eric motioned to the giant freaking espresso bar in his office. A new addition, one that had been brought in by Eric's wife, Piper. "Ms.

O'Shaughnessy," Eric said, his voice carefully polite. "Can I get you something?"

Her lips pursed. "Honestly, I could use a few shots of vodka."

He blinked. "So could I."

Kendrick stepped forward. "How about we save the drinks for *after* our little talk about the murder of Joseph Lucas?"

"Who?" Rick asked.

"I think he means Joey," Kat said as she rubbed her neck and headed for the nearest chair. She lowered into it. Kind of sprawled. Looked beautiful and exhausted. He wanted to scoop her into his arms and take her out of there. Maybe put her in a giant bed so that she could sleep and forget—

"Like that, huh?" Ben Wilde asked.

Rick's head shot up as he zeroed in on his friend.

Ben nodded. "Yeah, I've been there, too. I know that look."

"Shut it, man," Rick growled. He was glad to see some friendly faces—faces he could trust—but he was *not* about to go where Ben was leading.

Ben leaned close to him and, voice low, replied, "Consider it shut, for now. Though you might want to think about guarding your expression a little more. You're giving a whole lot away."

He flipped off his friend and dragged a chair closer to Kat. "I want an update on what's going on. Did the cops get Ghost?"

Eric took a seat behind his desk. "Cole called me right before you arrived. Yes, they've got him.

He's being transported to a hospital for treatment before they take him to the PD because...apparently, someone shot him." He looked expectantly at Rick.

Kat waved a hand in the air. "It was me. I shot him."

Kendrick strode toward her. He offered his hand to Kat. "Hello, Ms. O'Shaughnessy. My name is Kendrick Shaw, and while I knew your father, I don't believe we've ever met."

Her head tilted to the right as she peered up at him. "I know your name. You're a defense attorney." She shook his hand.

"No, I'm *the* defense attorney. As in, I'm *the* one you want. The only one you'll ever need." He pulled back his hand and straightened his already straight suit. "In the future, how about we don't just throw out statements like, 'It was me. I shot him,' when you're questioned? We don't just need to confess to every little thing."

"But...I shot him. Jimmy was going to stab Rick, and I knew that if I didn't shoot, Rick would have to fire his gun. I didn't want Rick to kill Jimmy. I didn't want that crime on him." Her shoulders squared. "So I did it. I shot Jimmy."

Kendrick's expression showed puzzlement. "You are *not* like your father."

"I hope not. But some days, I'm not so certain." Her hands twisted in her lap.

Kendrick turned his attention to Rick. "And who killed the guy at the motel?"

"Not me," Rick retorted. "I swear, he was breathing when I left him." Breathing but probably well on his way to bruising.

Kendrick's intent stare returned to Kat.

"I didn't shoot him," she said, frowning. "He really was breathing when we left him. And hey— we even have a witness to that."

Rick nodded. "Damn straight. Someone else saw that Joey was alive when we left him."

Excitement lit Kendrick's face. "Excellent. Then we can clear this all up fast. Who's the witness?"

"Yeah...about that..." Rick coughed. "The hit man."

Kendrick's neck and head jutted forward a little. "Excuse me?"

"Ghost. Jimmy. Whatever the hell you want to call him. He saw that the motel desk clerk was alive when we left the scene. He saw us leave *before* Joey was shot. He can tell you that."

Kendrick very, very slowly...nodded. "Right." He drew the word out so that it seemed to possess about ten syllables. "You think that a hit man who is after Ms. O'Shaughnessy...you think he is going to vouch for you? That he's going to alibi you?" His lips twisted. Not a smile. Not a frown. "I don't think so. Especially since Kat just confessed to shooting him. Something tells me that the fellow isn't going to feel the urge to cooperate with you."

True. The sonofabitch probably wanted his pound of flesh from Rick and Kat. *And he will never get near her again.*

"At the very least," Kendrick continued as he began to pace, "we'll need to sit you both down with Detective Lopez so that you can answer her questions." Kendrick always paced when he plotted.

Rick saw Kat glance over her shoulder, as if she was looking for someone. Her gaze lingered on the closed door to Eric's office.

He touched her hand. "What is it?"

Her head turned toward him, and Kat's lips curled down. "I was expecting the FBI to come bursting in. Seemed to be their cue." A sad shake of her head. "I'll go ahead and say it...they are not going to be down with me chatting with local cops about a murder."

Eric's fingers drummed on his desk. "She's right. Hell, they are not *down* with anything right now."

Rick narrowed his gaze on his friend. "What's the status with them?"

"The status?" The faint lines near Eric's mouth deepened. "I've lost contact with my closest ally there. The man who originally hired me for the job? Assistant Director Silas Evans? He's vanished. None of the higher ups are talking about him, and the staff below him is now taking orders from someone new. Silas was someone I trusted. A man who told it to you straight. But from what I'm gathering, he's gone dark, totally dark on everyone, and that's not good."

No, that shit *wasn't* good.

"What do you think happened to him?" Rick pushed.

Eric's gaze flickered to Kat. His mouth tightened.

"He thinks that Silas Evans is dead," Kat said into the silence that lingered a little too long in the office. "And he thinks Silas died because of me."

"Because he had *information* on you," Eric corrected.

Shit. Eric had corrected the reason why Silas might be dead, but he hadn't argued that the other man was, in fact, gone. Hell.

"I met Silas many times." Kat's voice was low. "He seemed like a good man. If he is dead, then I'm very sorry for your loss."

Eric's head inclined toward her. "Thank you."

Ben gaped at them. "Are you all serious right now? An FBI Assistant Director has been killed by the mob? And it's being covered up...*by the FBI?*"

"I doubt they are covering it up," Kat said, rolling one shoulder. "They probably can't find his body. Not unusual in a mob hit. And they don't know specifically who killed him. They won't go public until they have more. Especially not with me set to head into a courthouse in a few days."

Poor Ben. He was used to handling divorce cases, not mob hits. But he recovered fast. Squared his shoulders. Lifted his chin. And Ben asked, "What can I do?"

Kat pushed out of her chair and stood. "Don't die."

Ben's gaze darted to Rick.

"My apologies," Kat added quickly as she kept her focus on Ben. "But I didn't get your name. You kind of look like the other one..." A motion of her hand toward Eric. "You're another Wilde?"

"Ben." He approached her. Offered his hand. "I'm Ben Wilde."

She shook his hand. "Ben, please don't take this the wrong way, but I think you need to get the hell out of here." She let him go. "You, too,

Kendrick. I appreciate you coming in. I know my father probably had you on retainer or something before he died, but you don't need to be involved in this mess."

Ben seemed to take her measure. "I'm not going anywhere. My brother called me because he knew he could trust me. Don't let the pretty face fool you..." He flashed her a charming grin. "I can get shit done."

"I have no doubt." Kat backed away from him. "But don't you all see what's happening here? The people who are getting pulled into my world—those people are dying. And if an FBI Assistant Director can be taken out, then you can all be taken out." Her gaze slid to Rick. He could see tears pooling in her gorgeous eyes. Tears, dammit.

"Kat," Rick rasped her name.

She blinked the tears away. "The fewer people involved, the better. There are only a few days before I go into the courthouse. Just a few more, and then I vanish. You don't all need to put yourselves on the line for me."

Rick stood. He stalked to her. Reached for her hands. Held them carefully in his.

"You don't need to keep risking yourself for me." She licked her lower lip. "I know you promised to stay with me, but Rick...that was before I heard that an *Assistant Director* with the FBI had been taken down. Don't you see? They can get to anyone. They can hurt *everyone*."

His hold tightened. "I think I told you before, I'm not afraid."

Her gaze searched his. "Maybe you should be."

Eric cleared his throat. "Ahem, yeah, I think we need to take a moment and circle back to the FBI..."

Rick glanced over his shoulder at Eric.

Eric gave a little wince. "Because they are going to be here in about five minutes."

"*What?*" Rick snarled.

Looking glum and very uncomfortable, Eric nodded. "I'm sorry, man. I tried. Believe me, I did. But they have the power of the federal government behind them. Without my contact in the game any longer, my hands are tied. I've been ordered to turn Kathleen O'Shaughnessy back over to the Feds. They say that we're a greater threat to her than anyone else. The new boss in charge thinks she *never* should have been turned over to civilians, and his agents are going to be showing up to claim her." His gaze slid to Kat. "They'll be taking you to an undisclosed location, and you won't be seeing any Wilde agents again."

Rick couldn't breathe. His chest ached. His lungs *burned*. A red haze swam before his eyes. The Feds were coming to take Kat away from him? No, oh, hell, *no*.

***

James let out a ragged groan as he twisted his body on the stretcher. He was in the back of an ambulance, and two EMTs were fluttering around him. Okay, not fluttering. Hooking him up to shit. Checking out his wound. Since he was acting as if he was dying, he figured they were probably pretty panicked.

The female detective—he'd heard her name, Lopez—hadn't come along for the ride. She'd sent a uniform with him. He was sure a patrol car was tailing him while the ambulance hauled ass. The uniform watched the scene from the corner of the vehicle, and the guy's eyes were narrowed on James.

Detective Layla Lopez. He'd actually known who she was even before hearing her name. After all, he was a professional. It made sense to research all the players before you got involved in the game. Layla was tight with Eric Wilde, one of the members of his inner circle, so to speak. James had figured she'd be involved in Kat's world at some point.

That point was now.

James tugged his left wrist. It had been cuffed to a bar along the side of the stretcher. An annoyance, but one he could handle.

"How much longer until we reach the nearest hospital?" One of the EMTs checked James's pulse as she fired the question at the driver. "His pulse is thready and his blood pressure is dropping."

Was it? Hmmm...he wasn't that good of an actor. The last thing he needed was to require *actual* medical attention. That would slow down his escape goal.

"About ten more minutes," the driver shouted back.

Ten more minutes.

James closed his eyes. When he arrived at the hospital, he had to make his move. He needed to get the hell out of there.

Or else everything was going to be screwed.

CHAPTER FIFTEEN

The door opened and her two FBI suits walked in the office with slow and steady steps.

Kat sucked in a quick breath when she saw them. Suit Number One...he didn't look like his usual polished self. Bryan Brisk's black suit appeared wrinkled, his blond hair was mussed, and dark shadows lined his eyes. As for Tom Wayne—he was even paler than normal. There was what appeared to be some sort of red stain on his shirt, and she was really hoping that stain wasn't blood.

Neither man looked particularly thrilled to see her. The feeling was mutual. But Kat still pasted a smile on her face. "You missed me." She nodded. "I know you did. You couldn't wait to get back in my company again." She was going to keep her cocky persona in place until she was out of that office. No way would she let Rick see how much it was hurting her to leave him.

An Assistant Director at the FBI was dead? Or, rather, presumed dead? Hell, yes, this mess was a nightmare, and she wanted Rick out of it.

Because...*I care too much for him.*

He'd gotten to her. Gotten right past her guard. She cared so much for the man that she'd *shot* Jimmy. Sure, Jimmy was a lying douche so she didn't feel overly bad about that blast, but...

I would have killed him. To keep Rick safe, I would have shot Jimmy again and aimed straight for his heart. A staggering realization. One that made her sick to her stomach. Her father had warned her, long ago, that she'd be like this.

One day, my darling, you'll see. There will be something or someone that pushes you over the edge, too, and you'll realize that crossing the line between right and wrong is far easier than you might expect. His eyes—the same shade of her own—had held no emotion as he added, *And once you cross that line, you don't ever go back.*

She'd been ready to cross that line for Rick. *He* was her weakness, and she had to get away from him.

So Kat tossed her hair over her shoulder and kept her coy smile in place. She looked vaguely at the others in the room, never letting her gaze linger on anyone, but darting over Eric, his brother, Kendrick, and Rick as she said, "It's been real, everyone. But time to hitch out of here with my new ride. The FBI can't wait to get their hands on me again."

She took a few confident steps toward Bryan—

Rick stepped into her path. "No."

She faltered. He was blocking her view of Bryan. "I'm sorry." She didn't make eye contact. "I'm not good at good-byes. Let's make this short and sweet and—"

"No."

Again with the 'no' from him?

Kat sidestepped.

He moved with her. "Look at me. Look me in the eyes."

She did. Grudgingly.

"I told you that I wouldn't leave you. I promised."

Swallow. Breathe. Ignore the racing of your heart. "You're not leaving me. I'm leaving you. I didn't want to come to Wilde in the first place."

His dark and dangerous eyes narrowed on her. "I can tell now."

"You can tell what?"

His hand lifted and curved under her chin. "When you're trying to protect someone."

"I'm protecting myself." His touch was scorching her. "Good-bye, Rick."

"No."

"No?" Okay, her voice had gotten too high. She cleared her throat. "Uh, FBI agents, how about a little help here?"

Bryan and Tom moved to surround Rick. Bryan to the right. Tom to the left of him. "We're taking over custody," Bryan said.

She rolled her eyes at his words. Taking over custody? What was she? A child?

"Your agents can't be trusted," Tom added with a glare that he tossed at Eric. "So it's good that we're back to take over the job."

Oh, right. Never mind the fact that they'd been only too eager to ditch her at Wilde a few days before. *Now* they were acting all big and bad. Like that didn't flash RED ALERT in her mind.

"And we're going to be taking over custody of James Smith, as well," Tom told them all. "He's been wanted by the FBI for a long time, and while we appreciate the cooperation that Wilde and the local authorities have shown us, he's our perp, and he'll be held by our agents."

They were taking Jimmy, too, huh? Though Kat wasn't so sure that "cooperation" was the right word to use. She could practically feel the hostility vibrating in the room.

Bryan smiled at her. "You ready to go, Kat?"

"Yes."

"*No.*"

Of course, that denial came from Rick. Why was he doing this? Didn't he get that things were hard enough for her?

Bryan lost his smile. "Back up, buddy." He put his hand on Rick's shoulder. And pushed.

Rick didn't budge an inch. He did look down at the FBI agent's hand. "You'll want to move that, before I move it for you."

Bryan swallowed. "Assaulting a federal officer is a crime. I think you're already in enough trouble with the authorities, don't you? There's the little matter of the dead body you left back at that motel."

"I'm not in any trouble. Kat can back me up as far as the dead man is concerned. She saw me leave that guy—alive—in the motel. Your big, bad hit man knows the truth, too. So I'm not worried about that shit."

Tom laughed. "You think a hit man will back up your story? Hate to break it to you, but he's *not* the good guy."

"Never said he was. At this point, I think it's getting real hard to tell the good guys from the bad ones." Once more, Rick looked down at the hand on his shoulder. "Move it."

Bryan dropped his hand.

"Good. Now, Kat isn't going with you."

Kat opened her mouth—

"She's not leaving this office," Rick continued in his lethal growl. "Not unless I'm at her side. I signed up to be her bodyguard. My contract said that I was to stay with her until she walked through the doors of the courthouse, and that's exactly what I plan to do."

His contract? Had he actually signed a contract agreeing to those stipulations?

"We can do this the easy way..." Rick smiled. It was a rather chilling, but very sexy sight. "I walk out of here holding Kat's hand and place myself between her and any danger that comes her way..."

Bryan's face flushed red.

"Or we do it the hard way."

Tom's brow wrinkled. "What's the hard way?"

"I knock both of your asses out. I do it in about five seconds. Then I take Kat and I—"

Kendrick coughed. Or choked. Kat couldn't exactly tell what happened. He hurried across the room, waving his hands. "No, no, that is *not* what my client meant to say. He definitely didn't say he was going to knock anyone out."

"Yeah, I did." Rick nodded. He took Kat's hand in his. Held tight.

And maybe she inched a little closer to him. *Why* did she do that?

"We do have a contract, though," Kendrick continued, smooth as silk now, as if he'd never had his coughing/choking fit. "And that contract can only be voided by the man who signed it. Since the Assistant Director is currently on sabbatical—"

"The man is fucking missing," Bryan blasted. "Probably stone cold dead because he got caught in the hunt for *her*." He pointed at Kat.

Kendrick didn't even pause. "Since his whereabouts are unknown, technically, Rick does still have a job to do."

"Bullshit!" Tom's face flashed with anger. "The FBI trumps any contract. We trump—"

Kendrick shook his head. "Kathleen O'Shaughnessy is a free woman."

"No, she's a material witness," Bryan glared at Kendrick. "And you—of all people, Mr. Shaw—should know that means she goes where the government wants her to go."

"Ah, you know my name." Kendrick offered the agent a cold smile. "Then that means you know my reputation. You know you don't want to tangle with me because I will take *any* fight straight to the public. And the public loves me." He leaned forward. "Because I am fucking loveable."

He was?

"Save us all some time and effort," Kendrick urged. "Take Rick Williams with you. He has Kathleen's best interests at heart. He's willing to fight in order to keep her safe. He goes where she goes. Easy enough."

A flicker of hope stirred inside of Kat—

"No," Bryan snapped. "The FBI is taking over. Kat is a material witness, and we are done here.

No Wilde agents can come with us because that will just put her at risk. It's *not* happening."

The hope died.

She could feel Rick tensing, and she was very afraid that he was about to slip straight to his option two mode—kicking ass. And if he did kick the asses of the FBI agents, what would happen then?

He'd get tossed in a jail cell.

When Rick started to lunge at Bryan—

"No," Kat said softly.

Rick's head turned toward her.

"My turn to say no." She stared into his eyes. Her first good-bye. Or, rather, the first one that had hurt. "Thank you, Rick."

He shook his head. "Don't you do it. This *isn't* the end, I promised you—"

Her hands fisted in his shirt. She yanked him toward her even as she leaned onto her toes. She saw the flare of surprise in his eyes right before her mouth crashed into his. It was a fast, frantic kiss. She wanted one more kiss from him. Just one more.

His hands curled around her waist. He pulled her closer. Kissed her harder and deeper—

Someone cleared a throat. Was that Kendrick again?

She pulled away from Rick. Gazed up into his eyes. "I will miss you, and I will never forget you."

"Don't leave with them, princess, don't—"

"I don't have a choice, and neither do you. Thanks for looking out for me. It was nice. For a little while, with you, I think I got to truly enjoy life." She wanted to kiss him again, but she didn't.

Instead, Kat stiffened her spine and edged toward Bryan. "Let's go," she mumbled. "And by the way, I'm starving. I hope wherever the hell I wind up, there are brownies close by."

Bryan and Tom led her to the door.

"Kat!"

She stiffened at Rick's call and glanced back.

His eyes were so dark as they swirled with emotion. "It's not over."

No, it wouldn't be over for her until she went into the courthouse.

"*We* aren't over," he told her. "I promise."

***

Rick wanted to rush after Kat. He wanted to grab her, pull her into his arms, and never, fucking *ever* let her go.

"That didn't go so well," Kendrick allowed when the door clicked shut behind the agents. "Though I suppose it could've gone worse. I mean, no one was arrested. I always count that as a win."

Rick clenched and unclenched his hands. Kat had looked so sad after she'd kissed him. "I was supposed to stay with her."

"Yes, well, the FBI *does* beat out Wilde." Kendrick prowled around the room as he made this announcement. *Pacing and plotting again.* "But it's only temporary. We need to come up with a new strategy—"

"Or we could just let her go," Ben said as his brows shot up. "Um, I mean the FBI has her. She'll be okay."

Rick whirled to glare at his friend.

Ben shook his head. "No, no, that is a terrible plan, terrible," he corrected immediately. "I don't know why the hell I said that. What was I thinking? The FBI—"

"I don't trust them," Rick snapped. "Not for a minute."

Eric raked a hand through his hair. "Yeah, well, they don't trust us, either. That's the problem. Someone got in here at Wilde, someone hacked *my* system, and now the Feds have no use for us." His jaw hardened. "*Someone hacked my system*. How is that shit even possible?"

"The guy saved her life." The words were pulled from Rick. He frowned after he said them. But... "He did," Rick muttered. "He tipped us off and we were able to get out before Kat was taken. The guy who broke in here...maybe he wasn't looking to hurt her at all. Maybe he was looking to help Kat."

All eyes turned to Rick.

"Who would want to help her?" Ben asked.

Kat. Kat and her secrets. "She never told me who she called when she vanished from the Feds that first time."

Eric nodded. "The brownie run."

"Uh, do what now?" Ben squinted. "Can someone bring me up to speed? Because I feel lost as all hell."

"The Feds originally turned Kat over to us because she'd slipped away from them. She went on a brownie run." Rick would not smile as he thought of that first meeting with her. Would not. But his chest felt warmer. "Only while she was gone, someone found the hotel she and the Feds had been using. It got shot to hell and back. The idea was that the Feds had sold her out, so Eric's connection—"

"Assistant Director Silas Evans," Eric inserted with a worried frown.

"He pulled in Wilde. He wanted new protection for her. We were supposed to keep Kat safe until she went to court. She was supposed to stay with me." His time with her shouldn't have been over. He'd been promised longer. He'd—

"Uh, Rick?" It was Kendrick who studied him. "I have to ask, man. Just how involved did you get with Kathleen O'Shaughnessy?"

"Does it matter?"

"Shit. That's *not* the answer I was hoping to hear." Kendrick nodded briskly. "All right. You're in deep. Maybe you're not seeing everything in the clearest light, so let me shine some illumination for you. The fact that she's gone? That's not a bad thing. The Feds can take her. They can take the danger that trails her. You can go back to your normal life and you can just forget about her."

Forget about her?

"No." The same thing he'd told Kat. And suddenly...

It was just... *"No,"* Rick snarled again.

No, I can't lose her.

No, I can't let her go.

No, I can't risk Kat.

I need her too much.

He whirled and lunged for the door.

"Rick!" Eric yelled.

He didn't stop. Right then, he was only focused on one thing—*Kat*. She'd been in pain when she'd left. He'd *seen* her pain. And had he done a damn thing about it? No, he'd just let her walk away. He was supposed to protect her from everyone and everything—that was his job. Instead, he'd let her *walk.*

He rushed out of Eric's office and past the agents who were guarding the area. He turned and spared one glance for Eric's assistant, Dennis.

Behind the lenses of his glasses, Dennis gaped at him with huge eyes.

Rick just stared at him.

"They took the elevator." Dennis pointed. His finger trembled a little. "Their cars are waiting out front. They're going to the lobby."

What the hell? He jumped in the nearest elevator. They were just taking her out the front door? How was that safe? Rick had brought her into the building as quietly as possible, and the Feds were parading her around in front of everyone.

"Wait, dammit!" Eric hurtled into the elevator.

The doors shut a second later. Rick jammed the lobby button.

"Tell me what's going on here," Eric ordered him. "You are not like this, you are *not* out of control this way." A pause. "What has she done to you?"

Maybe she'd committed the worst sin of all. She'd made him care. "I'm not losing her. My job is to keep her safe, and that's fucking what I'm going to do."

"She walked away from you. She left *you.*"

Rick nodded. "And I'm going after her."

"The Feds aren't going to let you *near* her."

"We'll just see about that." Why the hell was the elevator so slow?

"Shit. You...you *like* her."

He glared at Eric. "Don't start with me."

"You had sex with her, didn't you?"

"Screw off."

"You're...you more than *like* her."

"I'm not a damn teenage boy, and we are not sharing shit. I'm not letting her go, and that's all there is to it. *Why the fuck is the elevator so slow?*" He slammed his fist into the wall.

"Yeah. Okay. Settle down, big guy. Don't go damaging the merchandise. Breathe, and you'll be in the lobby in a moment. They don't have that much of a lead on us, and—"

The doors opened. Thank Christ. Rick rushed out. Two guys in suits—guys he didn't recognize but who had the buttoned-down appearance of FBI agents—spun toward him. When they saw him charging forward, they shot toward him. Rick threw out his arms and knocked them both back.

"This is going to be so bad," Eric muttered from behind him.

Bad didn't cover it. He ran for the building's front doors. He could see Kat through the glass. She was being loaded into the back of a long, black car. For some reason, the car looked like a hearse to him. That was all he could think—Kat was getting in a car that looked like death.

No, no! He threw open the front doors, ignoring the doorman who tried to grab him. "Kat!"

He saw her head whip toward him. She was in the back seat now.

"Don't leave me!"

She was attempting to get out of the car. He could see her trying to push past Agent Tom Wayne. The guy was in the back with her. He was holding her back. The sight made Rick's fury even stronger. "Let her the hell go!"

The driver of the vehicle jumped out. The car was still on. Rick could hear its engine as it growled. He could even hear a strange little *click, click* beneath the growl.

The driver barreled toward him.

Bryan was running from another car, one that had been parked farther down the street.

Kat had finally gotten free of Tom. She stumbled out, with Tom right behind her. Tom grabbed her and they both crashed into the cement.

Rick bellowed as his fury erupted. Kat had hit the cement too hard. He grabbed her, yanking her away from Tom. He pulled Kat into his arms and cradled her. "I can't let you go. You need to know, I—"

The car exploded. The heat and force of the blast slammed into him. Rick flew into the air, holding tightly to Kat. They hit the ground and pounded into the cement even as screams and the crackle of fire filled the air. He could feel the heat all over his skin. Frantic, he lifted his body up so that he could stare down at Kat.

She blinked at him. A cut marred her right cheek, and blood slid over her skin. "Rick?"

Fucking, *no*. It had been a trap. He'd almost let her walk straight into a trap. Almost let her die. If he'd been a minute slower—a few *seconds* slower—his Kat would be dead.

Someone had blown that Fed car to hell and back. Someone could be out there right now, watching from one of the nearby high-rise windows, ready to take her out. Ready to finish the job he'd started.

Rick scooped Kat into his arms and ran back toward the Wilde building. He kept his body curved around her, protecting her as much as he could, running in a zig zag so there wouldn't be a straight bead on him.

Eric was there, waving him in and shouting something. His words didn't register. All Rick could hear was a pounding in his ears. The frantic pounding of his heart. Everything else was static. Madness. Chaos.

She's not dead. I got to her in time. She's not dead.

He flew through the open door. Met more chaos. Wilde agents grabbed for Kat, but he shoved them aside. No one was taking her from him. Not again.

Not ever again.

CHAPTER SIXTEEN

"Get her upstairs!" Eric shouted. "Get her back to my office—*now!*"

Rick ran into the elevator. He looked back to see Eric racing outside of the building. Debris littered the ground—burning debris. People were running around out there, and he could still hear screams.

Wilde agents he recognized closed in around him. They had their guns up, and they made a wall in front of him. Rick's shoulders pressed to the rear of the elevator. His hold on Kat was bruisingly tight.

He wanted to trust the men and women in front of him. He'd worked with them for years. But...

He didn't trust them fully. He couldn't, not with Kat's life on the line.

His body was tense, battle-ready. His gaze swept over her face. He hated the blood on her cheek. God, his Kat. She would have been blown to pieces.

"Baby, I'm sorry." His voice was a rasp.

She stared up at him. "Why?"

Her voice reached over the mad drumming of his heartbeat. *Because I let you down. Because I should have been there sooner. Because I should have been there the whole time.*

He bent his head. Pressed a kiss to her forehead.

When the doors opened moments later, the agents cleared a path for him. As he raced to Eric's office, he saw Ben rushing out to meet him. Ben and Kendrick. Shock covered the faces of both men.

"Dear God," Kendrick began, sounding as rattled as he looked. "The blast shook the whole building!" His gaze dropped to Kat. "Is she—"

"I'm okay," Kat said. Her voice was stronger. "He can put me down. I'm—"

Rick kicked the door to Eric's office. "Lock it," he snarled behind him. "No one else gets in this room—not unless it's Eric."

Ben and Kendrick had followed him back inside. Ben locked the door.

Rick lowered Kat to the couch. Or, he tried to lower her. His arms were just being all weird, though. They wouldn't let her go.

"Rick." Kat's hand rose and touched his cheek. "I'm okay. You can put me down."

The third time was the charm. He actually managed to let her go. "I need a cloth for her face. She's bleeding."

Instantly, Ben shoved a wet cloth into his hand.

Rick blinked at it.

"I got it from Eric's bathroom," Ben hurried to explain. "When you were, you know, trying to figure out how to stop holding her."

Rick slowly turned his head to stare at Ben. "She could have died." Even to his own ears, his voice sounded lost.

And afraid.

But he wasn't afraid of anything. Hadn't he told Kat that very thing? He didn't scare easily. He walked into fires. He faced down killers. He didn't get scared.

So why am I terrified right now?

Ben clamped his hand on Rick's shoulder. "She didn't die, man. You got her. She's safe."

"I'm safe, Rick." Kat's quiet voice. "I'm okay."

Her face was too pale. Her lips trembling. And blood was still on her cheek. He lifted the cloth and tenderly brushed it over her cheek. His Kat. Dear God, what would he have done if she'd been in that car when it ignited?

"The...scratch isn't that bad." Rick cleared his throat. "Are you hurt anywhere else?"

Kat shook her head.

His breath rushed out. "I'll get rid of the cloth. *Don't move.*"

He whirled. Marched into Eric's bathroom. That fancy-ass, too expensive bathroom that was probably bigger than some apartments in the city. Rick tossed the cloth into the garbage and caught a glimpse of himself in the mirror. Crazy eyes. Clenched jaw. Fury stamped on his face. He looked scary as hell.

He looked like he wanted to kill and destroy. Because he did. He wanted to destroy the person who'd set that bomb. And, hell, yes, he knew the work of a bomb when he saw one. He knew all about explosives. Back when he'd been a firefighter, he'd been called—unfortunately—to several bomb scenes in the aftermath of the explosions. And, God, they'd been bad. What had been left of those people...

Not much *had* been left.

And if he'd been on that street...with Kat blown apart that way...

I would have lost my mind.

Rick stormed out of the bathroom. He went straight to her.

Ben's eyes widened as he peered at Rick's face. "Uh, buddy, just take a breath. Calm the hell down for—"

"Get out," Rick snapped. "You and Kendrick— get out. I need to be alone with Kat. Right now."

Ben and Kendrick shared a long look.

"We'll be on the other side of the door," Kendrick assured him. "You need us, all you have to do is call out."

Ben was hesitating. "But we should ask Kat some questions—"

Kendrick grabbed him and pushed him toward the door. "Not now. Right now, he just needs her."

Rick didn't look their way. He was right in front of Kat. Her head tilted back as she stared up at him. Beautiful Kat. Eyes so deep and green. That long, thick hair. Her golden skin.

"Are you okay?" she whispered.

She was worried about him? *Him*?

He sat next to her on the couch. Pulled her into his arms. Buried his face in the crook of her neck and inhaled her scent. Okay? Hell, no. Hell, *no.*

***

"What happened?" Layla Lopez barked into her phone as she paced along the hospital corridor. She turned, her eyes locking on the man who was being examined in the room right across from her. She could see him easily through the nearby glass window. Two uniforms stood at attention beside the perp who had one hand cuffed to the gurney beneath him.

"An explosion," Eric Wilde told her. "Right in front of the Wilde building. Someone was trying to take out Kathleen O'Shaughnessy. Didn't succeed, but several FBI agents were injured. They're on the way to the hospital."

"What a coincidence," she muttered. "That's where I am."

"You've still got the hit man?"

"My eyes are on him."

"The bomb was *in* the FBI car. And if the fellow you have is really the guy who goes by Ghost, bombs aren't his style."

No, they weren't.

"Someone else put the bomb in place. Someone else in the line that wants Kat dead."

She knew it was a very long line. "Where is she now?" Layla asked.

"Safe," Eric responded flatly.

"Not a very specific answer."

"And I have no idea if this line is secure or not, so that's all you're getting. For anything else, we'll talk in person."

She definitely intended to talk with him in person. "You *and* Rick."

"He's occupied right now."

Through the window, she saw that the doctor was finished with the exam. Oh, poor hit man. He'd gotten stitches. Big freaking whoop. If she'd had her way, she would've dragged the perp straight to the station without pausing for the ER visit. But some FBI jerk had called her boss and given orders that Ghost had to be examined. Ghost was being treated like a freaking VIP. The FBI was saying they were in charge of him, and they were telling the PD how to handle the perp.

She didn't particularly enjoy following orders from Bureau bozos. Layla exhaled slowly. "I need to talk with Rick. I've got a dead body. He has answers that I need."

"According to Rick, your hit man has answers. Rick said the hit man can confirm that Rick and Kat left your vic alive at the motel."

A hit man as an alibi? Interesting. "Let me get back with you."

"*Layla.*" Her name burst from him.

She frowned.

"Be careful, okay? This is out of control. Bombs outside my building. A spy *in* here. FBI agents getting rushed to the hospital. The collateral damage in this case is insane, and I don't want you getting hurt."

"It's sweet that you care, but I can handle myself."

"This isn't like your usual cases. Don't trust anyone. You understand what I'm saying? Too many people are being bought. Cops. FBI. Maybe even my own agents...I don't even know who to trust. Watch yourself."

"I will." She shoved the phone into her pocket and squared her shoulders. With slow, calm steps, she headed into the exam room. "Status," she threw at the doctor.

"Blood loss, but nothing substantial. The patient's blood pressure dipped for a bit, but he's stable. Stitched him up, and he's ready to go."

"Thanks." She waved him away and headed closer to the "patient." Layla smiled at him. "Do we feel better? I mean, you did have a nasty scratch, and I can see how it would take down a big, tough guy like you."

His lips thinned.

"Time to head over to the PD. We need to get moving, before all those people from the bombing head in here. Place will be swarming with Feds." She motioned to the uniform on the right. "Let's—"

Her perp asked, "What bombing?"

Layla didn't let a flicker of satisfaction show on her face. "The one at Wilde."

His pupils flared. She was staring right at him, so she saw the dead giveaway. Then he rasped, "Kat?"

"I believe she was involved, yes." A nod. "Now, let's get you to the—"

"Get the idiots in uniform *out* of here. We need to talk."

The uniforms glared. Obviously, they didn't like being called idiots. Who did?

Layla winced. "You should be more careful. Words hurt."

"Screw that. We need to talk. *Alone.*"

What did he think? That if he had her alone, he'd be able to overpower her and get away? Oh, yes, she'd already figured out that Ghost thought he'd be able to sneak away. Ghost had never been arrested before. Never spent so much as a night in a jail cell. She was sure he'd be trying to get away.

But he wasn't escaping on her watch.

"You want information from me, Detective Lopez?" He yanked at the cuff. "Then you and I talk in here, *alone*."

She motioned to the cops. "Stand outside the door. Keep guard."

Reluctantly, they left. The doc had already high-tailed it out of there. She'd noticed that he'd seemed particularly jumpy after he'd spotted the handcuffs. If he'd realized he was treating a hit man, she thought the MD might have fainted.

When they were alone, she raised her brows. "Happy now?"

"*Is Kat alive?*"

"You know what...how about we play a game? I ask you a question, you answer it. And then, if you answer me *honestly*, I'll answer a question for you. Does that seem fair?" The antiseptic smell in that room was making her nose itch.

"Fine," he gritted out. His shirt had been removed by the doc—cut away and bagged as evidence. He was a muscled, very strong guy. If he thought he'd use that strength against her...

Think again.

"Question one..." *Let's get the big stuff out of the way.* "Were you present when Rick Williams and Kathleen O'Shaughnessy left the motel off of Highway—"

"They didn't kill the guy. Let's cut straight to it. That's what you wanted to know, isn't it? I'm pretty sure Rick knocked the guy unconscious." Ghost slid his jaw from side to side. "Trust me, big boy packs one hell of a punch. But Rick didn't kill the motel clerk. The fellow was still breathing when they drove away."

Well, color her surprised. She actually hadn't expected him to offer up that alibi so easily.

"What?" He blinked. "You think I'm lying? Why would I do that? You don't need to arrest Rick Williams. He didn't do anything wrong. Let him stay exactly where he is."

Now this was interesting. "Where do you think he is?"

Her perp shook his head. "It's my turn to ask a question."

Her lips thinned.

"Is Kat alive?"

"Yes. The bomb didn't get her. Some FBI agents were injured, but she's safe."

He released a low breath. Some of the tension seemed to slide from his body.

"Oh, I get it." Layla nodded. "If someone else kills her, you don't get paid. It must be like some giant hit man contest out there, huh? Who will claim the bounty? Hate to break it to you, but you won't be the winner. You'll be in a jail cell."

His brow furrowed. "Why? What crime have I committed?"

"*My* turn to ask the question."

He smiled. Ghost looked entirely too relaxed all of a sudden. She didn't like that. Not at all.

"What's your real name? I get that you go by Ghost, but I want an actual name for booking."

"Oh, I thought you already had that. Didn't the Feds tell you? My lovers call me Jimmy. Formal name is James. James Smith." A pause. "And your name is Layla Lopez. You're friends with Eric Wilde and Rick Williams. By all accounts, you're a stand-up cop. If such a beast exists."

"It does," she snapped back.

"You tend to have good judgment, you're respected by your peers—"

"Have you *investigated* me?"

"Yes...and that counts as another one of your questions, even though it was *my* turn."

That sonofa—

"I do have to wonder about the good judgment, though, since you've been secretly involved with defense attorney Kendrick Shaw for the last year."

No. No, he had *not* just said—

He made a tut-tut sound. "I mean, Kendrick reps some of the worst criminals out there. *You* are supposed to put the bad guys away. How does it work, sleeping with someone who should be your enemy?"

She lunged toward him. "You don't know—"

"*Ah, ah, ah.*" He wagged his cuffed fingers. "You're supposed to answer my question. *That* was my question."

She wasn't going to answer his question. *How, how* had he known about her and Kendrick? "Time for you to be transferred to the PD."

"Yes, I thought you'd say that."

She stormed away. Headed for the uniforms. They both had their backs turned to the door and observation window. What the hell? They should at least be watching to make sure the perp wasn't trying to make a run for it. Layla whipped open the door. "Get in there and get him ready for transfer," Layla ordered angrily. "Get him—"

There was a commotion at the end of the hallway. Her head whipped to the right as the ER doors burst open.

"FBI!" One voice yelled out as a throng spilled into the hallway. "These are FBI agents and you're damn well going to take care of them!"

Nurses and doctors were scrambling. Layla advanced on the chaotic scene.

A gurney shoved past her, and she caught a quick glance at a man's face—twisted in agony. A redheaded man in a dirty suit, one marked with blood and ash.

Another gurney followed. Then another.

The bombing outside Wilde Protection and Securities. She was staring at the vics. Her gaze flew over the agents and cops that now filled the ER. She recognized—"Agent Brisk?"

Bryan Brisk turned toward her. Yeah, their paths had crossed before. More than a few times. And he'd been the one demanding that her boss turn over custody of Ghost to him. He'd also been at the motel, nosing around *her* crime scene and telling her that the FBI had control. He and his redheaded partner, the poor guy she'd seen get wheeled back moments before.

"Detective Lopez?" He shook his head. "What are you doing here?"

"Getting my perp checked out—like *you* FBI guys insisted. I wanted to drag his ass straight to the PD because he barely had a scratch, but instead, I'm here." She jumped back as another gurney rolled past her. "How bad is it?"

"No dead. We're fucking lucky on that score." He rubbed the back of his neck. Appeared exhausted and hollowed out. "The driver and my partner were the two agents closest to the vehicle when it blew. Their injuries look bad and hurt them like hell, but the EMTs said they'd be okay." His hand dropped. He looked over her shoulder. "Where's your perp?"

She turned back. The two uniforms she'd stationed outside of Ghost's exam room were gone. Good—that meant they'd followed her orders and gotten him ready for transport.

Right?

Her stomach rolled, though, and Layla found herself hurrying—then running—back to Ghost's room. She peered through the observation window. "Shit!"

Layla shoved open the door.

Both of the uniforms were on the floor. She flew toward them, immediately checking to make sure they were still alive and—*yes*, thank God, they were. Pulse beating, breathing shallow, but alive. *Unconscious.*

Her gaze darted around the exam room, and she saw the handcuffs that had been dropped near the door. That tricky SOB.

A whistle came from the doorway.

Agent Brisk shook his head. "He got away."

She shot to her feet. "He can't be far!" She shoved Brisk out of her way. "I need help in here! Two uniforms are down!" She rushed down the corridor and slammed her hands on the nurse's desk. "We need to search this place, top to bottom! Get me your security—get me all hands that you've got!" Her breath heaved out. "A killer just walked out of his exam room."

***

The scrubs fit him perfectly. He'd snagged a surgical cap to cover his hair and donned a mask to hide the lower portion of his face. After getting the right clothes, it had been easy for James to join the crowd of doctors who'd swarmed around the downed FBI agent.

FBI Agent Tom Wayne. Yes, James knew the guy. He made a point of knowing everyone who could be a problem. James stayed with the medical crew as Tom was wheeled into an exam room. Damn, the Fed had a wicked burn on the left side of his body.

From the details he was hearing, things could've been a lot worse.

For Tom and for everyone else involved.

Some killers were so sloppy. They didn't care about collateral damage. They didn't care about anyone who got in their way. James wasn't like that. He had a code.

He took out the target, and no one else ever got killed. Simple enough. But then, he was a professional. He took pride in his work.

After a few moments, he slipped from the room. James made his way down some twisting hallways. Walked right past a few security guards and out into the sunlight.

His gaze swept the parking lot.

Decisions, decisions. Which car did he feel like stealing?

CHAPTER SEVENTEEN

Kat lifted her head and gazed at Rick. She'd never seen his face look so hard. So fierce. His body was like a rock, every muscle stiffened. "You saved my life."

"I couldn't let you go."

She should smile at him. Try to lighten the mood. Only she couldn't. "Are the FBI agents okay?"

"I...some of them were hurt, baby, and I don't know if there were casualties."

A knife stabbed into her heart.

"We'll find out. Eric is downstairs. He's going to report soon. Everything will be fine."

"That's a lie. Nothing about this situation is fine, and you know it."

His head inclined. "You're right. And I said I wouldn't lie to you, didn't I?" His breath blew out in a rush. "The situation is a four-alarm cluster fuck. You've got bad guys coming after you from every side. They all want you dead."

Okay, no sugar coating. But then, she already knew this.

"The Feds, Wilde agents, the cops...it's possible you've been compromised from all sides."

"I-I knew I was signing my own death warrant when I came forward with the evidence I had."

She choked down the lump that had risen in her throat. "There's nowhere to turn. Nowhere to go." She wasn't going to make it to the courthouse. The prosecutors would just have to use the evidence she'd already given them. They would—

"You turn to me. You run to me." His hand was so careful as it curled under her chin. "Because, baby, you can always count on me. I swear, I am not going to let you down."

She blinked away the tears that wanted to fill her eyes. She could still feel the heat of the fire on her skin and hear the screams that had filled the street. "Why are you risking so much for me? I'm not worth it. I'm a job you were hired to do. Walk away. Be done before *you're* hurt. Before you're the one in the street screaming."

He shook his head. "No."

"Rick, you need to know that you say that word far too much—"

"You're worth anything. Hell, I'm starting to think that you're worth *everything* to me."

He hadn't said that. She'd misunderstood him. Must have. Maybe her hearing was still messed up from the blast.

His mouth lowered and brushed over her lips. "Everything, Kat. That's what you are to me." Another soft, tender kiss. "Realized that very important fact right before a bomb exploded behind us both."

Her breath caught. She wanted to believe him. But another lover had once told her the same lie. Gage had sworn she was everything to him, and then Kat had learned she was only a means to an end.

"Believe me. Trust me." His fingers trailed tenderly down her throat. "You're not a job. You're everything."

She kissed him. Not some sweet, careful kiss. A frantic, desperate one because *she* was desperate. She was tired of being afraid. Tired of running. Tired of being used.

Rick was in front of her. The guy who was *good*. The man who had been hired to keep her safe. And he had—he kept coming through for her over and over again. He kept proving to her that all men weren't monsters. That there could be so much more in the world.

If only she'd met him a few years ago...or even last year...what would her life be like?

She clung tightly to him, truly wishing that she never had to let him go. Wishing that she could always keep him with her.

Slowly, his mouth lifted from hers. His forehead pressed against her.

"I called Gage Hollow," Kat confessed.

"Gage." Rick stiffened. "Your ex?"

"Yes, and he's the man who has taken over the power void left by my father's death." She was telling Rick everything. All the secrets she had. He wanted them? She'd give them to him. *Everything.* "I believe Gage was behind my father's murder. Gage likes to work a...a psychological game, I guess you could say. He seduced me. He tried to get secrets about my father's business from me, and when I learned the truth about him...when my father *told* me the truth, Gage promised he'd destroy my dad." Her voice trembled. She hated that. She wanted to sound strong and confident. "I called Gage because I had his private line. I had a way of cutting through the BS and the red tape that surrounded him. I told him that I had no evidence against him, nothing I could use in court."

"Why did you call him?" His gaze reflected his confusion.

"Because I suspect he's the one who put the heavy price on my head. I thought if I could get him to back off, everything would be easier. I was telling him the truth—I truly don't have anything I could use against Gage. I wish I did." She shook her head. "But Gage said it wasn't him. He told me that he wasn't gunning for me."

"And you believed him?"

"No." She held his gaze. "I didn't. Not for a second. You see, I learned what it sounds like when Gage lies."

"What does it sound like?"

"It sounds like he's talking."

His lips twitched.

"Gage always lies. That's what he does. I was hoping he'd slip up during our phone call. He didn't. I was also hoping he would back the hell off but obviously, he hasn't. When I walked away from him, Gage told me that he didn't give up the things that belonged to him."

"You don't fucking belong to him."

"No. I don't." A roll of her shoulders. "It was after I made that call to Gage that my hotel room was shot to hell and back."

His eyes were so dark and stormy. "Where the hell is he now?"

"From what I can tell, he's gone dark. Vanished from public sight. I doubt we'll see him again until after the court appearance, or you, you know, after I'm dead."

"You are *not* dying."

"Everyone dies sometime."

Rick kissed her again. Hard. Deep. God, she loved his kiss. Loved the way it could make her burn with need even when she felt as if she were breaking apart.

"Die when you're ninety-eight," he muttered against her lips. "Die curled in bed with me after you've had kids, grandkids, great-grandkids. Die after you've lived a life so full of happiness that you can't even remember the bad times."

Wait...She pulled back. Gaped at him. "What are you saying?" He couldn't be talking about a life together. Not a lifetime. No, no way.

"Princess, I'm saying I want to be in this for the long haul with you. When I tell you that you're everything, I mean it." His eyes glittered. "I could feel it with you, the first time I put my eyes on you. When you walked into this office and you barely glanced at Eric, instead you focused on *me*. You told me you loved the strong, silent type, and my fucking thought—my thought at the wrong time and at the wrong place...was...*what would it be like if she could really love me?*"

Her heart stopped.

"I know you don't love me." His smile was tender, and it made her heart ache. "But, princess, I fell fast and hard for you."

"That's...no, you don't even like me. I drive you crazy."

"I fucking *love* you."

"I'm a mob boss's daughter—"

"Who has more courage and conscience than anyone I've ever met."

"I hotwire cars—"

"And you make it look so damn easy and sexy."

"I..." She didn't know what to say. Kat was also afraid to believe him. She wanted it, wanted him, so much but... "There is no happy ending for us."

He brushed back a lock of her hair. "Who the fuck says so?"

"Even if I make it to court, I have to go into Witness Protection. Threats will always be there."

"Oh, princess, I know I told you this...why can't you remember? I don't scare easily."

Her heart was racing. Fast, so fast, and she was hoping. Daring to dream, just for a moment. Maybe...could he love her? Could they have a chance? "Rick—"

A fist pounded against the door. A moment later, the door flew open.

Rick surged to his feet.

But it was just Kendrick. Kendrick, with eyes that were blazing and a tight face that reflected his worry. "Big damn problem."

"Add it to the list," Rick groused back.

"Your hit man, Ghost? He escaped police custody. He's on the loose." Kendrick's gaze dropped to Kat. "Give you two guesses where he's heading."

She didn't need two guesses. Kat didn't even need one.

She darted a glance at Rick's hard profile. He'd said he loved her. How did she feel about him?

Come on, Kat. You know how you feel.

Yes, she did.

She knew, and she knew that they could *not* be together. Because the longer Rick was with her, the more danger he faced. He might say he was okay with a lifetime of looking over his shoulder, but she didn't want that for him.

She wanted more. She wanted *better* for him.

Because, dammit, she loved her big, bad beast of a bodyguard.

***

Hours later, Kat was in a penthouse. The rest of the building was empty, courtesy of Eric Wilde. He snapped his fingers, and, apparently, things happened.

She was being protected by the FBI and by Wilde. She was supposed to be in one of the most secure locations in the city.

Right, like Kat hadn't heard that line a time or twenty.

But at least she wasn't on her own. Rick was with her. A situation that both thrilled Kat to her core—*yes, more precious time to spend with him*—and terrified her—*no, he could get hurt being near me!*

Night had fallen. Getting her to the penthouse had been like participating in a three-ring circus. So many twists and turns. She'd been afraid that bullets would start flying or cars would explode on her during the trip there. She'd been *desperate* the whole time.

God, she was so sick of the fear.

The blinds and curtains were all closed. No looking out at the city. Instead, Kat stood before the fireplace. She didn't even know why it was lit. It wasn't particularly cold in the penthouse. The only cold she felt seemed to come from within.

"Kat."

Rick's low voice. She turned and saw him standing in the doorway, watching her.

"Why don't you try and get some sleep?"

She had tried, earlier. Only every time she closed her eyes, she heard an explosion. She felt the heat of fire on her skin. "You're sure the FBI agents are all okay?"

"Yes, baby..." He advanced toward her. "For the fourth time, I promise you, they are all out of surgery. They are all okay. Before you know it, your buddy Tom will be dodging your steps again."

"Tom didn't like me."

"You sure about that? I think he was starting to warm up to you."

"Before or *after* he almost got blown to hell because he was the lucky agent who got to be in the back seat with me?"

Rick stopped in front of her. "Want some wine?"

"No, thanks."

"Dinner? There's stuff in the kitchen, and I can—"

"I don't want food. I don't want wine. I don't want any sleep." She bit her lower lip. *Don't hold back.* "I just want you."

His eyes widened. "Kat..."

"I know, I know, it's not the time. Not the place. There's an army of agents outside our door and the last thing I should be thinking about is sex with you." Her words came out in a rush. "But I am shaking apart on the inside. I'm going crazy, and *you* are the only thing that calms me down. I don't want to use you, God, that's not what I mean, I just—"

He wrapped his hands around her hips and lifted her up against him. "Baby, use me any fucking day."

"What?"

"Use me. Need me. Want me. I'm here for you. I'll take care of you. *Anything* for you." His mouth took hers. The kiss sent desire surging through every cell of her body. She leaned into him, she wound her arms around his neck and just held on.

His tongue swept into her mouth. Licked and seduced. Stroked and claimed. Her hips were arching against him, and the adrenaline that had been driving her mad suddenly found a new outlet.

Him. Her need for him.

Rick's mouth slipped from hers. He kissed a path down her neck. "Baby, in case there is any confusion, I *always* want you." He carried her to the bedroom.

She didn't know how much time they would have before another attack came or before the

Feds decided that she needed to be dragged away or—

"Stop." He lowered her until her bare toes touched the thick carpeting. "Just think about me right now." He caught the hem of her shirt. She'd changed into fresh clothes at the penthouse. Changed. Washed away the soot and the grime from the explosion. She'd stood under the thunder of the spray, and she'd thought about him.

Just think about me right now.

His hand went to the snap of her jeans. He unsnapped the jeans, slid down the zipper, and she kicked the jeans away. She stood before him in her panties and bra, and his fingers trailed over the skin of her shoulder.

"You're beautiful."

Kat smiled at him. "I think you are."

A rough laugh broke from Rick as he yanked off his shirt. "No, baby, I am far from that."

The light fell on the hard muscles of his chest and shoulders. It lit the powerful strength in his arms.

He stripped quickly, no fuss, and it was the sexiest thing she'd ever seen. *He* was sexy. And to her, he was beautiful. He reached for her once more, but Kat shook her head.

"Kat?"

For all she knew, this was their last time together. "Tell me I can do anything I want."

"Baby, with me, you can do anything you want."

She slipped to her knees in front of him.

His eyes flared. "But if you're doing what I *think* you're doing, I am not going to last long. I'm already nearly insane for you."

"There are condoms in the nightstand. Checked earlier. Someone at your organization deserves a bonus."

"It was Eric, dammit, he told me that—"

She put her mouth on him. Closed her lips over the broad, thick head of his shaft, and Rick stopped talking. A primitive growl came from him as his hands closed over her shoulders.

She took him in deeper, moving slowly and truly wanting to savor him. Her tongue swirled over him and her head bobbed, hesitant at first, but then gaining confidence. Kat loved the taste of him. Loved the way his hands tightened on her as he bit out her name. She wanted to give him as much pleasure as he'd given to her. She could do it. She felt him swelling even more in her mouth. And—

And she was on the bed. He'd picked her up and spun her around and Kat blinked up at him.

"Yeah...we stop that, or I come right away."

How was that a bad thing? She loved that plan. Thought it was fabulous. She'd love to drive him so wild that he came right then and there.

"You first, sweetheart. *You.*" His fingers trailed down her body and caressed her through the silk of her panties.

She gasped at his touch and arched up against him. The first time—okay, and the *second* time— that they'd had sex, pleasure had consumed her. She'd wondered if it would be the same way this time.

Now she knew that yes, it would always be this way, with him. Because it wasn't only sex. Not with Rick. It might just be making love.

He kissed her as he stroked her. His fingers pushed aside the crotch of her panties and his fingers thrust into her. She was already wet for him. Going down on him had turned her on so much. Giving him pleasure made her hot.

He growled against her mouth. "So sweet..."

He kissed a path down her body. Used one hand to get rid of her bra while the other still stroked her sex. Part of her admired his skill and dexterity, but it was a really small part because she was mostly just having a hard time controlling her moans. Her hips jerked against him as she tried to get closer to his touch. When he was licking and sucking her nipple, her whole body warmed.

"Now, Rick. *Now.*"

He laughed and left her long enough to grab a condom. But when he came back to the bed...

Kat climbed on top of him. She took the condom from him, and her fingers were shaking a little as she rolled the condom onto his heavy length, but she got the job done. Heck, yeah, she did. Kat straddled him and the wide head of his cock lodged at the entrance to her body. She was on her knees, her hands braced on his broad chest, and her eyes held his.

He smiled at her.

She was a goner.

I love him.

God, how do I love him? How did this happen?

"Take your time, baby," Rick told her, all tenderness and care when she had his rock-hard dick at the entrance to her body and she knew he was as close to the edge as she was. "I'll wait for you. Always."

Oh, yes. That's how. That's why.

She eased down onto him, savoring every single inch that filled her, and there were lots of inches. Her breath heaved out as she tried to adjust to him. It was a tight fit—she was *full*. But his hand slipped between their bodies and he stroked her clit, moving his fingers over the nub again and again, and she found her body relaxing.

She pushed up on her knees. Came down. Her hands were still on his chest as she balanced herself.

Up and down.

Faster.

Harder.

"Hell, yes," Rick grunted. "You are so beautiful. Hell, *yes*."

Need was all she knew. She was moving so fast now, loving the way he filled her. Loving everything about him.

"I want to see you come, Kat. I love it when the pleasure lights up your face. Let me see—"

The orgasm tore through her, and Kat clamped down on her lower lip, trying to muffle any sounds because she knew there were guards right outside of the penthouse.

"*I can feel you, squeezing my cock...so good...*"

The pleasure went on and on as her heart raced. Every muscle in her body trembled.

Rick pulled her down toward him. Kissed her.

A tear leaked from the corner of her eye. Not because she was sad but because the pleasure was that good. She'd never cried because something was *so good* before.

Rick rolled her beneath him on the bed. "My turn." Another kiss. "God..." A thrust. "I." Thrust. "Love." Thrust. "*You.*"

Her arms clamped tightly around him. She didn't want to let him go. No, no, she *couldn't* let him go. He was saying that he loved her.

And, unlike when Gage had promised that he'd loved her and sworn that he'd cherish her forever...this felt different.

This felt real.

Rick was coming inside of her. His big body was shuddering, but even in his pleasure, he was being careful with her. He'd braced himself with his arms so he wouldn't crush her. He was always so careful with her.

She heard a wild drumbeat and didn't know if it was her heart or his. Such a fast, frantic beat.

Rick's lips brushed over her cheek. He stiffened. "Princess, you're crying." He cursed and immediately pulled away from her.

No, I didn't want him to pull away.

"I hurt you. God, I am so sorry. I will—"

She caught his hand in hers. "You didn't hurt me."

"You're crying."

"Because it felt so good." She brought his hand to her mouth. Pressed a kiss to his knuckles. "You feel good."

He felt right. It was hard to describe, but Rick just fit for her. Under the worst of conditions, he could make her smile, he could make her feel safe, he could infuriate her, yes, but...

I trust him. And the minute she'd trusted him...

That had been the minute she'd loved him.

The truth was unsettling, and she let his hand go. Love was frightening. Dangerous. She'd been burned in the past, and loving Rick—it couldn't end well. There was no easy way for them to walk off into the sunset together.

When *had* she first trusted him? When she'd told him about Jimmy and the pain that her seventeen-year-old self had felt? When she'd revealed those first secrets to him?

She'd wanted him before that. When she'd kissed him at the farmhouse, intending to use the kiss as a diversion so that he wouldn't run back into gunfire, her desire for her bodyguard had surprised her. She'd never wanted someone so quickly.

She'd thought the need was tied to adrenaline. To the crazy circumstances. But as she looked at Rick, Kat realized the truth. She'd want him the same way, with the same mad, passionate intensity, under any circumstances.

"I'll be right back, baby." He pressed a kiss to her forehead. He headed into the bathroom. She heard water running, and—a phone ringing?

Kat frowned. Her gaze darted to the nightstand. Rick's phone was there. She had no clue when he'd put it on the nightstand. He hurried back into the room, still naked. He grabbed the phone and shoved it to his ear. "Tell me what's happening."

Kat pulled the covers closer. Of course, danger time again. Because...why not? At least they'd had a few moments.

"Okay. Okay. Yeah. I'll be waiting." He hung up the phone. Hesitated, then gave her a smile.

"Don't." Kat shook her head.

His smile froze.

"Don't try to pretend like that call wasn't more bad news. You don't need to pretend with me."

Rick nodded. "It's not bad news. It's just Agent Brisk. Though, depending on your point of view, maybe hearing from him *is* bad news."

"What's happening?"

"He's in the lobby. Wanted to alert us that he's coming up. Said he needed to talk to us both in person."

Her hands fisted on the covers. Another face-off with the Feds. Great. "I'm going to get dressed." Not like she wanted Brisk to find her naked in Rick's bed.

Before she could get out of the bed, Rick curled his fingers around her wrist. He leaned toward her. "We're in this together, you know. I've got your six, baby. Always."

But who had his six?

Who was going to protect Rick while he was busy trying to save her?

CHAPTER EIGHTEEN

The police station was a madhouse. Typical, though, given all the shit that had been going down in the area recently. As a rule, police stations weren't exactly Cole's favorite place. Mostly because he and cops didn't get along.

With one notable exception...

"Detective Lopez!" He called her name and gave a wave.

She looked up—a circle of uniforms surrounded her—and if looks could've killed...

"Trust me," Kendrick Shaw muttered from beside Cole, "the woman is not in the mood to play."

She dismissed the uniforms and marched toward Cole and Kendrick. Barely pausing, she snapped at them, "Conference room two. *Now.*"

"Yes, ma'am." Cole gave her a salute, but she'd already missed it because she was four steps ahead of them. Her heels clicked on the scarred floor of the PD.

She threw open the door to conference room two, and they hurried in after her. Kendrick shut the door, then propped his shoulders against it. Cole just stood there.

Layla paced. "He escaped on my watch."

"Detective Lopez," Kendrick began carefully, "you were not the only law enforcement official at that hospital and—"

She whirled. "He *knows*."

Cole frowned. "Knows what?"

Kendrick stepped away from the door. "I don't understand. You'll need to be more specific."

"More specific? *More specific?*" Her voice rose, but she gave a brisk nod, as if catching herself. "Fine. That perp knew you and I were sleeping together, Kendrick."

Oh, *damn*. Cole's eyes darted between Layla and Kendrick. They had kept that hook-up on the very down low.

"How the hell did he know that?" Kendrick's voice had gone hard and low.

"Because he's obviously been watching us. Spying on us." She pointed to Cole. "I'm willing to bet he knows every secret you've got, too."

He hoped to God not. His secrets were ugly and blood-stained.

"Why would he watch us?" Kendrick asked. "That doesn't make any sense. Why dig into our lives? Especially if he's after Kat. She should be his focus."

"Yes, well, apparently, I'm his focus, too. I'm betting *everyone* tied to Kat is on this guy's radar. He's freaking thorough, I'll give him that." She blew out a breath. "But Kat only signed on with Wilde a few days ago. I asked Eric and he confirmed that for me."

Cole nodded. Yeah, that was true.

"So how does this guy already know so much, in such a short length of time?" Her lips pursed. "He has to be able to hack into our lives somehow. You and I—crap, Kendrick, we've shared personal texts and emails in the last few days. He must've gotten access to those."

Pieces were falling into place, and things were not looking good. "I'm sure Eric told you that Wilde was hacked, too," Cole noted.

She gave a stiff nod.

"What? You're thinking Ghost was behind that hack, too?" Kendrick's brow furrowed. "What are we dealing with here? A hit man hacker?"

"I guess his skill set isn't just about death." Cole considered angles and options. "He gets close to his vics without leaving a trace. Maybe that's because he does a lot of his work through hacking. He learns secrets, he learns weaknesses, and, if his targets are protected by security systems, he has the know-how to just turn the damn things off with a few clicks of the keyboard."

Layla jutted up her chin. "I hate this Ghost prick." Her shoulders squared. "But, yeah, you're saying what I've been thinking. He's a hacker. Eric reached the same conclusion when we talked. If Ghost could get into Wilde's secure systems, then it would be super easy for him to unlock the FBI's secrets and as far as the Atlanta PD's intel..." A laugh. "Well, I'm guessing he had access to that on day one."

Kendrick crossed the room to stand beside Layla. He lifted his hand, as if he'd touch her, but hesitated. His fingers fisted and fell back to his side. "How can I help?"

Her head turned toward him. "Use your criminal contacts. If anyone sees this guy, I want to know. An APB is already out, but wherever he's hiding, we need to drag him out. I don't think we've got a lot of time. He *will* be going straight for Kat."

"Rick is with her," Cole assured Layla. "He's not going to leave her unprotected."

But her expression just became even tenser. "I don't think Ghost would hesitate to kill anyone in his way. When he was in the hospital and he found out that someone had put a bomb in the Fed's car, he was frantic to find out if Kat was dead or alive. We all know there is a lot of money at play when it comes to her, and I got the idea that Ghost didn't intend to let anyone else take credit for her death."

Jesus. "I need to get to Rick." He wanted to be there for his friend.

"Agent Brisk is already heading to meet with him now. The Feds have tried and tried to change some of the court dates for Kat, but they were stonewalled at every turn."

The *Feds* were stonewalled? Weren't they usually the ones who did the stonewalling?

"I know she's given depositions," Kendrick remarked as he rubbed his chin. "Even if Kat is taken out—"

Damn but that sounded *cold.*

"The depositions she gave will still come into play," Kendrick finished. His lips tightened. "Unless the defense attorneys in those cases are very good." A pause. A cough. "I always can cast doubt on depositions. One of my best tactics."

"The prosecutors want Kat in the courthouse. They don't want depositions. They want her." Layla was definite. "And the word I've gotten is…if she's not present, they think several of their cases will crumble. Other witnesses will back out. It will be like a line of dominoes falling down."

"She's so close," Cole said as he turned away. "We just have to keep her safe for a few more days." He needed to get to Rick. He'd feel better when he was there with his friend.

"The Feds have a new strategy, you know."

Layla's words froze Cole.

"They aren't going to try and hide Kat any longer. They're going to put her location out there. They're going to see who comes after her. Their own men were hurt, so the Feds are out for blood."

Stunned, he glanced over his shoulder and gaped at her. "They're dangling Kat like some kind of juicy steak?"

"You could say that. The Feds think they are big and bad enough to stop the threats coming at her. Only I'm not so sure they are."

"You and me both," he mumbled.

"Ghost could be anywhere by now. I did my research on him. He's rumored to be tied to over thirty kills. *Thirty*."

"The Feds might not be able to stop him," Cole threw back. "But Wilde will. I'm personally not scared of a fucking Ghost." He grabbed for the door. His partner needed him.

"Maybe you should be…" Layla's soft voice followed him out. "One other thing…"

He glared back at her. "I'm kind of in a hurry here."

"It could be unrelated, but...too much of a coincidence for me."

Spit it out, Layla!

"The admin at the hospital reported a robbery. While we were all searching for Ghost, someone made off with a ton of drugs, including some sedatives that would be strong enough to take out a bear."

Just freaking dandy. "Any other bad news you want to deliver?"

"Not yet." A pause. "But give me some more time and I'll see what I can drag up."

He yanked open the door.

***

"You look like hell," Rick said as he opened the penthouse door to let Bryan Brisk inside.

The Fed grunted. "Yeah, you try sitting at your partner's hospital bed for a few hours and we'll see how *you* look." He raked a hand over the stubble on his jaw. His stare jumped around. "Where's Kat?" He lifted his hand to reveal a white, paper bag. "Brought her a little present."

Rick frowned. "She's getting dressed." He'd dragged on jeans, a t-shirt, and boots right before the Fed had arrived.

Bryan's hold tightened on the bag. "How is she?"

How the hell do you think she is? "Strong. Kat's a survivor. She's going to be just fine." He pointed to the bag. "What in the hell kind of surprise is that?"

Bryan blinked. "Brownies. They had them at the hospital. Went to the cafeteria. Saw them and..." His voice trailed off. "You have to find something good when everything goes to shit, you know? That's what my mom taught me." He ambled into the den. "I didn't grow up with much, but I promised myself I'd have more one day. My mom...she was always trying to get me to see the good in things. In people. You look for pain, you'll find pain. You look for good...shit, and I guess you find brownies." He dropped the bag onto an end table. His shoulders hunched.

Rick had followed him in the den. Now, he tilted his head and stared at the other man.

"I don't know if we can keep her alive," Bryan said softly, sadly. "My boss...the FBI Brass...you get why they allowed you to come and stay in this penthouse with her, don't you? You get what this whole set-up is about? No more running, but hunkering down..." He looked back over his shoulder at Rick. "You have to see it. You've worked enough cases that you *know*..." A twisted smile. "This isn't about keeping her safe any longer. It's about *using* her."

Rick's teeth ground together. "Yeah, I figured out the fucking scenario." But he hadn't said a word about it to Kat. What was the point?

"Assistant Director Silas Evans's body was found a few hours ago." Bryan blew out a long, hard breath. "We're keeping it quiet right now because that's the way Brass wants it, but the head honchos are losing their shit." A shake of his head. "An Assistant Director is taken out, a car bomb is planted in a vehicle belonging to Feds...several of our agents are hospitalized, hell, yes, the FBI Brass is out for blood now. So even if they want Kat to testify, they want her *more* so—"

"So they can use her to catch the people who've hurt the Feds," Rick finished, choking back his fury.

A glum nod. "They think it was Ghost. That he killed Assistant Director Evans. And maybe he did. Hell, he *probably* did. Cops think he's linked to thirty kills, but you want the truth? They should up that number. It's more like *one hundred.*"

Holy hell.

"*That's* why the game is changing so much right now. Yeah, the Brass still wants Kat to take down the others with the evidence she has, but if we can bag Ghost, that shit will be a game changer."

"You *had* Ghost. He was in custody—"

Bryan flinched. "Don't freaking remind me. When this crap is over, I see a demotion in my future. And poor Detective Lopez, she'll probably be writing traffic tickets somewhere."

The hell she would. The guy didn't know Layla well. She wouldn't rest until she got her perp. "There's no way Ghost planted the car bomb. He was in custody when it went off. Whoever set that bomb had to be close to Wilde—close enough to detonate it."

"Could've been on a timer." Bryan swiped a hand over his forehead. "Maybe Ghost planted it before he was caught and—"

"No timer. The guy wouldn't have known exactly when Kat was in the vehicle. *If* she would ever get in the vehicle. Too many variables." No,

Rick had analyzed that set-up in his head over and over again. "The bomb had to be set by someone else. And that someone was close by, waiting for Kat to get in the car. When she got in, he detonated, only there was a few seconds of a delay. That happens with some bombs. You hit the trigger and you've got just a couple of seconds before the world turns to fire."

"You seem to know a lot about fire."

"Once, that shit was my life." *Kat's my life now*. "If she hadn't jumped out of that car, she'd be dead."

"She got out because of you. You saved her."

And I'll keep fighting to save her.

Bryan took a step back. Sadness filled his gaze. "You saved her that time, but Kat is screwed to hell and back. We *both* know it. From day one, I expected to be burying her. I never thought we'd even make it this far. So close to the finish line, but Kat is never going to cross it. One way or another, she'll die."

CHAPTER NINETEEN

"So close to the finish line, but Kat is never going to cross it. One way or another, she'll die."

Kat pasted a smile on her face even as Bryan's words echoed in her ears and pierced straight into her heart. Her spine was straight as she walked into the den. "Agent Brisk, you are always my own personal Hallmark greeting card."

He winced and whirled to face her. "Kat, I didn't realize you were close enough to hear—"

"That I'm going to die? No worries. You weren't saying anything that I haven't suspected for a long time."

Rick hurried to her side and took her hand. "It's not happening. To get to you, any bastard coming will have to go through me first."

"Is that supposed to make me feel better? It doesn't. Not even a little bit. I don't want you dying for me." She stared into his eyes. Those deep, dark eyes. "I want you living an amazing life. Being happy. Laughing and loving and...and doing everything you want to do. I was born into this nightmare. You weren't." It was tearing out her heart to think of him being hurt.

Rick lifted their joined hands to his mouth. His lips brushed over her knuckles, the same way that she'd kissed his hand back in the bedroom. He stared into her eyes and told her, "You're worth any risk. Sweetheart, I'd fight anyone or anything for you."

Her breath caught. He meant it. She could see the truth in his eyes, and Kat didn't know what to say.

"This is all really freaking romantic," Bryan snapped. "But how about we all avoid dying, hmm? I think that's the best option. And looking toward that option, guess who your new roommate is?"

Both Kat and Rick swung their heads to look at him.

His smile was grim. "How about the FBI and Wilde team up together? Well, there's no 'how about' actually. We *are* teaming up. It's a direct order from above. I'm staying here with you. Agents outside, agents inside...you *will* be safe, Kat. And when Ghost comes for you..."

He'd said *when*, not if.

"We'll take the bastard out," Bryan said with deadly certainty.

She'd been listening to Bryan and Rick for a few moments, and she had to ask, "Has he really killed one hundred people?"

"That's what we suspect, yes. Having suspicions and proof, though, those are two different things."

She eased closer to Rick. "He wasn't always like that. When we were younger, I swear, he was *kind*. I-I couldn't have been that wrong about him."

Bryan rushed toward her. "Wait, back up. You *knew* the guy? Back when you were kids?" His eyes were suddenly hard and intent on her.

"I—yes." Had that info not been given to Bryan? She was having a hard time keeping track of everything. *That happens when you find out your ex is a crazy killer.* "When I was seventeen, we dated."

"Fucking fits." He spun away. "Fits and it makes sense...should have realized it all before."

Rick still held Kat's hand. "Realized what?"

Bryan looked back. "Kat was also involved with Gage Hollow. We believe he's the man who has one of the biggest prices on her head. Apparently, Kat, you leave one hell of an impression on a guy. First Gage, now Ghost." His gaze slid to Rick. "Wonder what you'll be like in the aftermath of Kat?"

She pulled away from Rick. "I'm going to bed." She needed to get away for a few minutes. To escape.

Both my exes want me dead. Great. Wonderful. What kind of track record was that? She was basically batting a hundred percent kill rate with her exes. *You date me, then you want to kill me.* Lovely.

"Wait!" Bryan curled his hand around her shoulder. "Hey, I brought you something." He pointed to the bag. "Brownies." A faint smile lifted his lips. "Your favorites."

"I can't eat anything right now, but thanks, Bryan. That was really sweet." She turned away. "Good night."

No. Stop. Kat pulled in a deep breath. She forced herself to slowly turn so that she could look at both men. "Thank you."

Bryan frowned.

"I appreciate the FBI's help, and I appreciate the help from Wilde. More than that, I appreciate you two." Her gaze darted between them. "So thank you."

Bryan didn't speak. His frown deepened.

Rick took a step toward her. "You don't have to thank me for anything. I want to be with you."

She wanted to be with him. That night and every night to come.

"I'll be joining you in just a minute, baby," Rick promised her. "Let me talk a little more to Bryan, and I'll come back there with you."

Kat nodded and hurried away from him. The thick carpeting swallowed her footsteps as she headed down the hallway. She turned toward the second door—the bedroom she'd used earlier. Kat stepped inside. Shut the door behind her.

The light was off.

No, that wasn't right. She'd left the light *on* when she'd slipped out before. *Oh, God.* Kat whirled for the door even as she opened her mouth to scream.

But a hard hand clamped down over her lips and muffled the sound.

***

"Pick up the damn phone!" Cole snarled as he rushed through the city. He'd been trying to get Rick, but the guy wasn't answering. Did Rick get how alarming that shit was? Did he understand that he was about to give Cole a freaking heart attack?

"Cole..." Rick's voice filled the interior of the car. Bluetooth was such a fabulous invention.

"We need to talk, man, I'm on my way to you."

"Bryan Brisk is here now. An army of agents are close by. I'm good. Why don't you go get some rest for the night? I know you've been working your ass off on this case, too."

Get some rest? He'd sleep when he was in the grave. "I'm coming to you. That's what partners are for." He took a hard right turn. Was he being followed? Those headlights behind him...

Turned right, too.

His hands fisted around the steering wheel. "You know the Feds want to use your lady to draw out Ghost? Do you know that shit? The authorities *lost* him, and now the Bureau guys want to use Kat to lure him back in."

"Yeah." Rick's voice was thick. "Heard that story. Can't say I'm a fan."

Cole figured that was the understatement of the century.

He took a fast left turn.

The headlights behind him...went left. "Sonofabitch."

"Cole?"

"I got company, man. Freaking on my tail."

"Shit, I'll call in backup for you—"

Crash.

Another car erupted from the darkness and slammed right into the front of Cole's car.

***

"Cole? Cole!" Rick roared his friend's name, but there was no response. Then the line died. He tried calling Cole back, but the phone just rang and rang.

"Problem?" Bryan asked as he edged closer.

Rick turned his back on the agent and hunched his shoulders. "Hell, yes, there is." He called Eric. His buddy answered on the second ring. "Trace Cole's location." All Wilde vehicles had trackers installed on them. "He was being tailed, and I lost contact with him. Ghost could be after him. We need to make sure Cole is okay."

"On it," Eric fired back immediately. "You stay with Kat. I've got him."

Rick shoved the phone into his pocket. He needed to go see Kat. Right the hell then. She was just down the hallway, but he was suddenly terrified for her. "Be right back," he told Bryan without glancing over at the other man. "I need—"

Something sharp jabbed into the side of Rick's neck. His hand flew up and he grabbed—a syringe?

Yes...a syringe. He stared at it, blinkingly slowly. An empty syringe.

He turned. Staggered.

"What you need..." Bryan told him, but the agent's voice was distorted, seeming to come from very far away. "Is to get the fuck out of my way."

Rick's knees gave way. He slammed into the carpet.

"Because I have a job to do," Bryan added as he walked over Rick. "And a very large payment to collect."

***

"I'm going to need you to calm down," he whispered into her ear. Darkness surrounded them, but she knew exactly who held her. *Ghost.* "I'm not here to hurt you. I get that you probably don't buy that line, but it's true."

No, she didn't buy the line. She didn't believe *anything* he had to say.

"If I move my hand and you scream, we're both going to be screwed, and I don't mean that in a good way."

She kicked back with her foot, aiming for his shins.

He grunted, but didn't let her go. "I got in too easily, Kat. I figured the Feds would be setting a trap to lure me to you, but it was too easy. *No one was even on this floor.* Do you hear me? There were no agents out there. No one waiting beyond the penthouse's door. They've been cleared out."

He was lying. She knew the agents were out there. They'd been with her and Rick the whole time.

"We need to leave, you and me. I need you to come with me and to stay dead quiet."

If she went with him, she was dead. He'd probably take her to Gage. Or he'd try to torture her for the location of that missing twenty million dollars. That missing money was just making everything *worse.*

"We can slip out. Just you and me. I want your cooperation, but if you don't give it to me..." A sigh from him. "I'll have to knock you out and carry you out of here."

Oh, wow. Wasn't he the gentleman?

"Nod if you'll be good."

Be good?

Not even on her best day. Or worst. But Kat nodded.

He hesitated. "Don't be trying to trick me, Kat, don't be—"

Her hand flew up. She grabbed his hand, managed to catch his pinky finger, and she snatched it back, breaking it instantly.

"Fuck!" His voice was still low. Still only carrying to her—

"Help!" While her own voice was a roar. Not some scream, but a roar. With his hand gone from her mouth, she roared with all her might, *"Help me!"* She turned around and drove her fist toward his stomach. But he was already moving, rushing back from her blow and fading into the darkness of the room, just like the damn ghost that he was.

She grabbed for the door. Her fingers flew over the knob, and she wrenched the door open. Kat leapt into the hallway.

Bryan grabbed her shoulders. His eyes were huge. "Kat! What is it?"

"Jimmy...Ghost—he's in my room!" Where was Rick? "We need to—"

"Get the bastard, that's what we need to do." He yanked out his gun and surged into her room. He flipped on the lights.

Kat rushed in behind him.

The bedroom was empty. The tousled covers were still on the bed.

Her breath panted out. "Where is he?"

***

"If I wanted you dead, I could shoot you right now."

Cole looked at the gun pointed directly at his chest...then at the man holding the gun. "I don't think we've been introduced." He cocked his head to the right as he leaned back against the side of his car. "And I really like to know the names of people who want to shoot me."

"Such a cocky asshole."

"I try."

"Why don't you try *thinking* harder? Because you know me. Our paths have crossed before."

Cole squinted, trying to see the fellow better in the darkness.

"Back when you used to offer out your...skill set...to the highest bidder? Before you got a conscience and started working for Wilde. You knew me back then."

What Cole *knew* was that he was in trouble. His gaze darted around. Empty road? Check. Goons surrounding him? Check. And the past coming back to bite him in the ass? Triple check.

"Though we never met face-to-face back in those days. Instead, you talked to one of my assistants."

"Look, we can dick around here all night or you can get to the freaking point. I kinda have places that I need to be," Cole gritted from between clenched teeth.

"I know exactly where you need to be...with Kathleen O'Shaughnessy."

Yep, he'd figured this conversation would steer in that direction.

"Kat's the reason we're here tonight." The guy backed up a little bit, and the street lamp fell on his face.

Aw, hell. "You're Gage Hollow." He'd seen photos of the guy. A very *higher-up* fellow in the criminal world. AKA a mob boss. A man who'd been the enemy of Kat's father. The guy who was suspected of ordering the hit on her dear old dad.

"Guilty." Gage grinned.

"Of a lot of things," Cole snapped, right before he made his move. Gage's mistake had been stepping back and moving his gun away from Cole's body. Cole leapt up and snatched the gun right out of the SOB's hand. He flipped it around and aimed it at Gage's chest. *See how you like it, shitwad.*

Gage's thugs immediately yanked out their own weapons and aimed them at Cole.

"I can shoot before they can," Cole promised. "So tell the attack dogs to stand the hell down."

"Stand down," Gage ordered, but his voice wasn't tense or worried. It was too calm. A bad sign.

"You wannabe tough guys..." Cole shook his head as he took Gage's measure. "I bet you don't usually get your hands dirty. You hire out work to others, don't you? That's why it was so easy for me to take your weapon—"

"I do often hire out work to resourceful fellows like you, Cole." Still not worried. Still far too calm.

"I'm not working for you."

"Are you sure? You haven't even heard my job offer yet. Why not listen? My offer might be too good for you to pass up."

"I have a job, thanks, and the last thing I'd ever do is take freaking blood money from someone like you." Once, yes, dammit, he had. But he was atoning. Getting his life and shit straight. He would never go down that dark path again. "What did you think? You could toss money at me and I'd hurt Kat? Not going to happen. I'm here to keep her safe. *That's* my job."

Gage glanced down at the gun pointed at his chest. "Leave us," he said, voice finally tense.

His men backed away. Then climbed into the waiting cars. Shut the doors.

Okay. Cole hadn't expected that order. His eyes narrowed. "What is it you want?"

"I want you to keep doing your job," Gage said, voice low and only carrying to Cole's ears. "*I want you to protect Kat.* Because I'm not the man who put a price on her head. I'm not her enemy."

***

"He was right here," Kat said as her gaze jumped around the bedroom. "I swear it."

Bryan stood in front of her with his gun still out. "I believe you."

"Maybe he's in the bathroom. Or hiding in the closet, or—"

"Come out, come out, wherever you are!" Bryan shouted.

She flinched. "I need to get Rick." Kat whirled. Why hadn't Rick come in there with her already? Where—

"No, sorry. He's busy." Bryan grabbed her and yanked Kat against his chest.

Kat twisted in his hold. "Bryan! Shit, let go!"

"Kat...*shut the fuck up.*" He jabbed his gun into her side. "Or I will have to hurt you."

Shock froze her.

"*You hear that, Ghost?*" Bryan raised his voice even more. "If you don't come out, right now, I'll have to hurt her. I'll start with a few shots that won't damage anything too vital. You know, the shots that just make her scream."

"You are crazy!" Kat heaved in his arms. "Stop it! Let me *go!*"

"*Kat.*"

She blinked.

Ghost had just appeared—in one blink, he was standing in the middle of the bedroom.

"Kat, he means what he's saying," Ghost told her as he rocked onto the balls of his feet. "I think he killed that kid at the motel. He'll hurt you, too. So stay calm."

The *hit man* was telling her to stay calm?

Bryan laughed. "I *knew* you weren't gunning for her. I mean, I read your file. You never miss targets."

"No, I don't miss." Ghost stared straight at Bryan. She couldn't even think of him as Jimmy anymore. Jimmy had been the smiling, charming boy she knew at seventeen. Ghost was the man with the dead eyes and the cold voice.

"When she kept living after being around you at the farmhouse, I knew the truth. You weren't there to kill her. You were there to protect her."

Bryan's gun still jabbed into her side. "Where's Rick?" Kat whispered.

Bryan laughed again. "Oh, don't worry about the big guy. He's not going to be rushing to interrupt us. He won't be doing a damn thing."

Silence. That was all Kat could hear. Thick, enveloping silence. She was pretty sure that Bryan's mouth was still moving, but she couldn't hear anything else he said.

He won't be doing a damn thing.

Bryan had hurt Rick. He might have killed him.

Kat felt something break inside of her. Her father had always told her, he'd warned her...one day, there would be something that made her cross the line. He'd told Kat that she'd see it was easier than she thought to take a life.

Her soul seemed to break away in that moment. To just shatter.

Rick?

Her lips parted. Her throat burned. Kat was pretty sure she was screaming, but she couldn't even hear that sound. She slammed her elbow back into Bryan. Threw up her fist in the same instant and rammed it into his nose. Then she whirled and drove her fingers right at his eyes. They both slipped and tumbled onto the floor. The gun flew out of his hand. She scrambled for it, her fingers reaching out, so close—

Something jabbed into her neck. Sharp. Deep. An icy cold seemed to immediately shoot through her body. "What...?"

She couldn't get the gun because she couldn't feel her fingers.

She couldn't feel anything but the cold.

Bryan hauled her against him, dragging her onto his lap. She saw him put the gun against her forehead, but she couldn't feel the muzzle. She could barely keep her head up, and her eyes wanted to sag shut. He glared across the bedroom. "Make one move toward me, Ghost, and I'll put a bullet in her head."

"No, the fuck you won't!" Ghost snarled back. "Because you think she knows where the money is. You won't do a damn thing to her until you find out—"

She couldn't hear what he said next. Mostly because Kat couldn't hear a damn thing. She passed out.

CHAPTER TWENTY

He felt like he'd been hit with a sledge hammer. Rick slowly cracked open one eye and found himself staring at the freaking floor. His hands were twisted behind him, and he could feel metal biting into his wrists.

Cuffed. I'm cuffed and on the floor.

He didn't move, not wanting to alert—

"You're going to die, you know that, Ghost?"

Rick's back teeth clenched.

"There is no way you walk out of this penthouse," Bryan continued. He was close—just a few feet away, so Rick knew he had to play this scene very carefully. "You tell me where the money is...and *maybe* I won't hurt you too badly before I send you to hell."

Ghost laughed. Then there was the sound of a fist hitting flesh. A groan.

"I'll beat the shit out of you and never break a sweat," Bryan promised with a savage kind of glee. "I can do this all night. I mean, you deserve it, don't you? After all those people you *killed*..."

Rick moved his head the slightest bit. A fast movement would alert Bryan. He didn't want to tip off the sonofabitch. He could see Bryan's back. The man had Ghost secured in a chair. Looked like Ghost was cuffed, too, with his hands behind his back. His face was bloody. One eye swollen shut. Blood covered his mouth and dripped onto his shirt.

How long had Bryan been working him over? *How long was I out?*

Rick tried to wiggle his fingers. Everything still felt numb, his body too heavy. What had Bryan dosed him with?

Cole...Cole was supposed to be coming over. Shit, his friend would either bust in to save the day...or Cole would walk in to his own execution.

Where is Kat? Rick didn't hear her. His head angled a little as he tried to see her. When he thought of Kat, terror clawed at his insides. He had to keep the fear at bay. He couldn't let it take over. But if Bryan had done anything to her. If he'd *hurt* her...

Rick knew he would lose his freaking mind. His head shifted more to the left. His mouth was bone dry, from the drugs that Bryan had given him and from the fear—the stark terror—that something had happened to Kat.

Then he saw her.

Kat was slumped in a chair near Ghost. Her arms were pulled behind her back, and her thick hair fell over her face. Her neck tipped forward like a broken flower stem, and he wanted to *destroy*. His teeth clamped together as he willed his body to obey him and fucking *move*...

Kat moaned. Her breath shuddered out. "S-stop..."

Bryan turned toward her. "Figured you'd be coming around soon. Didn't give you as much as I gave the bodyguard." He grabbed her by the hair and yanked her head back.

You are a dead man. Rick knew he'd be killing the agent. Just a matter of time.

"You're back with us, but your jackass lover over there..."

Rick knew the guy was going to look his way, so he shut his eyes.

"Gave that sonofabitch enough to knock out a bear. Fitting, don't you think?"

I think I'm going to make you sorry you were ever born.

"If it makes things easier for you, Kat, when I kill him, he won't feel a thing. I'll slit his throat, and he'll just never wake up. See, I can be kind."

You can be a sonofabitch.

Kat whimpered. "You're...hurting me..."

I will destroy you. Rick's eyes flew open.

Bryan was busy fisting his hand in Kat's hair and wrenching her head back.

"I don't want to hurt you, Kat. I wanted your death to be as painless as Rick's, but you have something I want, and if you don't tell me where the money is, I will make you scream and scream until you beg for death."

You'll be the one screaming. Rick's fingers flexed. Feeling was coming back into his hands— pinpricks. In his hands and his feet. He sucked in a breath. He needed Kat to hold on for a few more moments. Rick tried to pull his legs up, tried to push down with his knees. Fuck, he couldn't move them yet....

Hold on, Kat. Just a little longer.

"No one will come to save you, Kat. The agents outside? I sent them away. Told them that another team was taking over. Of course, there is no other team. I just wanted you all to myself. They didn't question things. I mean, most of them wanted to leave. The Feds don't particularly love watching a mobster's daughter, anyway. As for the Wilde agents, I informed them that their services were no longer needed. FBI orders beat private cop wannabes any day of the week."

You don't beat anything, dickhead.

"You didn't even look in the brownie bag I brought you. That was rude. Sure, the brownies were laced with drugs, but you didn't know that."

"I don't have the...the money." Kat's voice was groggy. "T-told you...from the beginning...*don't have it...*"

"Yes, but you're a liar, Kat. Just like your father. Twenty million doesn't simply vanish. You must have it. All stashed away for a rainy day, hmm? Guess what? It's raining outside. *Storming.* I want the money. I need it."

"Dirty Fed..." Ghost spat blood on the floor. "You are so wrong."

Bryan let go of Kat.

"*I* have the money," Ghost snarled at him. Then he laughed. "Had it...all along."

The hit man had to be lying, of course, but at least his words had gotten Bryan to let go of Kat.

"Her dad *hired* me," Ghost told Bryan, sounding almost gleeful. "Twenty million...all mine, if I did just one job for him." His head turned, and he stared at Kat. "Know what that job is?"

A tear leaked down her cheek. "He wanted me dead. He...he knew I'd go to the authorities eventually. He w-warned me once...if I betrayed him again..." Another tear. "He paid you to kill me?"

"No, Kat," Ghost's voice was thick. "He paid me to protect you."

Bryan burst into laughter. "You're shitting me!"

"No, I'm not, dammit! He sent instructions to me, had the whole thing set up...in the event of his death, my job was to make sure no one hurt Kat. So I have the money and—"

Bryan bent and jerked out a long, thick rope from a black bag. The Fed didn't even glance Rick's way. *So sure of yourself, are you, asshole?* Bryan turned to Kat, smiled at her—

No, don't!

Then he wrapped the rope around her neck. "This shit just got so much easier." More laughter from Bryan. "Your job is to keep her safe, Ghost? Fine. Tell me where the money is. Tell me where you hid it, and I won't kill her."

He tightened the rope around her neck. Kat gasped.

"*I don't have it on me, dumbass! It's in a bank in the Cayman Islands!*"

"Either I get the money or she's dying right now." He tightened the rope. "So much for protecting her—"

Rick roared as he leapt to his feet. He staggered because the drugs were still coursing through his veins. But no one—*no fucking one*—was gonna put a rope around Kat's neck and threaten to kill her.

Bryan gaped at him. "You...you should be out cold—"

Rick surged toward the bastard. His arms were still cuffed behind his back, but so what? He didn't need his hands. He rammed his head into Bryan's face. *Slam.* Bryan staggered back at the impact, moving away from Kat. He didn't go down, though.

He would.

Rick angled his body and rammed his shoulder into Bryan. *That's right, you asswipe. Guess who was all-state back in his football days?* He drove into Bryan again, hitting him even harder, ready to rip him apart. Bryan was trapped between the wall and Rick. Hunching his body down, Rick went in for another hit—

Bryan pounded his fisted hands into Rick's back. A hard blow right on the spine.

Rick snarled and hit harder. He slammed Bryan with his head and his shoulders and he kicked the bastard, over and over and—

"Rick!" Kat's scream. He realized that she'd been screaming his name, over and over, but a red haze and the frantic beat of his own heart had consumed him.

"Rick!" Her voice, so desperate.

Kat, his Kat. Rick released a shuddering breath.

"Yeah, big guy, he's not fighting back now," Ghost called out. "This is the time to *uncuff* us!"

Rick stumbled back. His whole body was swaying, but Ghost was right. Bryan wasn't fighting back. And when Rick stopped pounding him, the FBI agent fell to the floor and collapsed.

No threat. For the moment. Rick whirled. *"Kat!"*

She was twisting and jerking in her chair.

He lunged for her. His legs gave way, and he wound up falling before her. Rick rose onto his knees and Kat surged toward him, bringing her chair tipping forward as her mouth slammed onto his. They were both still cuffed, but the rope had fallen off her. She had tears on her cheeks. He had Bryan's blood on him.

So the fuck what?

She kissed him.

He feasted on her. Wild, hard, desperate. His Kat. *No one hurts you. I will kill anyone who tries.* She was his, he was hers, and he'd fight anyone who attempted to take her from him.

Then Kat's arms were around his neck. Her body pressed hard to his. "I thought you were dead," she whispered against his lips. "When I first saw you on the floor, you weren't moving at all, and I thought you were dead. Everything stopped for me. *Everything.* Until I saw your chest rising and falling."

He blinked at her. "You got out of the cuffs."

She lifted a hand. The cuffs dangled from her fingers. "Was working on it the whole time. You think I was going to let him slit your throat?"

Still on his knees before her, still with his hands cuffed and with an unconscious FBI dick against the wall, Rick told her, "I love you so much."

She kissed him again. Her hand slid behind his back. Her fingers danced over his wrist. Her body pressed even tighter to his and then Rick's cuffs gave way. He felt the release of pressure even as he heard a soft snick of sound. He whipped his hands up and around and held her as tightly as he could.

"*Cough, cough,*" Ghost snapped, saying the words and not actually coughing. "Could you two get your hands off each other and *uncuff me*? I'm not like Kat. The guy frisked me and took all my weapons and picks before he left me in this chair, so I could use some *help!*"

Rick turned his head and glared at the hit man. "I'm not uncuffing you. You're wanted for a shit-ton of murders, and the last thing I'm going to do is give you the chance to run again." He pushed up on his feet. Almost slammed down face-first, but Kat rose with him. They both wobbled, but straightened.

"Oh, *come on!* I wasn't lying to that jackwad FBI agent! I'm here to keep Kat safe."

Rick's hold on Kat tightened. "Kind of got that covered..." Each word was stronger as more of the drugs wore out of his system. "So fuck you." He looked down at her. "Baby...you okay?"

"I love you."

His heart pounded faster. "God, I love you, too." He bent to kiss—

"I am *choking* on the frigging sweetness here!" Ghost shouted. "Look, we need to send a message. One big, bad, *bloody* message to anyone else who wants to come after Kat. You can't let that FBI agent live. We need to carve his ass up and hang him from a window."

Kat shuddered.

"Ignore him. He's a psychopath." Rick kept one arm around her as he lifted his head and glared at Ghost. "Not happening. Bryan's going to be arrested and—"

"And he'll get out. He's a Fed! That means he has powerful friends." Ghost heaved in his chair. "Even if he doesn't get out, there will be others in line. We have to send a message. We have to make an example of him. A *bloody* example."

Rick shook his head. "That's not who I am."

Ghost stopped heaving. His eyes glittered. "What-the-hell-ever. If you can't do the job, uncuff me and I'll get the shit done."

Rick didn't move toward him. "I'm not letting a murderer go free." He gently pushed Kat forward. He wanted her out of there. He needed to call Eric and get people he could trust in that penthouse. His gaze slid toward Bryan's slumped form.

Rick stiffened.

He was sure that he'd just seen Bryan's eyelids flicker.

Playing possum? Bastard, I just used that same trick.

"You don't have the balls to do what needs doing!" Ghost was raging. "You're too scared that if you let go of that freaking beast you keep chained inside and Kat sees the real you—you will lose her. Because she'll realize you're just as much of a bloodthirsty, violent bastard as the rest of—"

Bryan lunged up. He'd grabbed a backup gun from his ankle holster. Like Rick hadn't seen that move coming from a mile away.

You should have stayed down.

Rick pushed Kat out of the way even as he grabbed Bryan's wrist—and he twisted. He twisted hard and shoved the weapon back at the FBI agent. *Bam*. The bullet tore through Bryan's throat.

Bryan's eyes bulged.

"Your first mistake...was coming after her," Rick rasped.

A gurgle came from Bryan.

Rick yanked the gun down and aimed it at Bryan's heart.

"The second..." Rick moved his mouth near the bastard's ear. "Was not killing me when you had the chance." *Bam*.

He backed away. Once more, Bryan slumped onto the floor. But this time, blood was pouring from the wound in his neck and soaking the front of his chest. Bryan wouldn't be attacking again.

Rick's head turned toward a gaping Ghost. "Any other fucking comments? Or did shit just get done?"

Ghost shook his head. "I think I'm good. Uh, don't worry about uncuffing me. I'll...just...wait here. You know, for the cops. There's a really pretty detective who I *think* won't blast a bullet into my throat. I'll wait for her."

Rick grunted. He dropped the gun. His hands clenched and released. And he made himself look at Kat.

She stared at him with wide and terrified eyes. *Jesus. Baby, no.*

"I love you," he told her. The truth. The stark, consuming truth.

Her lips quivered.

The front door shattered. The wood flew inward and thudded into the wall. Rick surged forward, ready to charge at the new threat.

"Rick!" Cole bellowed. "The freaking agents aren't outside! Where the hell are you? What is—" He stopped. His gun was drawn as he stood there, gaping.

"FBI agent...was bad guy." Rick swallowed. The adrenaline had helped him to stay upright, and while he was feeling better, his body still had a wee bit of a tendency to weave. "Took care of him."

Cole blinked. "Yeah, I can see that." His weapon turned to Ghost. "What about him?"

Sirens wailed in the distance. Rick realized that Cole had brought backup with him.

"Would you believe..." Ghost gave a weak smile. "That I'm *not* as bad as they say?"

"Not for a minute." Rick nodded toward him. "Keep your gun on him. Guy has a...tendency to vanish."

Cole would make sure Ghost didn't get away. Right then, Rick had to focus on Kat.

She wouldn't look him in the eyes. Oh, God, that *shattered* him. "Baby, I'm sorry. He was going to keep coming after you." And, Rick knew, dammit, that Ghost had been right. A message needed to be sent.

Rick had sent one.

You fuck with my woman, I will destroy you.

"I'm not like your father," he whispered.

Her hands twisted in front of her.

"I don't want you hurt. Not ever. All I want to do is keep you safe. I just want to make you happy." He wanted to touch her. Wanted to curl his hand under her chin and tip her head back.

But he didn't touch her.

This was Kat's life. Kat's choice.

"You're what I want. I will do *anything* for you. Know that. I'd lie, cheat. I'd kill—"

"That's not you." A fast shake of her head. "You wouldn't even let me steal a phone, remember? You—"

"All bets are off when it comes to your safety."

Her gaze lifted. Held his.

Only he couldn't read the expression in her gorgeous eyes.

"I would do anything for you." She had to understand that. For her, there was no law he wouldn't break. No line he wouldn't cross.

Her lower lip trembled. "I don't want you losing your soul for me."

"Baby, you *are* my soul."

She glanced over at Bryan's body. Shuddered.

She's going to turn away from me. I've shown her I'm just as violent and brutal as the others. She's going to—

"I was going to kill him, Rick. I was going to kill him the moment he said he would slit your throat." Her chin lifted. "What does that say about me?"

"Kat—" He could feel Cole and Ghost watching him. He didn't care. This moment with her was too important. They didn't have long, though, before the cops would be coming. Those sirens were so loud now.

"Can you love all of me?" Kat asked him. "The good parts and the bad?"

"You are good, baby. You always have been. Even good people can be pushed too far."

She licked her lower lip. "You *are* good, Rick. I knew that from the beginning. Good, with a little bad thrown in...and I kind of think that makes you perfect for me."

She still wanted him?

"When I said I loved you...I meant it." Her gaze stared straight into his. "Every part of you. And I'm not scared of anything that you throw at me."

He pulled her into his arms. His mouth locked on hers.

He was still kissing her when the cops stormed in.

CHAPTER TWENTY-ONE

A million reporters seemed to have swarmed outside of the courthouse. Kat could hear their shouted questions even from the interior of the car.

"You ready?" Rick asked her.

They were in a limo. Some bullet-proof ride that had come courtesy of Wilde. Rick was at her side. His fingers curled with hers.

He'd been at her side the whole time.

After she walked into that courthouse, what would happen?

They hadn't talked about *after,* not yet. She'd been too busy living in the moment.

Now she glanced at their linked fingers. She'd be going into Witness Protection soon, and there wasn't a place for Rick there. *That* was why she hadn't talked to him about the *after.* She didn't want to ask him to give up his life.

She loved him too much for that.

"You made me happy," she told him. His hand was so big that it swallowed hers. "You made me feel...so much." More than she'd ever expected. She looked into his eyes. "Thank you."

"Ah, princess, why does it sound like you're telling me good-bye?"

"Because you were only supposed to walk me to the courthouse." *Do not cry. Do not.* "You weren't supposed to change my life, but you did."

"You changed mine."

She sucked in a breath. "I'm not going to forget you."

"It's kinda impossible to forget a woman like you."

Her gaze turned toward the window once more. To the crowd that waited.

"Ask me to come with you."

Her hand jerked in his. "I-I thought you had to walk me to the courthouse." They weren't there yet. She still had a little time with him.

"That's not what I mean." A pause. Then, voice low and tender, he repeated, "Ask me to come with you."

Her lower lip was trembling. She bit it, trying to stop that tremble. Kat shook her head and glanced back at him.

His brows lowered. "You love me."

"I do." Her words came out so softly. "That's why I'm not asking. I want to be selfish. I want to keep you with me forever. But, always looking over your shoulder, having to give up your life and pretend to be someone else...that's not what I can ask the man I love to do." She *wouldn't* ask. Not that. "So I'm going to ask you to do this instead. Live a life that makes you happy. Don't look back. *Don't.* Go forward. Laugh and love and have a family and get *every* moment of joy that you deserve." She pressed a soft kiss to his lips. "Because you're a wonderful man, Rick Williams.

The best man I ever met, and I need to know—I *have* to know—that you're safe and happy."

The privacy screen lowered. The driver announced, "It's time to go." The driver—another agent. She was surrounded by them.

She pulled away from Rick and reached for the door.

Rick tugged her right back into his arms. His mouth crashed onto hers, and he kissed her with a feverish intensity. A desperation. As if he never wanted to let her go.

And I don't want to let you go. She kissed him back, took that moment to have him and to memorize every detail of his mouth on hers. There would never be anyone else like him.

Her hands curled around his shoulders, and Kat held on tight. She wished they were other people. Wished they were far away. A different place, a different life.

His mouth lifted from hers. "I'm taking you inside. I'll stay with you at the courthouse, every day, until it's done."

She could still taste him.

"And I will love you, every day, for the rest of my life," Rick promised her.

He slid out of the limo first, then turned back for her. His hand extended toward her.

Kat took his offered hand. The reporters shouted.

Rick led her into the courthouse.

***

"I don't really need a lawyer." James Smith smiled at Kendrick Shaw. "But I wanted you here because the detective just refuses to update me on Kat, and I have it on good authority that *you* know what's going on with her."

Kendrick sat beside him at the small, wooden table in the police department's interrogation area. James hadn't been taken through the normal police booking procedure. Mostly because he didn't think the PD knew what to do with him *and* because they were too afraid that he'd slip away. So they'd kind of left him in limbo. A very boring place to be. Not legal, either, but, who was he to argue when the situation had suited his needs?

But, while he had a lawyer there..."I'm pretty sure they've broken lots of laws by just holding me for so long." James nodded as he considered Kendrick. "I bet a guy like you could have a field day with all of that. But, hey, if they'll just let me walk out of these doors in the next twenty minutes, I'll forgive and forget. I can be the bigger person."

Kendrick cocked his head. "Are you trying for an insanity defense?"

"Is Kat at the courthouse? Is she good to go?"

"You *aren't* going to be released anytime soon. The Feds are coming for you. *That's* why you've been kept here. You're wanted in connection with over—"

James held up his hand. His cuffed hand. Seriously, what a joke. Why did they keep cuffing him? He simply kept getting loose. "Let's not name numbers. It seems braggy."

"Braggy." Kendrick's stare could have melted a lesser man. "Murder isn't a joke, and I don't think I am the right defense attorney for you." He rose. "We're done—"

"Is Kat in the courthouse? Is she sealing the deal, so to speak?"

Kendrick flattened his hands on the table. "Kat is at the courthouse. She'll be testifying on a number of different cases, as you well know. She has quite a force of guards, and since the last attack on her—"

"Oh, there won't be more attacks. The message was sent. Loud and clear. Rick Williams is a bloodier bastard than I expected." He had to admire that. And to think, he'd almost shot the guy back at the farmhouse. A little friendly fire, so to speak. He hadn't intended to kill Rick, only to make sure the fellow stayed on his toes.

Kendrick's jaw clenched.

"I'm sure your buddy Cole informed you of his little chit-chat with Gage Hollow." James smiled. "Gage isn't interested in Kat dying. Truth be told, he likes Kat. She's *likeable*. Has that trait about her, know what I mean? She kinda gets under your skin when you least expect it. First, she drives you crazy, then you find yourself liking the crazy."

"We're done."

James sighed. "Gage was never trying to get Kat killed. He wanted her safe, too. She's not testifying against him. He's not linked to any of the crimes that she's talking about in court. Why would he need her to die?" He waved toward the one-way mirror on the wall. "Is the detective watching in there? Or is she supposed to be staying away since I'm conferring with my lawyer?"

"I'm *not* going to be your lawyer."

James sighed a second time. All long and dramatic. "Then that makes it so much harder for me to spill my secrets to you. And here I thought we were friends."

The door opened. Detective Layla Lopez marched inside. Cole Vincent was right behind her.

"The band's all here!" James laughed. "Well, with the exception of Kat and Rick. But I get that they are occupied."

Layla crossed her arms over her chest.

Cole glared.

"You guys are *not* a fun crew." His gaze darted to the clock. "Okay, time is running out, so I'll try to answer some questions because I am a great guy like that. One, I never wanted Kat hurt. As you all know, I was hired to protect her."

"*Where's the twenty million?*" Layla demanded.

"In the Cayman Islands, waiting for me. Next question." He twisted his hands in the cuffs. "Hurry. Time is running out."

Cole stepped forward. "Why doesn't Gage Hollow want Kat hurt?"

"Because I suspect he fell for her. You know, when he was trying to use Kat against her dad. Like I was telling Kendrick, Kat works her way under your skin." A shrug. "Or maybe she didn't get under Gage's skin. Maybe he doesn't want her dead because she saved his ass once. That explanation might be more believable since most folks know Gage Hollow doesn't actually have a heart."

"How'd she save his ass?" Layla stared at him, her whole body tense.

"Well, when Kat's dad was still alive, she went to the cops...you know about that? Anyone? No? Huh. She did, she went to them and told them her father was planning a hit on someone. She wanted that hit stopped. But the cops she went to see..." He winced. "They were not like you, Detective Lopez. Not good, up-standing citizens. They were on the take. They turned Kat right back over to her father and made her evidence disappear." He leaned forward and lowered his voice, as if imparting a secret. "The man who was supposed to be the victim of that hit? It was Gage Hollow. Even though he'd broken Kat's heart, betrayed her...she still was ready to save him. Word about the hit leaked from the PD, and Gage was able to take steps to protect himself."

Layla nodded. "And he felt grateful to Kat..."

"So *he* won't be gunning for her. When she called him a few days ago, Kat was under the impression that Gage was the one leading the pack to kill her. Wrong. He was busy eliminating threats to her. Paying his debt, if you will. The real threat to Kat was the FBI. Greedy-ass Agent Brisk wanted her money. By the way, Agent Brisk is the one who killed the Assistant Director. You *did* figure that out already, didn't you? No? Well, the AD found out about Brisk's side jobs for the mob—oh, yeah, the dick had been on the take for years—and Brisk had to eliminate the AD."

Layla's eyes narrowed.

"I just helped you solve a case." James exhaled. "You're welcome."

Cole laughed, but it was an angry sound. "You are a twisted sonofabitch."

True. "Takes one to know one."

Cole raked him with a hard stare. "You were involved with Kat once."

Ah yes, the good old days of his youth. "A life-altering involvement, I assure you."

"Why protect her if she's the reason you—"

Suddenly serious, he snapped out, "Kat put her body between me and a bullet when she was just seventeen years old." His words were hard and flat and time was up. "You don't forget shit like that. Maybe Gage and I aren't so different. We both pay our debts."

"Why would Kat's father turn to you?" It was Kendrick's first question since Layla and Cole had entered the room. He'd been watching in silence.

"Because he knew I would do the job."

"He's dead, though. Why don't you just walk away?"

"Because that twenty million is only released in my account when Kat walks into the courthouse." He smiled. "Kendrick Shaw recently let me know that Kat has made that final walk. So I am all clear now. Thanks so much for your help." He stood up.

"Where the hell do you think you're going?" Cole barked. "I have more questions! I want to know who killed Kat's father—who put out that hit on him—"

"Ah, you think I know that? Sorry to break it to you, but I'm not the all-knowing Oz."

"That shooter went in that restaurant and *only* fired at Kat's father. He could've killed her, too, but he didn't." Layla's eyes glinted. "Does that mean it was Gage Hollow? *Paying* back his debts? Her father tried to kill him, so Gage took out the old man? And he let Kat live because he was still paying his debt to her?"

"That's an interesting theory. You should run with that. See where it takes you." It was a brilliant theory, but he wasn't about to confirm or deny it. He wanted to keep living, after all. Gage *looked* pretty clean on paper. The guy was good at covering his tracks, but he never forgot or forgave those who targeted him. Never. James shot another glance at the clock. "And that ends our fun question and answer session."

"We aren't done," Layla fired at him. "We're only getting started. Until the FBI takes you out of—"

The door opened. A man and a woman stood there, both in boring, black suits, and flashing badges.

"We're here to take him," the lady announced.

James dropped his cuffs on the table. He flexed his now free hands. "Great. Thought you'd never arrive."

Layla grabbed for one of the badges. "You're not FBI."

"No, we're not," the man agreed. "We work for an entirely different branch of the government." A nod toward James. "So does he."

"Well, I did," James allowed, keeping his voice modest. "But I have recently come into a bit of retirement money, so I'll be leaving my job with Uncle Sam. It's been real."

"What the fuck?" Cole burst out. "You're a killer. You don't walk away! You don't get to—"

"My exploits have been way exaggerated." Some had been exaggerated. Not all, though. "Sometimes, it's hard to tell who the bad guys are and who the good guys are. I'm sure you understand."

Layla was reading the paperwork she'd just been given by the female agent. "This is bullshit. *Bullshit*. I'm supposed to believe you were working undercover? That you are a government—"

"Shh..." James put one finger to his lips. "The door is open. And this intel isn't for everyone."

She looked up. Glared.

His grin stretched even more. "Time's up. Like I said, it's been real." He motioned to the two agents in suits. "Let's get the hell out of here."

***

A new home. A new city. A new state.

And a new name.

Weeks had passed since Kat first stepped foot into the courthouse. Rick had been at her side as she walked through the marble hallways.

Her fingers rubbed together as she stood before the front door of her new home. She could almost still feel his touch.

But Rick wasn't there. He was back in Atlanta, and she was in Colorado. Far, far away from life on the East Coast.

The marshals were leaving. They'd just gone over the long list of rules they had for her.

Their list made her think of Rick and the rules he'd given her when they'd first met.

"Okay, that's everything." The female marshal cleared her throat. "You know how to reach us if there's an emergency."

Yes, she knew all the contact steps to take.

"You should be safe here." The marshal smiled. "You can be happy, too."

Happy? Kat just wanted the marshals to leave. She wanted to go inside her house and break down into tears while she was all alone. Was that too much to ask?

"You want us to come inside?"

"No, I'm good. Thanks." *Go, please go. Go now.*

They finally left. Kat shoved the key into the lock. Opened the door. The place was freaking gorgeous, but she barely spared the surroundings or the killer view a glance because tears were already leaking from her eyes and—

"I think we need to make some new rules."

Rick.

Rick was standing in front of the giant picture window that overlooked the mountains.

His arms were folded over his massive chest. His dark eyes were on her. He looked gorgeous and sexy and she was about to faint right then and there.

"Rule one...you don't try to disappear from my life again because that shit rips out my heart, princess."

He stepped toward her.

"Rule two...if you want me to be happy, then you need to be *in* my life. You make me happy, Kat. *You.* You're the best thing I've got, and I sure as hell don't intend to be living on the other side of the country while you are here."

She was smiling. Hoping...

"Rule three...you understand that I'll love you forever. You let me spoil you and love you and you—"

She threw herself against him. Held on as tightly as she could. "I love you!"

His arms closed around her. Rick lifted her up and held her against him. She felt the tremor that worked over his body. "I love you, Kat, so fucking much."

He kissed her. She kissed him. She couldn't believe he was there, and she never, ever wanted to let him go.

They didn't talk about any other rules. Not right then. It wasn't exactly talking time. He was yanking off her clothes. She was yanking off his. Her shirt hit the floor. His flew toward the couch. He pretty much tore off her bra, and his mouth locked around her nipple. He licked and kissed and need poured through her.

"I've missed you!" Kat cried out.

"God, baby, I was insane without you." He lifted her higher, held her so easily. Her legs were curled around his hips, and Kat rocked against the thick erection she could feel shoving against the front of his jeans.

"Never leave me again," Rick rasped.

Did she look crazy? "I tried...to do what was...right..." Her words were panted out.

He carried her into the bedroom. Stripped off the rest of her clothes. She sprawled on the bed while he stood there and stared hungrily down at her. His face was so tense and hard and sexy. "We're right," Rick told her. "We're right together."

He ditched his jeans and shoes and socks. He came back to her, and his cock shoved toward her. She reached out, curled her hand around his heavy length, and stroked him. Again and again.

He caught her hands and pushed them up on the pillow. "I missed the way you taste."

"Rick—"

He put his mouth on her. Worked her with his tongue and fingers and lips, and she fisted her fingers around the pillow. Pleasure pulsed through her as Kat came on a scream.

She could scream now. No one else was listening. It was just them.

"Let me get a condom—"

"No." She stared at him. Straight into his eyes. "I want you. Only you. Nothing between us."

"Kat?"

"Forever. Me, you. And kids? God, yes, I want kids." But she shivered. "Will...will they be safe? Will someone come after—"

"No one will ever hurt you or our kids. I'm with you. I'll keep you safe. You'll keep me safe.

We're a pretty fucking awesome team." He kissed her. "I pity anyone who comes after us."

She smiled at him.

He thrust into her.

Kat arched her body up against him. So good. So thick. So full. "I missed you." She grabbed for him. Her nails bit into his shoulders.

"Baby, I was lost without you."

He withdrew. Thrust. The rhythm was uncontrolled and savage, and she loved it. Loved him. They tore that new bed apart. The wooden posters shoved into the wall, pounding over and over again. Kat came, and she shouted his name as loudly as she could.

She felt his release inside of her. Kat squeezed him even tighter and knew she wasn't going to let him go anytime soon. She'd found her forever. She'd found the man who would always stand with her.

The past was over. Their future waited.

His head lifted. His lips brushed over hers. Then...his eyes twinkled. "Something I should tell you..."

She stared up at him and couldn't believe how happy she was. He'd chosen her. He'd given up everything else...for her.

"I came bearing gifts, sweetheart." Another light kiss to her lips. "'Cause I didn't want you to turn me away..."

As if she ever could.

One more soft kiss.

He slid away from her and headed back into the den. She sat up in bed and frowned. "Rick?

Naked, he walked back to her. He held a small, black box in his hand. He perched on the edge of the bed and offered it to her.

Her fingers shook a little as she opened the box. Earrings. Pearl earrings.

"Your mom's," he said gruffly. "I had them made into earrings for you."

She looked up. Got caught in his eyes.

"I felt like shit the day I destroyed your necklace."

Kat had to swallow the lump in her throat. "The tracking—"

"There's nothing in those pearls. They're real, they're your mother's, and I wanted to give them back to you. Hell, princess, I want to give you *everything.*"

"All I want is you." She kissed him. Loved him. "Though the earrings are amazing," she whispered against his lips.

He gave a soft laugh. "Well, I *did* come with a few other things, too."

She eased back. Stared a little suspiciously at him.

"I also brought your two favorite things to you..."

He was her favorite thing, didn't he get that?

"They are still in the den, but..." Rick kissed her again. A slow, sensual kiss. "I brought you...brownies," he murmured. "And handcuffs."

Laughter spilled from her. Real, happy laughter. She couldn't remember when she'd laughed so freely. Curled with her lover, with the man she loved. Free and happy.

So happy.

Huh. It was unbelievable but...maybe mob princesses did get happy endings, too. Maybe everyone could get them.

If you fight for them. Rick had fought for her. She'd spend the rest of her life fighting for him.

"Get the cuffs," she told him. "And the brownies..."

EPILOGUE

Eric Wilde was at his desk when his late-night visitor appeared. The guy didn't follow the normal procedures for scheduling a meeting. He just waltzed his cocky ass in shortly after midnight.

Eric had been expecting the meeting, though. He'd known the fellow would show up sooner or later.

So Eric just lifted his brows when the man stepped out of the shadows. "Ghost, I presume?"

The man smiled.

"Not your first visit to my office, is it? You love to walk your ass in as if you own the place."

Ghost lifted one shoulder in a shrug. "Is it my fault that your security is a little lax?"

"Lax?" Eric jumped to his feet. *I'll show you lax.* He waved his hand, and Cole surged from the darkness. They'd been waiting for this little meet-and-greet.

Cole aimed his weapon at the back of Ghost's head. "Freeze, asshole."

But Ghost laughed. "Is that anyway to talk to your new partner?" He glanced back at Cole. "Word on the street is that your old partner vanished. Just went poof and now you need someone to take his place."

"Are you crazy?" Cole asked, sounding genuinely curious.

Eric was curious about the same thing.

"Some days." Ghost nodded. "Other days, I'm boringly sane. Tonight, I think you hit me when my crazy was stirring."

Cole swore. His gaze slid back to Eric. "Want me to call the cops?"

"Why?" Ghost asked before Eric could respond. "What will they do?"

"Uh, arrest you?" Eric supplied.

Ghost shook his head. "If you dig into my past now, you'll see that I am nothing but an upstanding member of society. A former intelligence specialist for Uncle Sam, in fact. I mean, how does one get more upstanding than that?"

Eric's eyes raked him. "You had your background scrubbed. Whatever. I don't employ killers here. Get your ass out—"

"Don't lie. You employ all kinds of people. Besides, we both know you could use a man with my skill set."

Cole hadn't lowered his weapon. "Don't you have twenty million dollars to go spend?"

"Um, blood money." Ghost seemed dismissive...*of twenty million dollars.* "Why would an upstanding guy like me want to use blood money? But don't you worry, I'm sure most of that money was donated to a charity."

Most of it?

"Think about my offer," Ghost said, all encouraging and polite. "I'll be around if you need me." He turned on his heel and strode for the door.

"Should I stop him?" Cole still had his weapon at the ready.

Eric shook his head. "We both know all charges were dropped against him." Mysteriously dropped because *someone* had pull high up in the government. Eric suspected Ghost had been working undercover for a very long time.

Yet now he wanted to come out of the shadows? He wanted to work for Wilde?

They'd see...

Eric *did* need a new agent. His head cocked as he slanted a glance at Cole. "You up for a training job?"

Cole blanched in horror. "No, no, *tell* me that you're kidding! He's wanted for murder—"

"Not anymore," Eric pointed out. He'd been doing plenty of his own research on James Smith. After all, when someone was good enough to get past the alarm system at Wilde...*you get my attention.*

"I need a drink," Cole declared. "No, correction, I need a lot of drinks. He *can't* work for Wilde. He's an asshole. He's—"

"I'm still here," Ghost said from the doorway. "And I accept the job."

Eric swept him with a stare. He still wasn't so sure about Ghost. "It wasn't offered yet."

The guy grinned. "Not yet...but it will be."

THE END

A NOTE FROM THE AUTHOR

Thank you for reading FIGHTING FOR HER. I've had such an incredible time writing the "Wilde Ways" books. Just when I think I've completed the series, a new character appears, and I find myself wanting to do another book! As I was writing FIGHTING FOR HER, Ghost kept sneaking into my head. What do you think? Should I write a book for him? (GHOST OF A CHANCE is now available) Let me know—drop me a line at info@cynthiaeden.com. I love hearing from my readers, and I'm always curious about the characters you enjoy.

If you'd like to stay updated on my releases and sales, please join my newsletter list.

https://cynthiaeden.com/newsletter/

Again, thank you for reading FIGHTING FOR HER.

Best,
Cynthia Eden
cynthiaeden.com

ABOUT THE AUTHOR

Cynthia Eden is a *New York Times*, *USA Today*, *Digital Book World*, and *IndieReader* best-seller.

Cynthia writes sexy tales of contemporary romance, romantic suspense, and paranormal romance. Since she began writing full-time in 2005, Cynthia has written over one hundred novels and novellas.

Cynthia lives along the Alabama Gulf Coast. She loves romance novels, horror movies, and chocolate.

For More Information

- *cynthiaeden.com*
- *facebook.com/cynthiaedenfanpage*

HER OTHER WORKS

Death and Moonlight Mystery

- Step Into My Web (Book 1)
- Save Me From The Dark (Book 2)

Wilde Ways

- Protecting Piper (Book 1)
- Guarding Gwen (Book 2)
- Before Ben (Book 3)
- The Heart You Break (Book 4)
- Fighting For Her (Book 5)
- Ghost Of A Chance (Book 6)
- Crossing The Line (Book 7)
- Counting On Cole (Book 8)
- Chase After Me (Book 9)
- Say I Do (Book 10)

Dark Sins

- Don't Trust A Killer (Book 1)
- Don't Love A Liar (Book 2)

Lazarus Rising

- Never Let Go (Book One)
- Keep Me Close (Book Two)
- Stay With Me (Book Three)
- Run To Me (Book Four)
- Lie Close To Me (Book Five)
- Hold On Tight (Book Six)

- Lazarus Rising Volume One (Books 1 to 3)
- Lazarus Rising Volume Two (Books 4 to 6)

Dark Obsession Series

- Watch Me (Book 1)
- Want Me (Book 2)
- Need Me (Book 3)
- Beware Of Me (Book 4)
- Only For Me (Books 1 to 4)

Mine Series

- Mine To Take (Book 1)
- Mine To Keep (Book 2)
- Mine To Hold (Book 3)
- Mine To Crave (Book 4)
- Mine To Have (Book 5)
- Mine To Protect (Book 6)
- Mine Box Set Volume 1 (Books 1-3)
- Mine Box Set Volume 2 (Books 4-6)

Bad Things

- The Devil In Disguise (Book 1)
- On The Prowl (Book 2)
- Undead Or Alive (Book 3)
- Broken Angel (Book 4)
- Heart Of Stone (Book 5)
- Tempted By Fate (Book 6)
- Wicked And Wild (Book 7)
- Saint Or Sinner (Book 8)
- Bad Things Volume One (Books 1 to 3)
- Bad Things Volume Two (Books 4 to 6)

- Bad Things Deluxe Box Set (Books 1 to 6)

Bite Series

- Forbidden Bite (Bite Book 1)
- Mating Bite (Bite Book 2)

Blood and Moonlight Series

- Bite The Dust (Book 1)
- Better Off Undead (Book 2)
- Bitter Blood (Book 3)
- Blood and Moonlight (The Complete Series)

Purgatory Series

- The Wolf Within (Book 1)
- Marked By The Vampire (Book 2)
- Charming The Beast (Book 3)
- Deal with the Devil (Book 4)
- The Beasts Inside (Books 1 to 4)

Bound Series

- Bound By Blood (Book 1)
- Bound In Darkness (Book 2)
- Bound In Sin (Book 3)
- Bound By The Night (Book 4)
- Bound in Death (Book 5)
- Forever Bound (Books 1 to 4)

Stand-Alone Romantic Suspense

- Never Gonna Happen
- One Hot Holiday
- Secret Admirer
- First Taste of Darkness

- Sinful Secrets
- Until Death
- Christmas With A Spy

Made in the USA
Las Vegas, NV
26 April 2023